BLUE SHIFTING

18 · 1 · 96

Eric Brown
BLUE SHIFTING

To Keith

Very Best

Eric B.

PAN BOOKS

First published 1995 by Pan Books

an imprint of Macmillan General Books
25 Eccleston Place, London SW1W 9NF
and Basingstoke

Associated companies throughout the world

ISBN 0 330 33590 1

The Death of Cassandra Quebec first published in Zenith 2, 1990; *Piloting* first published
in Interzone 44, 1991; *The Art of Acceptance* first published in Strange Plasma 1, 1989;
The Disciples of Apollo first published in Other Edens 3, 1989; *Elegy Perpetuum* first
published in Interzone 52, 1991; *Song of Summer* is original to the collection; *Epsilon
Dreams* first published in Interzone 59, 1992; *Blue Shifting* is original to the collection.

1 3 5 7 9 8 6 4 2

A CIP catalogue record for this book is available from
the British Library

Phototypeset by Intype, London
Printed and bound in Great Britain

This book is for
Robyn Cannon & Madeleine Dunnett
With love.

And for Stephen Baxter
and Keith Brooke –
A token of gratitude for
your friendship, criticism
and encouragement over the years.

Contents

Contents

The Death of Cassandra Quebec

I came to Sapphire Oasis in search of experience, or so I thought at the time. I had made my home on Nova Français for almost two decades, the last few years a repetition of café-life, parties and second-rate exhibitions where even my best crystals failed to sell. I was getting old and lonely and my work was suffering, and some vague desperation drove me to Earth to experience that which I might synthesize, through my skill, into art.

The famous crystal *The Death of Cassandra Quebec* was being exhibited for the first time in ten years, and I made this my excuse to revisit the planet of my birth. I took a bigship through the interstellar telemass portal to Timbuktu and caught the mono-train north to Sapphire Oasis.

I had seen many a lavish illustration of the colony – had even admired Tyrone's famous hologram of '37 – and as a result I was overcome with a sense of *déjà vu* at first sight. The oval oasis, perhaps a kilometre from end to end, was surrounded by a great leaning series of golden scimitars, their hilts planted in the sand of the desert, their arching blades supporting the pendant globes that comprised living quarters and spacious studios with views across the artificial lake.

That first night I dined alone in the revolving restaurant on the island at the centre of the oasis. I ate synthetic gazelle and yam, with chutney and Moroccan wine. The panorama was magnificent: beyond the illuminated orbs of the individual domes, and the fringe of surrounding palm trees, the desert extended in dark and sultry swathes the size of Europe. Across the dunes to the south stood the telemass portal. As tall as a mountain, its blank interface was braced in a glowing frame like a hexagon of colossal fluorescents.

It was through this portal that I and a thousand other tourists had journeyed today from Nova Français, and tomorrow it would be opened to the world of Henderson's Fall, 61 Cygni B. The talk in the dining-room was of nothing else but Nathaniel Maltravers, and his arrival tomorrow evening at Sapphire Oasis.

I ordered a second bottle of wine.

As I drank I thought about another famous artist, a woman this time. Cassandra Quebec had inspired more women than just myself to seek expression through the medium of fused crystal. She was the artist who had shown the world her soul, who had taken the fledgling form and proved it as a legitimate means of self-expression. At the height of her career she was the world's most celebrated artist. Then she spoiled it all by announcing her betrothal – I was young; I wept when I found out – to the minor laser-sculptor Nathaniel Maltravers. A year later she was dead.

I finished the second bottle and contemplated a third. I had known when I booked the bigship to Earth that Maltravers – who was indirectly responsible for his wife's death, after all – had decided to return to Sapphire Oasis for the twentieth anniversary commemoration of her passing, but I had not let it put me off the idea of making the trip. Tomorrow, I would visit the Museum of Modern Art and request a private viewing of the Maltravers/Quebec crystal.

I retired early and lay on my bed, staring at the stars through the dome. A party was in progress on the lawn beside the lake, one of the interminable soirées that gave the place more the air of a luxury resort than that of an artists' retreat. Artists, their rich patrons and guests, mixed with a social ease I found enviable; snatches of cultured conversation drifted to me through an open vent in the dome.

Unable to sleep, and reluctant to join the gathering below, I took refuge in a memory-tape. I placed the crown – more like a skull-cap – on my head and selected a tape. As I shed my own identity and slipped into the programmed persona, I could not help feeling a twinge of guilt at my escape. Memory-tapes were a spin-off from a device known as mem-erase, illegal on Earth for almost two decades. Mem-erase, the process of self-selected amnesia to which I had once been addicted, had been proven to have certain adverse psychological side-effects. Not only had their private use been proscribed, but even law enforcement agencies, who had used mem-erase to access the minds of suspected criminals, had been denied its advantages. As a result of the ban, the simulated scenarios of memory-tapes were viewed in some circles with a certain stigma.

I selected the ersatz memories of a fictitious vid-star, lay back and for the next hour lived a life of success, fame and love.

I awoke early the following morning, booked some time alone with the crystal and strolled along the palm-lined boulevard to the museum.

On the few occasions when the crystal had been exhibited in the past, I had been loath to experience it – the mere fact of Cassandra Quebec's death had been painful enough, without subjecting myself to the emotional reality of it. But twenty years had passed since the incident; I was older and perhaps wiser now, and I considered myself ready to have the experience.

Not that I was without misgivings. I held, perhaps irrationally, a fierce dislike for the man who had married

Quebec and who was ultimately responsible for the accident that killed her. Added to which, Maltravers' production of the crystal had elevated him from the minor artisan he was to the status of a world celebrity. Perhaps what had prevented me from experiencing the crystal before now, quite apart from the emotional trauma I would have to undergo, was the thought that I would be participating in the metaphorical aggrandizement of man at the expense of woman.

That morning at breakfast in the revolving restaurant I had been invited to the table of a group of Hoppers – rich artists and their hangers-on, who skipped the globe from one colony resort to the next. They were shrill and opinionated, and I sought the protection of silence, offering nothing to the debate about Maltravers and the reason for his return. I heard one claim that he was returning to seek artistic rejuvenation from the locale of his wife's horrific death; another, that he intended to end his life here, as befits the artistic temperament.

The truth, I suspected, was neither. It was my guess that Nathaniel Maltravers was staging the spectacle of his return for no other reason than that, in the years since Cassandra Quebec's death, his own artistic and popular success had floundered. The dozen or so 'major' works he had released upon the universe had flopped abysmally. His return was probably nothing more than a cheap ruse to gain publicity.

The Death of Cassandra Quebec remained his first and last great work.

The museum, which housed the crystal and a thousand other works of art, was an onyx cathedral raised above the desert on flying cantilevers and approached along a sweep of gently ascending steps. It was cool and hushed within, and I took my time and strolled towards the crystal wing. I paused at the arched entrance, showed my pass to the security guard and stepped inside. The chamber was empty; I was quite alone. Before me, in pride of place in the centre of the room, was the crystal – in fact, a thousand alien stones fused into one faceted, centimetre-thick disc perhaps two metres across. Visually, it was a mere swirl of colour, a coruscating vortex of argent and indigo. Only to the touch would the crystal discharge the stored emotions of its creators.

I must have heard a hundred different reports about Cassandra Quebec's death, and staged and re-staged the tragedy in the theatre of my mind. I was on Nova Français when I first read about the accident; the article was in a journal almost two years old, and the shock of the news was compounded by the fact that I had learned about it so late.

Her arrival at Sapphire Oasis, with her husband and new-born baby, made world news. It was her first public appearance since the birth of her daughter; the film of their approach in an open-top vintage Mercedes, smiling parents and babe-in-arms, is famous – a scene imprinted on the collective consciousness by the tragedy of the events that followed. The fact that the instrument of her death was travelling with them makes the short clip all the more grotesque. As a wedding present, Quebec had bought her husband a bird-like alien known as a Pterosaur from a newly discovered planet in the Serendipity Cluster. It was an ugly, featherless creature, had a beak like a scythe and was reputedly empathic – a suitably bizarre pet for the world's most famous couple. It could be seen perched on the back seat, maintaining its balance with edgy adjustments of its vast, leathery wingspan as the automobile swept through the gates of the colony.

Quebec and Maltravers argued often during their first year of marriage. It was reported that their differences of opinion, because they were artists, were all the more vituperative. Maltravers, the rumour went, was jealous of his wife's talent and success; Quebec, for her part, despaired that her husband's constant envy would prevent him from ever attaining greatness for himself.

The one known truth of their relationship was that, however violent their arguments, their *rapprochements* were just as intense. They were hailed, in media hyperbole, as the planet's greatest lovers – how jealous I felt when I read this! – and as evidence the news-media offered up the fact that, as well as sharing a bed, they also shared a studio.

It was in this studio, three days after her arrival at Sapphire Oasis, that Cassandra Quebec met her end.

They had argued. Quebec was part-way through a crystal that would stand as testimony to their love, and as such it had to contain *everything*, their imperfections and flaws of character as well as their strengths. Maltravers was loath to subject himself to so public a scrutiny, and his protestations which began their final argument were overheard by their daughter's nurse.

They were in the studio, facing each other across the sunlit chamber. The volume of their recriminations was noted by several other artists, who paid no heed as this was nothing new between the husband and wife. The nurse reported that she had glimpsed the alien pet, flapping in agitation beside Maltravers, before she departed to attend the crying child in another part of the living quarters.

According to Maltravers, they had reached an impasse in their disagreement, a temporary cease-fire, and Cassandra remained staring at him from across the work-strewn room. Maltravers admitted to feelings of anger, and it was this anger, experts testified at the inquest, that the Pterosaur must have picked up.

Before Maltravers could move to stop it, the Pterosaur left its perch, swooped across the room and attacked his wife with claws like sickles. Maltravers fought it off, but so savage was the attack that within seconds Quebec was lacerated beyond hope of resurrection. He realized – he said later, in sworn testimony – that his wife was dying and that nothing, not even the latest surgical techniques, could save her.

The events that followed were bizarre to say the least.

Beside Quebec was the fused crystal, empty but for touches of her love for Maltravers. What he did then, in his grief and regret and overwhelming sense of loss, was to lift his wife and place her on the slab as if it were a catafalque, and then lay his brow against its faceted surface and impress upon it his turbulent emotions. She died in his arms minutes later, and the crystal recorded the moment for eternity.

For three days the world's media vilified Maltravers as a monster, until the coroner reported at the inquest that nothing could have saved Quebec. Then his agent released the crystal, and over the next year or so public opinion swung in Maltravers' favour – the vilification turned to sympathy and appreciation.

In the silence of the museum I steeled myself, stepped forward and laid my palms on the crystal's surface. Warmth ran up my arms, the warmth of Quebec's love for her husband, with which she had begun the work. This joy lasted only seconds, though, for as I moved my hands from the edge of the piece towards its centre, pain swamped me, physical pain – the scream of every nerve slit through and through again. Beyond this, on some deeper substrata of the crystal, was Quebec's bewilderment, and then her sudden comprehension as she realized what was happening, that life was ebbing from her, that everything she had ever experienced, the hate and the joy and the everyday miracle of existence, was draining away, becoming faint as she approached the terrible point of total annihilation.

Her end was a crescendo scream of terror as oblivion descended.

Then my touch encountered Maltravers' pain at his loss. The howl of desolation that communicated itself from his soul to the crystal, and then to my senses, was almost more unbearable than the pain of Quebec's death – for it continued long after her dying, a lament for his wife, a scream of despair at the knowledge of his existence without her.

Unable to take any more I tore myself away, and the sudden cessation of pain was an exquisite relief. I had no idea how long I had been standing before the crystal, so captivated had I been by the raw human emotions. I realized then that I was in tears.

As I made my way slowly from the museum, I knew that I no longer resented Maltravers. The act of creating the crystal had been instinctive, born of pain and the need to share his grief, and not the opportunistic bid for fame I had assumed for so long.

Within a week of his wife's death, Maltravers took his daughter and sought refuge on the colony world of Henderson's Fall, as if by doing so he might distance himself from the pain of the tragedy.

And tonight he was returning to the source of that pain.

That evening I attended the party thrown by the President of Mali to welcome Nathaniel Maltravers to Sapphire Oasis. It was held in the President's own dome – he dabbled in photo-montage – with a view across the desert to the telemass portal, through which Maltravers was due to arrive at midnight. The dome was packed with eager guests. I recognized the two dozen or so serious artists who made up the nucleus of the Sapphire colony, faces familiar from Earth to the furthest settled world. Also present were the flamboyant Hoppers, attendant sycophants, and sombre-suited officials from the countries of Northern Africa and Europe.

I drank by myself beside the alcohol dispenser and thought about returning to my own dome. There was an atmosphere of excitement and expectation about the gathering that smacked of voyeurism. I was on my fourth drink when I admitted that the only reason *I* was here was to see for myself how the passage of years had treated Maltravers, and perhaps learn the real reason for his return.

At midnight we spilled out on to the balcony and marvelled at the exhibition of interstellar *son et lumière* enacted to the south.

Until its activation, the portal was nothing more than an illuminated hexagonal frame, through which could be seen a continuation of the starlit African sky. Within minutes all that had changed. The frame flickered, as if affected by a power-drain; then a thunderous report rolled across the desert, and the scene through the portal was transformed. The guests gasped and applauded as an alien landscape appeared: a busy spaceport, distant blue mountains, and binary suns in a pink sky. As we watched, a bull-nosed bigship eased its way through the interface and entered the atmosphere of Earth. The ship came to rest on the apron of the spaceport at the foot of the portal.

We returned inside. As the flier carrying Maltravers raced across the desert towards the oasis, the conversation in the dome had about it a charged expectancy. Around me, guests quipped, exchanged stories and looked frequently to the gates in anticipation of Maltravers' arrival.

I was thinking about my experience with the crystal that morning when a sudden hush fell upon the company. I stared through the diaphanous, curvilinear wall of the room as the flier slipped through the gates and settled beside the lake.

Two figures climbed out, were met by the President and his entourage, and disappeared into the scimitar shaft that supported the dome. The conversation started up again, self-consciously, all eyes on the entrance. Seconds later the door opened and applause rippled through the room.

I can recall very little about Nathaniel Maltravers as he made his entry – I was too intent on watching the person who entered with him. While the guests flocked to congratulate Maltravers on his return, I had eyes only for his daughter.

Corrinda Maltravers surprised me on two counts. The first was that I had never thought of her as a young woman – if I thought of her at all, it was as a babe-in-arms, a cypher in the tragedy, untouched by the passage of time. The second was that she was as beautiful as her mother.

Maltravers moved from one group of guests to the next, and his daughter followed in his wake. This was the first time she had returned to Earth since the tragedy, and she appeared shy and bewildered at the reception. She was small, slim, wore a black tube dress that left her shoulders bare, hugged her hips and finished just above the knees. I caught only a glimpse of her large green eyes and isosceles face – *so* painfully like her mother's – before she disappeared into an admiring throng of guests. I wondered how long it would be before she found herself waking up beside the next self-professed Picasso.

My reverie was interrupted by the arrival at my side of Maltravers and the President of Mali. They sipped their drinks and the President regaled Maltravers with a short history of his country.

Nathaniel Maltravers was in his middle-fifties, tall and silver haired, with the well-groomed, distinguished appearance of someone who has forgone the life of an artist for that of a sybarite. I could not reconcile the man beside me with the artist who had suffered the anguish of his wife's death and communicated it so harrowingly.

Then I noticed the distant, blitzed look in his grey eyes. I recalled the report that, during his self-imposed exile on Henderson's Fall, Maltravers had taken the easy way out. Before the possession of mem-erase became an offence, he had duly self-administered the process of wiping from his memory the entirety of his stay at Sapphire Oasis. His only knowledge of the tragic event was what he read in factual accounts, stripped of all emotion and pain.

Now he glanced my way, his eyes measuring me for size in the places he thought important. His gaze was less lecherous than professional, as if he were seriously considering me as a prospective model.

'Aren't you Eva Hovana?' he asked. 'The creator of the *Persephone* crystal?'

I admitted that I was; it was an early piece and not one of my best.

'If I may say so' – he smiled – 'I have always found your work rather derivative.'

I was quick with the riposte, and immediately regretted it. 'At least I don't get other people to do my work for me, however derivative it might be.'

Stung, he moved off instantly. 'As I mentioned earlier,' he said to the President of Mali, 'my next piece will be influenced by my obsession with symmetry.'

The President hurried him across the room. 'Ah . . . meet my friends from the Council of Europe . . .'

I escaped on to the balcony.

I gazed out over the body of water, glittering in the moonlight, and wondered what was keeping me at Sapphire Oasis. After all, I had experienced the crystal I had come to see. I was contemplating a trip to Europe when I sensed someone beside me. I felt a hand on my arm, and turned.

Corrinda Maltravers stood before me, even shorter than she had seemed in the room, almost childlike. She had quickly withdrawn her hand when I started, and now regarded me uncertainly.

'I'm *so* sorry. My father . . . He . . .' She gestured.

I smiled. With her shock of sun-bleached hair, her green eyes, she was so much like the picture of her mother I had kept at my bedside during my uncertain youth.

She smiled in return, relieved at my acceptance. 'My father *hates* women and artists. It's bad luck if you happen to be both.' She had the habit of emphasizing certain words, as her mother had done.

I shrugged. 'I can live with the hatred of men,' I told her, and cursed myself for being so obvious.

She regarded me shyly. There was a diffident look in her eyes that could *not* be what I believed it to be. 'I think your best work is the *Goddess of Lesbos*,' she whispered.

My stomach fluttered. 'You do?'

There were a thousand questions I wanted to ask her, about herself, about her mother . . . but I was frightened of being seen to be too forward, too eager.

Maltravers called her name ‾and Corrinda almost winced.

'I *must* go. I'll see you again?' She smiled shyly. 'I really meant what I said about your work.'

She slipped through the sliding door with a small wave and disappeared into the crowd.

I decided to remain at Sapphire Oasis for a while.

Over the next few days I saw Corrinda on a number of occasions; but she was always with her father and it was obvious that she felt she could not leave him to join me although, I thought, she gave the distinct impression of *wanting* to do so. Or was I kidding myself? I was pushing fifty and desperate, still searching for that which most people have either found at my age, or have given up hope of ever finding. Besides, I had to admit that it wasn't Corrinda I was attracted to; rather, I was obsessed with Cassandra Quebec and the tragedy of her death.

However much I tried I could not bring myself to start work. I had brought with me several miniature crystals in various stages of completion, with the notion of dabbling with them should no new project inspire me. Not only did nothing come to mind, but I found it impossible to complete the crystals already begun. My thoughts were too occupied with Maltravers, his daughter and the death of Cassandra Quebec. I was afraid of corrupting the unfinished work with my turbulent and unresolved emotions, and reluctant to begin a fresh crystal, perhaps on the subject of Quebec, for fear of being unoriginal. It had all been done before, and how might I bring some new and stimulating insight to the drama?

I spent more and more time beside the sparkling oasis, sipping long drinks and wondering whether my assumption the other night as to Corrinda's preferences had been nothing more than a drunken fantasy. Certainly, she did not join me as I sat in full view with my drink. But then, I told myself, perhaps this was because her father was in evidence so much of the time.

Maltravers spent a few hours each morning in his studio. Around noon he would emerge, showered and suited, and hold court in the bar. He had found himself lionized by the clique of Hoppers, and had proved himself a competitive drinker and an able raconteur. From my lounger by the water, I took the opportunity to watch him as he drank and illustrated his spiel with expansive gestures. I recalled the way he had eyed my body at our first meeting, and during the course of the next few days I realized that he was, likewise, sizing up the women in his crowd.

He soon found what he was looking for. Within a week of his arrival he was escorting a willowy Nigerian Princess, a laser-sculptress with a penchant for scarlet gowns that emphasized the absolute ebony of her flesh. They spent the mornings in his studio, afternoons in the bar and the evenings partying at various other oases scattered about the desert. I heard one rumour that they were creating a crystal together, another that they were producing a sculpture.

As much as I disliked seeing a beautiful and talented artist used by him, it did have the advantage of keeping Maltravers occupied and out of the way. I lived in hope that Corrinda might take the opportunity to seek my company.

Then, one evening, as I watched the sun set and the moon rise, and was contemplating whether to go to the bar for another drink or to return to my dome, a shadow fell across my outstretched legs.

Corrinda smiled uncertainly. 'Miss Hovana . . .?'

'Eva, please. Won't you sit down?'

She perched herself on the edge of the chair across the table and gave a shy smile in lieu of words. She wore a spacer's silversuit, chopped at shoulders and thighs. I could not help but notice, on the tanned flesh of her limbs, white scars like tribal striations.

In mutual nervousness we both began speaking at once. We stopped, and I said, 'Please, you first.'

She shrugged, reddened. She seemed younger than when we first met. 'I just . . . I wanted to *apologize* for not meeting you sooner. I was working.'

I reached across the table and took her hand. 'Working?'

She reacted to my touch with characteristic nervousness. 'Didn't I tell you that I'm an artist?' she whispered.

'An artist?' I was surprised and delighted.

'Shhh! Not so *loud* – if it ever got back to my father . . .

You see, he hates women and artists. What do you think it's like being his daughter?'

I made a small sound of commiseration.

She looked up from our hands. 'That's what I wanted to see you about – my work. I've just finished a piece. I . . . I was wondering, *would* you like to see it?' She watched me with eyes so soft it seemed they could be bruised by rejection.

I said that I'd like nothing more, and she led me around the curve of the oasis, talking earnestly by my side in relief at my acquiescence. She took me through the lounge of her father's hanging dome and into her bedroom.

'I must keep it in here,' she explained, hardly able to meet my gaze, 'so that Father doesn't find out. There's no telling what he'd do.'

She stood beside an angular object covered by a silken sheet, and unveiled it so shyly that she might have been uncovering her own nakedness. 'What do you think? *Honestly?*'

I approached it slowly, aware of some choking emotion in my throat. It was a sculpture in some kind of glowing, off-world wood; perhaps half life-sized, it was of a naked woman seated on the ground, hugging her shins.

Corrinda was watching me. 'It's you,' she said in a small voice.

I touched the wood, caressed it. I wanted to cry, and yet did not want Corrinda to see me doing so – which was ridiculous. I wanted to cry because Corrinda had produced in the carved representation of myself all my loneliness, all my desire to want someone who wanted me.

The invitation was obvious, but I was too scared to trust her. She was so young, I told myself, while another voice asked what did age matter beside the fact of her compassion.

I bit my lip in a bid to stop the tears, turned to her. 'And your father would put an end to this?'

'He's ruled by his hatred. Success makes him jealous.'

'You should leave him!'

'He wanted me with him when he returned. He said that by returning here he could come to terms with what happened – then I *will* leave.'

'You must hate him,' I said.

Corrinda looked away.

In the silence that followed, I heard a sound from beyond the open door: the leathery creak and swoop of wings. I recognized the shape that flapped across the lounge and alighted on the back of the chesterfield.

I screamed.

Corrinda took my arm. 'It's OK, Eva. It's not the same one, and anyway it's quite tame.'

'But even so . . . !'

'I know. It's sick. But, you see, my father is quite insane.'

She reached out and pushed the door shut. 'We'll be alone for the rest of the night,' she said.

For the next week, at every available opportunity, Corrinda would leave her father's dome and visit me, and we would make love in my bedroom beneath blue Saharan sky. I blessed each minute that Maltravers spent in the company of the Nigerian, creating his work of art.

The day before the twentieth anniversary of her mother's death, Corrinda sat cross-legged beside me on the bed. I stared at her naked body, her torso a sun-browned canvas on which a pattern of pale striations had been inscribed. Some incisions were more recent than others, and the tracery of mutilation was too symmetrical to be the result of an accident. I wondered what had driven her to this masochism that masqueraded as art.

I stared through the dome at the clear blue sky. It was as if all week our love-making had been a rehearsal for what we had just shared. I had gone as far as I could, taken carnal knowledge towards an intimacy beyond which only a verbal declaration of love remained. Perhaps my circumspection, my refusal to match with words the physical commitment I had shown, communicated itself to Corrinda.

She traced a scar on her thigh, and said, 'Do you love me, Eva?'

I made some tired remark to the effect that we hardly knew each other, and that when she was my age she would come to doubt if anything such as love existed.

'I'm sorry – that's cynical. I like you a lot, Corrinda. Perhaps in time . . .'

For so long I had hero-worshipped Cassandra Quebec that, having her daughter, I could not be sure if the girl I wanted to love was no more than an illusion of my fantasies, a substitution for the love that was impossible.

'I love you,' she whispered.

I kissed her projecting knee. I wanted to tell her that she longed for a mother, and as I was both the right age and an artist . . . I glanced across at the statue, now installed in my bedroom, and convinced myself that even this was her subconscious grieving for her mother's absence, with myself as the transferred subject.

Ours was a union born of tragedy, and I kept asking myself how such a union might succeed.

I said: 'Tomorrow we could visit the Museum of Modern Art. We could experience your parents' crystal.'

Corrinda regarded me with a shocked expression. 'My father would never allow it.'

'Why are you so imprisoned by your father's wishes?' I asked harshly.

Corrinda just shrugged, ignored the question. 'I've read about the crystal, Eva. I *want* to experience it, to understand what my father went through. Then I might come to understand what makes him like he is. I might even be able to sympathize with him, instead of hating him.'

'Then come with me tomorrow.'

She shook her head. 'He wouldn't like it.'

In the silence that followed I realized that it was because of her father that Corrinda was so pathetically shy, her experience so circumscribed.

She changed the subject. She leaned over me and stared into my eyes. She could see, in my distant, shattered pupils, the tell-tale sign of addiction.

'You've used mem-erase!' she declared.

I told her that I had used it often in my twenties.

She shrugged. 'But why? What did you need to erase?'

'Oh . . . I suspect periods of unhappiness, old lovers . . . Of course, I can't remember.'

'But didn't you know it was dangerous?'

I shrugged. 'Not at the time,' I told her. Mem-erase was withdrawn from sale only when it was discovered that memories could never be truly erased. They were just blanked from the conscious, pushed into the subconscious, and could resurface at any time as trauma, psychosis.

'Have you ever thought of *replaying* those memories, reliving those affairs?'

'No, I haven't. Anyway, I destroyed all the tapes. I always thought that if the memories were sufficiently terrible for me to erase in the first place, then perhaps I shouldn't relive them. Then again, perhaps I was mistaken. How can I claim to be an artist if I can't face my past and make something of it?'

Corrinda smiled timidly. 'Would you erase *me* from your memory?' she asked.

I pulled her to me. 'Of course not,' I said, and I wondered how many times I had made that promise in the past.

I touched the scars that covered her body. 'You still haven't told me, Corrinda.'

'Please, Eva,' she said, and would say no more.

That evening, as the sun sank beyond the dunes of the Sahara and a cool night breeze tempered the heat of the day, the entire colony turned out to witness the ceremonial unveiling of Maltravers' latest work of art. There was a full moon shining, and above our heads the bulb of his studio hung like a replica of the ivory satellite. There was no sign of the great work, and I was not alone in wondering just what form it might take. Corrinda had chosen not to join me; she said that she *absolutely hated* her father's latest production, but had refused to tell me why.

There was a patter of applause as Maltravers appeared on the balcony, resplendent in white suit and cravat. He raised his hands to damp the reception, then gave a short speech. His latest creation, he claimed, represented living evidence of his contention that all art attempted to attain the symmetry of nature. I found the monologue vain and pretentious, but I had to admit that it did have the desired effect of creating a considerable air of anticipation.

He came to the end of his speech and gave a slight bow, the minimal courtesy suggesting a certain contempt for his audience. His Nigerian escort joined him on the balcony. She wore a scarlet gown, fastened at the throat and gathered at the crotch to form a pair of voluminous pantaloons.

Maltravers kissed her hand and, as we gazed up in expectation, he stepped behind the woman and unfastened the choker at her neck. The gown whispered down the black curves of her body to reveal her terrible nakedness.

She struck a demure, Junoesque pose and the crowd gasped.

Her flesh had been sliced and flensed, the incisions opened, pulled back and pinned to reveal the inner organs in their precise, geometrical arrangement; the kidneys were displayed in positional harmony, the lungs likewise. The muscle of her abdomen had been turned back to form an elliptical orifice, through which could be seen the opalescent coils of her intestines. Her arms and legs had also undergone the depredations of Maltravers' scalpel: the ebony skin was scored and folded in a baroque series of curlicues and scrolls, repeating the motif of red on black.

But Maltravers' ultimate abomination – or masterstroke, depending on one's point of view – was the woman's heart. It perched between the orchids of her segmented breasts and throbbed like some grotesque alien polyp.

I recalled the scars on Corrinda's body and almost retched.

Maltravers stepped forward and took the woman's hand. She twirled. 'The Symmetrical Goddess,' he announced.

The stunned silence extended itself for several seconds, and then someone whooped and clapped, and immediately the acclamation was taken up by the rest of the crowd. Maltravers and his model disappeared into the dome. Minutes later they strode out across the lawn, and there was a mad scramble to be the first to congratulate the pair.

I took refuge on the patio outside the bar and anaesthetized myself with alcohol. I alone seemed to understand that Maltravers' macabre violation of the woman's body had its source not so much in his desire to create new and outrageous art, but in some deep-seated psychological need known only to himself.

It was not long before my thoughts returned to Corrinda. I recalled her scarred body – her diffidence, which amounted almost to shame, at my insensitive questioning – and her refusal to attend the exhibition. I pushed myself unsteadily to my feet. I wanted suddenly to find her, to comfort her as best I could.

A party was raging in Maltravers' dome. The guests filled the various levels with a buzz of conversation, debate as to the man's genius and the occasional burst of laughter. I pushed through the groups of drinkers and searched for Corrinda, my desire to be with her increasing with every passing minute. I felt a surge of panic take hold of me, as if fearing that Corrinda, provoked by the extent of her father's latest perversion, might take it into her head to do something stupid. I wondered how much she hated Maltravers . . .

I found myself on a small, railed gallery overlooking a sunken bunker of loungers, which in turn overlooked the darkened desert. The mutilated Nigerian stood on a coffee table in the hub of the bunker, striking a series of extravagant poses. Light flashed off her exposed internal organs. 'He took my heart,' she was saying drunkenly to a posse of admirers, 'and did with it that which no man has ever done.'

I was overcome with revulsion and hurried around the circular gallery. The only place I had not yet looked for Corrinda was in her bedroom. I was about to make my way there when, across the lounge, I saw a door swing open and Maltravers stagger from his studio. His sudden appearance silenced the gathered drinkers; he became the focus of attention as, in evident distress, he pushed his way through the crowd. He paused at the rail, breathing heavily, saw his model and hurried down the steps into the bunker. He grabbed the woman by the arm, dragged her from the pedestal and pushed her across to the outer membrane of the dome. The circle of admirers hastily evacuated the bunker; already, a crowd had gathered along the gallery rail opposite me. I stood directly above Maltravers and the woman, and I alone overheard what followed.

'Where is it?' Maltravers sounded all the more menacing for the low pitch of his question. He still gripped the woman's patterned arm, and she grimaced at the pressure and raised a hand, palm outwards, as if to protect herself from a blow.

'I have no idea what you're talking about!'

I noticed that, for all the violent intimacy of the assault, Maltravers could not bring himself to regard the woman. Her organs were highlighted, the line of liver and kidney duplicating the overhead fluorescents – but Maltravers stared past her at the desert outside, as if ashamed of his creation.

'You were the only person in the studio when I opened the locker.' He was shaking with rage. 'Where is it?'

Pinned inelegantly to the wall of the dome, the woman nevertheless affected disdain. 'Where is *what*, exactly?'

Then he brought himself to regard her. He hissed something too low for me to hear, and the woman looked shocked. I could guess, from my knowledge of his past, from his haunted eyes, the reason for his secrecy.

I pushed myself from the rail and hurried through the dome to Corrinda's room. I opened the door without knocking and slipped quickly inside.

She was curled on her bed in the foetal position.

I paused by the door. 'Your father still uses . . .' I began.

She looked up and stared at me through her tears. 'After every session with the Nigerian and me,' she whispered. 'He didn't want to remember how much he enjoyed cutting us up . . .'

I could barely make out her words. She seemed traumatized, present only in body. Her eyes stared through me.

Then I saw the mem-erase crown beside her on the bed.

'Corrinda . . .'

'I had to!' she said. 'I had to know what it was that made him do these things. I knew he was ill, but I didn't know *why.*' She struggled into a sitting position, picked up the crown and held it out to me. 'So I took this and accessed his past.'

I accepted the crown. The access slide was set at its very first tape. I looked at her.

'I replayed his memory of the death of my mother.' She began to cry. 'Take it! Access it for yourself!'

From another part of the dome I heard Maltravers, calling his daughter. Corrinda looked up at me and smiled a terrible smile. I quickly kissed her and hurried from the room, at once eager to learn the reason for Corrinda's horror and yet dreading what I might find. I left the dome as dawn touched the desert sky. The party was breaking up, the revellers leaving and making their way around the curve of the oasis.

In my own dome I poured myself a stiff drink, and then another. I sat down, picked up the mem-erase crown and re-checked the setting. I placed the crown on my head, connected the probes and pushed the slide to activate the programme.

Instantly, I was inside his head. I saw what Maltravers had seen that day twenty years ago, experienced everything he'd heard and said. But his thoughts, as they were not my own, remained in the background, blurred and indistinct, full of nebulous anger.

He was in the studio, facing his wife – oh, so much like Corrinda! – across a floor littered with slabs of crystal, frames and crystal-cutters. The Pterosaur, hunched and menacing, regarded him down the length of its scythe-like bill.

Cassandra stood in shirt-sleeves next to her fused crystal, sunlight falling on her golden hair. 'I don't understand your objection,' she was saying. 'The crystal will show my *love* for you. I want you to collaborate—'

'I want no part of it. It's your crystal, not mine.'

'But you're part of me. How can the crystal be anything other than *both* of us?' She stared at him. 'Are you frightened? Is that it, Nathaniel? You don't want the world to see you as you really are.'

Maltravers turned at a sound from the door, and the nurse hurried away to tend the crying baby before he could find the words to censure her.

He slammed the door and turned to his wife.

'How can you talk of love like that, after what you've been doing?'

Cassandra stared at him, stricken. 'What do you mean?' It was barely a whisper.

Maltravers tried to laugh, but the sound he made was desperate. 'How did you think you could keep it from me?'

She was staring at him, shaking her head.

'How long has it been going on? Before we came here?'

Cassandra was silent for a second, then said, 'Two days – no more. I met her here. But she means nothing to me.'

(Paralysed, on the edge of consciousness, I screamed.)

'Then why have an affair with her?' Maltravers cried. 'It isn't even as if ... as if she's a good artist. Christ, the woman's third-rate. She isn't even as good as me!'

(I wanted to hit the release stud, retreat into the safety of ignorance; but some other part of me, fascinated and appalled by this vision of the past, would not allow me so easy an exit.)

'Oh, Eva's much better than you, Nathaniel. That's what attracted me – her talent. But, please believe me – I don't love her. It was only a physical thing, an infatuation.'

Maltravers' anger welled; I could feel it massing in my head like a thundercloud.

'Then if you think she's so good, why don't you stay with her!'

The Pterosaur hopped from foot to foot in agitation. At

any second, I thought, it would swoop across the room and tear Quebec to shreds.

'Because I love you!' Cassandra yelled through her tears.

'I don't want your love – I want your respect for the artist I am.'

She broke; the walls of her reserve crumbled and she was no longer able to lie. She bent almost double and screamed at him.

'But, Nathaniel – *you are no artist!*'

His anger exploded, rocking me.

I knew, then, what was about to happen. I suddenly understood the reason for Corrinda's terrible smile.

The Pterosaur remained on its perch.

Maltravers rushed at his wife.

He lifted a crystal-cutter and in a blind rage attacked, slashed at her again and again as she stood before him and offered no resistance.

(I tried to shut out the vision as Cassandra Quebec was transformed before my eyes into a lacerated carcass – but the image played on in my head.)

Then Maltravers ceased his attack and Cassandra slipped to the floor, and realizing what he'd done he fell to his knees, and his remorse swamped me. He saw the crystal, and something – perhaps some insane idea that this was the only way to immortalize his wife *and* her talent – moved him to gather her up and lay her to rest on the slab of crystal. She died and gave her dying to the world, and Maltravers was overcome with a weight of guilt and regret that I was slowly coming to realize was my burden also.

I hit the release, tore the crown from my head and sat staring through the dome, weeping at the new order of reality revealed to me. Then I realized what day it was – the twentieth anniversary of Cassandra Quebec's passing – and something, some vague and disturbing premonition, reminded me of Nathaniel Maltravers' obsession with the symmetry of art. I could see, across the oasis in Maltravers' studio, the evil flapping form of the Pterosaur. I pulled myself upright and staggered from the lounge.

I crossed the lawn in a daze of disbelief. I seemed to take an age to reach Maltravers' studio, aware of the terrible fact that my affair with Cassandra Quebec had brought tragedy upon two generations.

Just as I, denied the emotion of grief by my use of mem-erase all those years ago, had been brought here by my subconscious for motives of its own – to empathize with Quebec's death on its anniversary, to fall in love again with her through the medium of her daughter? – Maltravers too had been delivered here by his subconscious for its own sinister reasons. He hated women and artists and – as Corrinda happened to be both, as well as a substitute figure for his wife – what greater act of artistic symmetry might there be than a *second* celebrated Nathaniel Maltravers' crystal, twenty years on?

I came to the scimitar support of Maltravers' dome and, sobbing with desperation, hauled open the door. I ran inside and up the escalator, numbed by the knowledge of what I might find.

I was crossing the lounge when I heard Corrinda's scream from the direction of the studio, and my relief that she was still alive was tempered by the knowledge that soon, if her father had his way, she would not be. I heard Maltravers curse, and the din of things being overturned from within the room. I reached the communicating door and tried to yank it open – but it was locked. Corrinda yelled my name, pleading with me to hurry. I called in return that I was coming. Through the frosted glass I could make out two indistinct figures circling each other with extreme wariness, and above them the Pterosaur in flight.

I scanned the lounge for something with which to smash the door when I heard another cry: Maltravers, this time – though whether in victory or defeat I could not tell. Then silence. I hefted a carved statue, pitched it through the glass and stepped in after it.

The scene that greeted my eyes was a grotesque tableau, the aftermath of tragic events played out to their conclusion. Maltravers lay on his back on a slab of crystal, his throat slit and his torso, from gullet to abdomen, opened to his spine. Beside him, Corrinda braced herself against the faceted crystal, as if in exhaustion or in silent prayer.

Still gripping the crystal-cutter, she stared at me with eyes burning like emeralds.

'He attacked me,' she whispered. 'He had it all planned, the crystal set up . . .'

Only then did I notice the rip in her one-piece and the bloody gash across her stomach. She stared at the cutter as if seeing it for the first time, then dropped it and reached out to me. 'Eva . . .'

'After all I've done?' I said.

'I *need* you!'

As I took her in my arms, the Pterosaur swooped through the air, alighted on Maltravers' corpse and began picking at the bloody remains.

Corrinda looked at me and, together, we reached out to the crystal and experienced Maltravers' death. We shared his initial shock at the realization of his end, and then his profound relief that his jealousy and guilt were drawing to a close. We experienced his macabre satisfaction in the symmetry – not quite that which he had planned – that the crystal would come to represent.

Then, in a subtle underlay of emotion, I became aware of Corrinda's contribution to the crystal. I felt her joy that, at last, she was free, her delight in the irony of creating a work of art at her father's expense.

I came to Sapphire Oasis in search of experience, or so I thought at the time.

Piloting

Abbie covered light years in an instant.

She stepped into the telemass portal on Earth and emerged on Nea Kikládhes without breaking her stride. She hurried from the Acropolis and paused at the top of the thousand steps carved into the slope of the mountainside. From this elevation she had a perfect view of the archipelago stretching towards the horizon of the waterworld, and the lambent sunset which lasted for hours and was the time when all work ceased and play began. Abbie started down the steps, her ease giving no hint of her apprehension.

She strolled along the illuminated boulevard, set with tables at which the Altered, the Augmented and the Omegas disported themselves, waited upon by boosted-primates, chimpanzees and gibbons. She hurried past a group of Altereds, humans who had assumed the partial forms of beasts, extinct or mythical. Zebra-men traded gossip about celebrities with unicorn-women. Other Altereds had kept their human form but for the affectation of fur or scales.

She found a vacant table beside the sea, among a group of her own kind. To a soul, these sophisticates were handsome and well-dressed, of human form and proud of the fact, disdainful of their loud and frivolous neighbours. They wore tasteful cortical implants, spinal addenda which showed only as a knife-edge ridge beneath gown or robe.

Along the boulevard, at some remove from the cyber-assisted clique, sat the dignified Omegas. They were neither Altered nor Augmented, and had about them the appearance of great age without infirmity: they were ancient and yet youthful. At the sight of their white gowns, Abbie drew a breath and looked away. Never before had she witnessed so many immortals together in one place.

While she waited, she watched a fish-boy sporting in the shallows. Sleek and silver, he stitched the calm surface of the ocean with dives and leaps. He saw her watching, sprang from the water and landed like a single, errant wave. He was beautifully muscled, with a shock of silver hair, a chevron of gills at his neck and a fin concertinaed against his spine. He sat at the table and drew his thighs to his chest, hugged his shins and regarded Abbie over his knees.

He smiled. 'Are you requiring a guide?'

'I'm here on business, not pleasure.'

'Are you an artist, here for the Contest? Would you like me to take your proposal to the judges?'

'No,' she said, 'and no . . .'

The boy opened his gills and shunted air, as if in derision. 'Immortality is the prize. Did you know that? I can't claim to be an artist, but come the Contest I'll be diving.'

Abbie nodded politely. She had heard that the caste of immortals occasionally sponsored artistic contests, offering increased longevity for the artists they deemed the finest. Omegas themselves could not create, and she wondered if the sponsorship was an act of amendment for their inability.

The fish-boy cocked his head prettily. 'Then why are you here?'

'As I said, on business.'

He frowned and scanned the exposed areas of her flesh for sign of augmentations. 'Your facility?'

She lifted her dark hair to reveal the plates at the base of her skull. 'I'm a Pilot. I've been hired by the artist, Wellard.'

His large eyes registered surprise. 'Wellard? Mad Wellard, the Primitivist?'

'You know his work?'

'His *work*?' The fish-boy flung back his head in a burst of raucous laughter. 'He's a Primitivist! A true primitive – un-Altered, un-Augmented . . .'

Abbie disliked his arrogance. 'The work by him that I've seen – his early work – communicates true emotions, unlike so much art today, clinical, emotionless, without soul.'

He rejoined: 'Do you understand today's art?'

'Should one have to *understand* art to appreciate it?'

'Today's art is a science, for the literate. Surely, as an Augmented . . .?'

She began to explain that her facility did not endow her with increased intellection, and in doing so cursed herself for sounding as though she were making excuses for her lack of knowledge.

'Be careful with Wellard,' the fish-boy warned. 'The rumour is that he keeps his daughter locked in a dome on his island.'

Abbie glanced at her watch. Wellard was late.

The fish-boy smiled intuitively. 'Wellard drinks heavily,' he informed her. 'You'll probably have to make your own way there.'

He looked out to sea. 'Behold, the opening ceremony . . .' His large eyes regarded the darkening sky with fascination. 'See – the Supra-sapiens.'

These beings – Abbie had never actually seen one before, merely heard stories – were one step beyond the Omegas. They had divested themselves of their physical forms and assumed identities of pure energy. They were sparkling points of light as capricious as the wind, beholden to no one and to no state or planet.

'Tonight they dance for the Omegas,' the fish-boy breathed. 'Aren't they . . . aren't they *beautiful*?'

They choreographed intricate manœuvres against the indigo heavens. Never still, they trailed images of themselves through the night like comets' tails. Abbie understood that the performance was more than just a display of calculated aesthetics, which at first was all she had assumed it to be. According to one commentator, the trajectories of the dozen Supra-sapiens were, taken in total, the representational maths of universal quantum verities.

Then the lights disappeared along every point of the compass, streaking away around the curves of the planet, and their exit presaged the fall of night and the appearance of the Core stars overhead like the brilliant spread of a chandelier.

Wellard arrived one hour later.

He approached in his launch from his private island, one of the chain that curved away into the distance like the vertebrae of some great fossilized saurian. He moored his vessel at the end of the jetty, then walked towards the boulevard and paused half-way, hands on hips, a sturdy and intimidating silhouette against the starfield. Or was it Abbie alone who divined the threat in his posture as he gazed down at the assembled artists? His arrival had occasioned a murmur of comment.

'From the sublime,' the fish-boy said, 'to the ridiculous.'

Abbie stood. 'I must go.'

'If you do decide that you need anything . . .' He held up a communicator on his wrist and gave his code.

Abbie made her way to the jetty. She was aware, as she

approached Wellard over the creaking boards of the pier, that she was the centre of attention. It had the effect of making her meeting with the artist all the more fraught.

He glared at her. 'Are you the Pilot?' It was almost a roar.

She nodded, unable to look him in the eye. He was squat and powerful, and seemed to emanate a raw animal emotion – in this case animosity – unchecked by the sophistication of alteration or augmentation.

'I requested a male Pilot.'

'I was allotted the job' – which was a lie; she had bribed her superior to give her the commission – 'I assure you that I can do what you want just as well as—'

'I've no doubt,' he said. His misogyny, according to rumour, had increased during his self-imposed exile on the planet.

He nodded grudgingly. 'Very well . . .'

As she followed him back to the launch and climbed in beside him, Abbie wondered whether her physical revulsion of Wellard was merely because he was a primitive.

The engine fired, lifted the launch and shot them away from the jetty on a long curve paralleling the diminishing islands of the archipelago. Wellard sat at the tiller, staring ahead. In marked contrast to the artists on the boulevard, he was dishevelled and shabbily dressed. It was as if he affected the bohemian persona of an artist from myth to score some personal point against those he regarded as no more than artisans and technicians. His forearms scintillated with crystal dust, like gauntlets, and his square, ruddy face was streaked with belligerent dabs of war-paint. Abbie knew that he was almost sixty, though he appeared older.

Wellard's studio and living quarters comprised three domes suspended over the ocean on a series of cantilevers. He ran the launch aground on a beach beneath the projecting hemisphere of the first dome, and led the way to a spiral staircase which accessed the flat underside.

Abbie was not prepared for the sight of the work of art which rose from the deck to the apex of the studio. The hologram stood perhaps five metres high, a light-sculpture of a beautiful woman. She stood demure and at ease, a Greek Goddess in a flowing gown. Other pieces littered the room, but none so stunning as the raven-haired Mediterranean beauty.

'My wife,' Wellard said briefly. 'She died almost thirty years ago, giving birth to my daughter. We were living in the wilds of Benson's Landfall at the time, in retreat from contemporary trends.' He stopped himself and regarded Abbie, as if resentful at having imparted this information.

She moved around the room, laying hands on crystals, regarding light sculptures. He even worked in the ancient medium of oils on canvas. He watched her from the exit to the second dome, as if impatient to usher her away. 'Don't bother telling me what you think – I already know. You Augmented are all the same. You have no appreciation of the truth of the work by the artists you call Primitivists.'

It was a moment before she could bring herself to reply. She found his attitude of injured pride rather pathetic, like a chided child convinced of his worth. She sought to subdue him with praise.

'On the contrary, I find your work very powerful. I'm moved by it. Few artists these days are so honest, so open – few would admit to their faults and weaknesses. Your guilt is very apparent.'

'Art is the communication of true emotion.' He regarded her with what might have been new respect, hedged with suspicion. 'Regret and guilt constitute so much of my past. Perhaps by trying to come to terms with the guilt through my work I might cure myself—'

'To find you can no longer create?'

He gave a grudging smile. 'Isn't all art a striving for an elusive cure?'

She gazed around at the work in progress and tried to calculate the hours invested in creation. She gestured. 'Don't you ever feel like . . . like giving in?'

His regard of her changed; from wary respect, his eyes showed hostility. He became businesslike. 'I am employing you not to ask questions, but to follow my orders to the letter. What I will be asking of you over the next day or so is highly unconventional.'

She was surprised. 'Piloting?'

'And more. But we'll discuss this later. I will pay you well to undertake my instructions, but you can resign if you so wish.'

Abbie smiled, hoping her trepidation was not obvious.

'You must be tired. I'll show you to your room. Tomorrow,' he went on, 'you will meet my daughter.'

Abbie smiled again, conscious of her heartbeat.

She awoke the following morning to dazzling sunlight. She had slept well and without interruption, and it was a while before it came to her where she was and what she was doing here.

She showered, found her gown and stood before the clear curve of the dome. She slid open a panel and leaned out, and the beauty of the view was some compensation for her anxiety. In the foreground, below her dome, was Wellard's studio; projecting from it was a semi-circular patio like a stage, directly above the sea. Across the bright blue waters, the next island in the chain was a verdant knoll dotted with residential domes. The sun burned low on the horizon.

As she gazed down, Wellard stepped onto the patio. He was barefoot, wearing only a shapeless pair of trousers.

Abbie was about to wave in greeting, but something about his attitude stopped her: he was talking to himself and making wild, angry gestures as if drunk. He leaned over the palisade that encompassed the patio, shook his fist at the sea and shouted something incomprehensible. From a tray on a table beside him he picked up something wet and red and dropped it over the rail. He followed it with another strip of what Abbie took to be meat. This and Wellard's semi-nakedness filled her with revulsion.

As she watched the meat shimmer through the clear blue depths, it was overtaken on the way up by a chain of dancing bubbles. They broke the surface, followed by others. Dimly she made out a dark shape, rising; foreshortened at this angle, it broke the surface and torpedoed towards the overhanging deck. Only when it stood on its tail, its teeth snapping at the strip of meat Wellard held in his fist, was she aware of its full size. It was about five metres long and jet black, with the hydrodynamics of a shark and a mouth perhaps a metre wide. The teeth snapped shut on the meat and the monster backflipped gracefully into the sea. It circled and prepared to launch itself again. Wellard was laughing like a maniac, leaning out over the ocean with another length of meat.

'Soon!' he cried, as the shark-thing rose, hung in suspension at the zenith of its climb, snapped and backflipped. 'Soon, you will have your way. Be patient!'

The meat consumed, Wellard turned and made his way unsteadily back into the studio. Abbie ducked out of sight.

She jumped as the chime sounded and Wellard's voice paged her. 'Are you awake? Would you care to join me on the patio?'

She found the speaker and, controlling the tremor in her voice, answered that she would be down right away.

*

'It's been light for a good two hours!' Wellard greeted her. 'I've been up since dawn. I always do my best work before breakfast.' He waved for her to be seated. He had started his meal already. The table was piled with fruit, bread and cheese. Wellard drank from an oversized goblet; he was more than a little tipsy.

'You've been working today?' She thought it wise not to mention the episode with the sea monster.

He winked at her enigmatically. 'Just putting the finishing touches to a little project.'

As they ate, Wellard expounded on the history of Nea Kikládhes, its discovery and subsequent exploration by the telenauts, and how it became the haunt of the galaxy's richest artists.

Abbie listened politely, sipping fruit juice and taking small bites of honeyed bread. Wellard had changed from the sombre, embittered artist of last night; he was animated now, almost excited. She wondered how much this transformation was due to the wine, how much to a residual elation from his encounter with the shark-thing.

She became aware that he had been staring at her for a time in silence. She looked up and saw that his gaze was fixed on her forehead just below the hairline.

'I didn't see that last night,' he said.

'Oh.' She raised a hand to the tattoo.

He smiled tipsily. 'I'm sorry – I don't keep up with the latest Augmented shorthand.' His tone was sarcastic. 'But doesn't that denote a second body?'

Abbie nodded, watching him.

'I must admit . . . to a Primitivist, the thought of having a second body – I mean, not content with your first . . . I find it rather amusing . . . and pathetic.'

'To many an Augmented out there in the real world,' she said, 'your reactionary attitude would be considered pathetic. Bodychange is established practice, Mr Wellard.

This,' she gestured from head to foot, 'is a somatic simulation.'

He was staring. 'You're a computer?'

'I'm wholly biological, I assure you.'

He shook his head. 'Who were you before . . . before the change?'

'The same person I am now, of course. All that is different is the body and the name.'

'But *why* did you change?' He seemed to find it hard to believe that anyone should want to discard the body with which they were born. 'Were you diseased?'

She shook her head. 'I . . . I found myself in an intolerable situation. I had to get away without being traced.'

He seemed to have sobered a little. He cleared his throat. 'I find it hard to imagine how someone so . . . so Augmented can possibly appreciate my art, as you claim to.'

'I am still human,' she replied. 'Your work speaks to me.'

They ate in silence for a while.

Abbie changed the subject. 'Do you intend to enter the Contest?'

Wellard snorted. 'As if they'd look twice at anything I submitted! And anyway, the Omegas have a bias for dramatic presentations, plays and tragedies of old.'

'I was told that immortality is the reward for the winners.'

He laughed. 'What hell! Do you really think I desire all eternity in which to contemplate and regret the deeds of my past?' He cast her a stricken look. 'And, anyway, how might I spend eternity, unable to create?'

'Immortals have no *reason* to create,' Abbie said. 'They have time to answer every question; they're no longer slaves to psychological conflict. Imagine being free of the devil that drives you . . .'

'I can imagine other ways,' he said, more to himself than

to Abbie. Then it was his turn to change the subject. 'Come. It's time for you to meet my daughter.'

Abbie followed him through the studio to the third dome, sick with apprehension.

The dead woman lay naked and very still, cocooned in a crystal catafalque above the computer system. Subdermal electrode implants showed as raised discs beneath her pale skin. She was very much like the hologram of her mother, and just as beautiful. Her chest rose and fell with measured breaths. Wellard stood beside her, stroking hair from her brow, and Abbie almost cried aloud at the poignancy of the father and daughter tableau and all it represented.

Wellard emerged from his reverie. 'Technically, Zoe is dead. This system has kept her body alive for fifteen years. Her mind is empty, blank.' He smiled. 'Thanks to the system, she is capable of limited motion.'

He hit a command key; the electrodes fired and Zoe spasmed. The contrast between the sleeping woman as she was and this helplessly jerking corpse was painful to behold. Abbie winced, turned away.

Through her fingers she watched the woman sit up, drag her legs from the catafalque and stand clumsily. She took half a dozen faltering steps, her father in close attendance. What was so tragic about this woeful parody of a marionette was that the technology at Wellard's command was over a decade old. A modern system could fit unobtrusively at the base of her skull and give her the swinging gait of a mannequin. There was such a thing as respect for the dead.

And there were Pilots . . .

Wellard returned his daughter to her resting place and glanced at Abbie. 'Well?'

'If you could leave us alone for a time . . .'

When Wellard had finally departed, after lovingly arranging his daughter's hair, Abbie approached the dead woman and stared down at her. A regime of regular, computer-assisted exercises had maintained her muscle tone, but her moribund eyes suggested a similar deterioration of mind. Abbie kissed the woman on the lips, fighting to control her emotions, and slipped into a sitting position on the floor. She reached behind her head and activated her occipital system.

The sensation was as if she had suddenly switched off her senses. She existed in a lightless limbo, unaware of her own physicality. What happened next had a perfectly rational scientific explanation, but the process always came to Abbie in the image of a dispossessed awareness (her own) floating into a vacated seat of consciousness (her subject's). She insinuated herself into the derelict neural pathways of Zoe's brain, exploring the intricate matrix of the dead woman's nervous system. She was aware of an extreme weariness, the leaden weight of a body fifteen years dead. There would be much that she would be unable to do with Zoe, and more that she would only be able to make function at a much reduced capacity. In normal circumstances her subjects were newly dead and easily manageable. Zoe would be a test of her abilities.

She opened Zoe's eyes, made out the sunlight beyond the dome as if through a fathom of ocean. With care, she flexed the right leg, then the left. She sat up, and her misted vision swung from the upper curve of the dome to the far wall. She was swamped with nausea, dizziness. She gripped the edge of the catafalque and pushed herself to her feet. Swaying, she took a tentative first step, then a second. She glanced down and noticed herself sprawled across the tiles, her eyes vellicating behind closed lids, a soft moan escaping her lips. Then she looked down at Zoe's body, the small breasts, the curving thighs, and although she wanted more than anything to cry, the dead woman's tear ducts would not oblige. She walked across the dome, her first faltering steps giving way to a more confident stride. She moved her arms, fingers and neck in the prescribed routine of rehabilitation, not unlike the precise choreography of a Balinese dancer. Sounds came to her, but distant, muffled. Likewise the sense of touch relayed objects to her as if they were wrapped in fleece. She stared at the dead woman's reflection in the dome. She opened her mouth, expelled air, then a scrap of sound. 'Hell . . . hell . . . hello. Hello. I . . . am . . . Zoe. Wellard is . . . insane.' The words came one by one, creaking from a larynx redundant for years. She experimented with complex sentences, wry observations, obscenities directed at Wellard, and then she relented: 'Wellard cannot help . . . himself. He is a victim of . . . circumstance. I am Zoe Wellard. How do you . . . do?'

She returned to the catafalque, sat carefully and lay down. She closed her eyes, allowed her awareness to drain slowly from the body.

Abbie opened her own eyes and found herself lying on the floor. She lay blinking up at the dome, disorientated at the shift back to her own body. She stood wearily, touched the Zoe's brow and wept.

She had known, when her agency had received the commission, what Wellard required, but his precise motives now, as then, were a mystery.

Wellard was seated on the patio, staring out across the ocean, when Abbie stepped from the studio and joined him. He looked up. 'Well?'

She did not realize, until she sat down opposite him, how much the transfer had drained her. She felt physically weak, emotionally unstable. She had the urge to snap: 'Well, what?' But it was obvious what he wanted to know.

'I can pilot her,' she replied. 'She can walk, talk, hear, see. I could maintain control for an hour, maybe more.' She watched him closely.

Wellard smiled, a paradoxically boyish grin on a face so rugged. 'That should be quite long enough.'

'For what?' she asked.

He reached out to the table and picked up a sheaf of paper, an antique medium appropriate to Wellard's Primitivism. He passed it to Abbie.

She leafed through the sheaf. It was an old fashioned play-script, a dialogue between two characters. She scanned the top sheet, bearing the title *Atonement*, and the opening. Time: fifteen years ago. Setting: the patio of an artist's dome, Mikonos, Earth. Dramatis personae: Benedict Wellard, an artist; Zoe Wellard, his daughter.

Wellard: The love I had for your mother was unique.

Zoe: Please, father . . .

Abbie looked up from the script and stared at Wellard.

His smile, the light in his eyes, suggested more than just enthusiasm for the entertainment he had planned. 'It is the transcription of my final meeting with my daughter. It's verbatim up to a certain point, at which I have allowed myself a degree of artistic licence. Please, read on . . .'

Abbie regarded the opening lines, a constriction in her throat, then slowly read her way through the following pages. Her heart hammered and gradually she became less aware of herself; she was wholly captivated by the words on the page as the drama unfolded its terrible logic.

She was only peripherally aware of Wellard, watching her.

She lowered the last page and stared at the artist, seeing only the tragic finale, the denouement that Wellard had fashioned to stand as testament to his overwhelming guilt.

'Well?' he smiled.

She shook her head. 'It's sick . . .'

His expression became grim. 'Whether it is sick or not does not detract from its fundamental truth. Tonight's re-enactment will bring the cycle to a close with my fitting punishment—'

'But you don't deserve . . . *this*.'

'Who are you to say what I do not deserve?' he snapped. He stood and paced to the edge of the patio, then sat side-saddle on the rail and regarded her. 'What I did fifteen years ago – and it isn't in the script – was . . . unforgivable. It brought about my daughter's demise and plagued me ever since.'

Abbie sat without moving, shocked at the thought of the role Wellard wanted her to play. 'But even so—'

'Please, allow me to explain.' The artist drew a long breath and stared into the ocean. 'My daughter, Zoe, was a telenaut. Fifteen years ago the science was still in its initial stages – the telemass process was crude, compared with the system as we know it today. The only people who 'massed were the telenauts, and the incidence of fatalities was high. Back then, the body of a telenaut was duplicated and fired to its destination, the planet under investigation. Then the telenaut's cerebral identity was beamed after it. This way, even if the duplicated *doppelgänger* was injured or killed, the telenaut's identity could be retrieved and restored to its original body. At fifteen, Zoe was a veteran of some dozen missions to the planets of stars within a radius of twenty light years from Earth. On the occasion of our final meeting she was contemplating the commission to be 'massed here, Nea Kikládhes, then an unexplored world. No one had ever before been telemassed thousands of light years through space. It was highly dangerous, and, needless to say, I did not want her to go.'

Abbie whispered, 'You can't hold yourself responsible.'

Wellard ignored her. 'We had an argument, more or less as set down in the script. Then I did something terrible. I was desperate at the time – some might say unbalanced – though I'm not pleading this as an excuse . . . Zoe fled, vowing that she intended to take the commission and saying that she hoped she died. She was my only daughter, so much like my wife . . .' Wellard took a breath, glanced from the sea to Abbie. 'Less than one week later I heard from her private clinic in Athens that her body was await-ing collection. She had bequeathed it to me in the event of an accident. It was kept alive – if you can call it that – by a sophisticated computer system. I had her moved to my studio . . .'

'What do you think happened to her?' Abbie murmured.

The sun was beginning its long fall towards the horizon, bringing to a close the short Kikládhean day. Overhead, the Core stars were coming out. Wellard returned to his seat across the table from Abbie and smiled to himself. 'Zoe never said much about her work, but I do recall something she told me once. She said that one of the exercises involved entering the mind of a hummingbird, viewing the world through its consciousness. She told me that for the period of an hour, she *was* that humming-bird.' He shrugged. 'This appealed to my primitive imagination . . .

'A number of years after receiving my daughter's body, I learned that Nea Kikládhes was being opened up as a resort complex for artists. I had my studio duplicated and moved here with my daughter.' He poured more wine, took a mouthful and paused before continuing. 'During my first year here I used my launch to ferry provisions from the telemass station to my studio, and on every trip I was followed by a leviathan – a deep sea monster like a shark, though larger. It attacked me several times. I know it was the same monster – I once scarred its flank with an ill-aimed harpoon, and the distinguishing mark was clearly visible. It struck me as obvious,' Wellard said, staring at Abbie with total conviction, as if to forestall her incredulity, 'that, when she was beamed here fifteen years ago, the consciousness of my daughter had found itself somehow trapped in the monstrous form of the sea creature.'

Abbie wanted to laugh, and then to cry, but Wellard stared at her with frightening certitude, his knuckles white where they gripped the goblet.

He indicated the script. 'Now, you appreciate the symmetrical perfection of my final work?'

Abbie stood and moved to the rail, her back to Wellard so that he could not see her tears. Across the curve of the ocean, a sparkling troupe of Supra-sapiens performed pyrotechnic aerobatics above the largest island, entertaining the gathered artists.

'Well?' Wellard said. 'Will you take part in my little finale?'

Abbie gripped the rail. On the horizon, the will-o'-the-wisps described symbols of infinity.

She nodded. 'Very well . . . yes.'

They drank a toast, and Abbie hurriedly excused herself and retired with the script to her dome. For a long time she lay on the sunken sleeping pad, memorizing the stilted dialogue. Later she stood and walked to the clear wall of the dome, stared out across the ocean to the island on which she had arrived the night before. Lights illuminated the length of the sea-front boulevard. The Supra-sapiens played – or communicated universal verities, meaningless to her – in the darkening sky. Abbie reached beneath her hair, opened the communication channel and arranged to meet the fish-boy. Then she returned to the sleeping pad and with a stylus struck out Wellard's original title and replaced it with her own: *Redemption*. Then she turned to the final pages, where the scenario diverged from the original dialogue, and rewrote the ending to her own satisfaction.

Later, when the fish-boy emerged from the sea and sat awaiting her on a rock, the starlight illuminating his wet nakedness like some fabulous figure from myth, Abbie left the dome and joined him. She passed him the revised dialogue, along with her instructions, and he placed the script in his pouch and dived gracefully into the sea.

Abbie returned to the dome and lay down, her pulse accelerated. Overhead the stars burned with a rhythmic pulse. She could almost hypnotize herself, watching them.

Beside her, the speaker crackled. 'Abbie . . . are you ready to begin?'

The transference was easier this time, the precincts of Zoe's sensorium no longer unfamiliar territory. Also she could control the body with relative facility, co-ordinate the movement of the limbs so that Zoe could perform with grace. She wore an ankle-length gown and facial cosmetics, as prescribed in the script; she presented to the world a calm composure, a neutral expression and a steady gaze. Inside, though, Abbie was numbed with fear. She had memorized Wellard's script, but it was not the recall of the lines that worried her so much as his reactions to her amendments. The satisfactory outcome of the imminent drama depended wholly on her delivery, on the degree to which she could convince him.

She walked Zoe through the studio; it was in darkness, but the hologram of Zoe's mother was illuminated, and had been turned to overlook the performance area of the patio.

Abbie stepped through the sliding door. The patio was bathed in silver brilliance, surrounded by the night. She thought she could see the occasional flicker of a Suprasapien, but could not be sure: her attention was wholly taken by the dominant figure of Benedict Wellard, centre stage.

He was attired in a smart grey suit, and with his hair combed back he presented a substantially altered figure to the dishevelled bohemian of that afternoon. The sight of him like this caused Abbie's pulse to race. She took up her position, stage left, staring out into the night with her back to him, awaiting his opening line.

There was a pause before the performance began. Then:

'The love I had for your mother was unique.'

The words caught in her throat. She managed, 'Father, please . . .'

'I don't think I've mentioned this to you before.'

'Yes you have – many times.'

'I must tell you how we met.'

Abbie turned Zoe's sluggish corpse. 'Father!'

Wellard smiled. 'It was at the Saharan artists' colony of Sapphire Oasis . . .'

He proceeded to describe that first meeting, his initial infatuation, which turned in time to love and respect. Cornelia Bethany was an accomplished artist, a Primitivist like Wellard. They shared similar techniques, theories. They became inseparable. Wellard recounted all this, and announced with a reflective smile that one month later they were married.

Abbie spoke her lines: 'I've heard this so many times before!'

'One more time will do you no harm.'

'*No!* I've heard enough.' She raised her hands to her ears in histrionic denial of his words. He continued, regardless.

'For two years we worked together on joint projects.'

He described their work, how they planned to construct Primitivist crystals and holograms, synthesized from their unique harmonic perspective, the like of which the world had never seen before. With their creations they hoped to storm the insular sensibilities of the critics, who favoured the clinical minimalist work of Augmented and Altered artists. Their aim was to bring humanism back to art.

'It was ironic that your conception came at the very height of our creativity . . .' Wellard continued, with a trace of sarcasm. 'We planned great things for you. We would educate you ourselves, and in time you would join us in a Primitivist triumvirate. We found a remote colony world, set up a studio and awaited the joyous day. You know the rest.'

'I know I'm a disappointment to you, Father.'

'I never really recovered after your mother's death – but I did regain my senses sufficiently to know what I wanted for you. I trained you in all the artistic techniques . . . You had a fine future ahead of you.'

'Some would say that I still have.'

'As a *telenaut*!' He almost spat the word. 'Did I tell you that your mother detested Augmented humans?'

'Often—'

'She considered their mechanization a denial of human sensibilities. I agreed with her, and still do.'

Wellard claimed that since her Augmentation she had become heartless – more, soulless. He told her that she had thoughts for no one but herself.

Abbie rejoined with the line that she had grown up so much under his influence that it was inevitable she assumed his selfishness. She cried that she had to make her own decisions, even if those decisions were the result of mere defiance.

Wellard crossed the patio and paused before her. 'I don't want you to accept this latest commission.' He was trembling with emotion.

She stared at him. 'My life is my own!'

'But think of the danger.'

Abbie, through Zoe's eyes, saw the empty meat-tray on the table.

Wellard reached out and cupped her tear-streaked cheek. 'I love you too much to lose you, Zoe.'

His other hand stroked her hair, and the light of helplessness in his eyes told Abbie that he was no longer acting, that he was back on the patio of his studio, fifteen years ago, with his daughter in his arms.

'You're so much like your mother, Zoe.'

He broke away and stared into the darkened sea.

Beyond the patio, Abbie could hear the surge and splash of the leviathan as it whiplashed from the ocean. She stared at Wellard as he cried out in self-disgust.

'Zoe!' His eyes pleaded with her to follow through the business of the script. He stood beside the rail, directly above the ocean and the thrashing leviathan, awaiting the gesture from his re-animated daughter that would avenge his treatment of her and bring about the end of his guilt.

This was where the re-enactment diverged from Wellard's scenario.

Abbie said, 'You don't deserve to die!'

Behind Wellard, the shark-thing leapt and snapped.

'I forgive you – can you hear me?' Abbie cried. 'You're forgiven!'

Wellard stared past his daughter's eyes and addressed

Abbie. 'How can you forgive me? You have no idea what happened! Push me!'

'I know,' Abbie said. 'You attacked me, beat me until I was half-conscious and then raped me, calling me all the while by my mother's name. You almost killed me – perhaps maybe you intended to, to avenge my birth. That's why I left.'

He shook his head. 'Abbie? How can you know this? Who are you?'

Abbie gathered herself. 'I'm your daughter – Zoe!' she cried, and all the hurt and frustration she had suppressed for years now overwhelmed her. 'When I left that night I vowed to avenge you. I thought at first that I *would* accept the commission, to spite you – and I hoped that I'd be killed. Then I had a better idea. I bought a somatic simulation from an Augmented mart in Cairo, had myself downloaded and my emptied body returned to you. For years it delighted me to think of your grief . . .'

'Zoe . . . is it really you?' He reached out feebly. 'Why did you come here?'

She stared at him. 'I came back to kill you. I wanted *true* revenge.'

He raised his arms in a gesture of defeat. 'Then why not take it?'

'Because I saw your art. I saw how much you suffered, how guilty you were and how much you regretted doing what you did. Then I read the script . . . How could I bring myself to kill you when you had already decided to kill yourself?'

She finished her dialogue and held out her arms to him, and the performance was complete.

Lasers bloomed in the darkness above the dome, and Supra-sapiens materialized and turned tight spirals of delight. An open air-car bearing six Omegas hovered above the patio rail. A venerable immortal stood, smiled at Zoe and held out a hand. In sombre tones he communicated their judgement, and bade Zoe and her father step aboard.

Abbie allowed herself to more fully accommodate her body of old, felt the last tenuous link with her somatic simulation break like a silken thread. She inclined her head and stepped towards the air-car. Then she turned and held out her arms to her father – who was standing mute in the cone of a spotlight, between one life and the next – and awaited his decision.

The Art of Acceptance

I curled in the window and watched the rain come down in the darkened boulevard. It was the graveyard shift in Paris for the next thirty days, party-time for suicides and psychopaths. Next month we were scheduled a classic spring, and Gay Paree would be thronged with lovers and poets and artists – and I'd do my best to hibernate until night came round again.

Dan sat lotus on the battered, legless chesterfield. Leads fell from the lumbar-socket under his shirt, and a bootleg tantric-tape zipped ersatz kundalini up his spinal column. He'd told me to go home at midnight, but I liked being around him, and anyway I had to be on hand in case the fountain of pleasure hit jackpot and blew the chakra in his cerebellum. I'd told him he was playing Tibetan roulette with his meatball – bootleg tapes had scoured the skulls of many a novice – but Dan just laughed and said he was doing it all for me. Which he was, in a way, but I still didn't like it.

When I got bored I tidied the office, stacked Zen vids, cleared away *tankas* and Confucian self-improving tracts. Then I felt-tipped *mahayanan* aphorisms backwards on his forehead, the only part of his face free from beard and hair, and inscribed his arms and palms with that old number, 'He who has everything has little, he who has nothing has much,' just to show him what I thought of all this transcendental malarkey.

I was getting bored again when the building began to

shake and flakes of paint snowed from the ceiling. The clanking downchute signalled the approach of a customer.

I yanked the jack from his socket and winced in anticipation of his wrath. He jerked once at the disconnection, then slumped. 'Shit, Phuong.'

'Visitor,' I said. I prised open his eye and peered in like a horse-doctor. 'Jesus, you look wrecked.'

He was all hair, bloodshot eyes and bad temper. I pulled him to the desk and sat him in the swivel chair, combing my fingers through his curls and arranging the collar of his sweat-soaked khaki shirt. The adage on his brow accused me, but there was no time to remove it – footsteps sounded along the corridor. 'Pull yourself together, Dan. We need the cash.'

I switched on the desk-lamp, made sure my *cheongsam* was buttoned all the way up, and sat in the shadows by the wall.

She strode in without knocking. I like style – being possessed of none of it myself – and everything, from her entry to the way she crossed her legs and lighted a cigarillo, whispered sophistication.

'Leferve?' she enquired, blowing smoke.

'How can I be of service?' It was his usual line. I was pleased to see that her elegance left him unaffected; he was doing his best to disdain all things physical.

Even so, we needed this commission.

The woman relit her cigarillo and fanned the offending smoke. It crossed my mind that all this was an act.

She was white, but throwback African genes gave her face the exaggerated length and beauty of the Masai. The lasered perfection of her features was familiar, too. I was sure, then, that I'd seen her somewhere before.

'You charge by the hour?'

'Five hundred dollars per.'

She nodded. If she was aware of the ridiculous scrawl on

his forehead she did not lose her cool and show surprise. She wore a silver lamé mackintosh, belted at the waist, and when she leaned forward to deposit ash in the tray on the desk, with a single tap of a long-nailed finger, the lapels buckled outwards to reveal tanned chest and the white sickle scars of a double mastectomy, the latest thing in body fashion.

'I want to hire you for one hour, for which I will pay you twenty-five thousand dollars.'

'I'm not an assassin,' Dan said.

'I assure you that I want no one killed.'

'Then what *do* you want?' He reached out to the chess-board on the desk and pushed white bishop to queen's four: *follow her.*

'That was a rash move, Leferve.' She advanced a pawn, and smiled.

Dan toppled his king. 'Now, perhaps you could supply me with a few details. Who are you, and what kind of work do you have in mind?'

She glanced around the office. 'This is hardly the place to do business. Perhaps we can discuss these points later, over lunch.'

Below the level of the desk, Dan gestured for me to go. He saw the writing on his arm and, instead of showing anger, he smiled to himself at this childish exhibition of my affection and concern.

I slipped from the office without the woman noticing me.

I took the downchute to the boulevard, ran through the rain and rode up the outside of the opposite towerpile to the flier rank. I found Claude and slipped in beside him. Claude was a boosted-chimp, an ex-spacer with the Canterbury Line, and in his retirement he piloted a taxi flier part time. He sat back in the seat with his fingers laced behind his bulky occipital console and his feet gripping the steering wheel. 'Action, Phuong?'

'When it shifts, follow that flier.'

I pointed across the gap to the landing stage. The woman's flier was an ugly Soviet Zil, two tons of armoured, bullet-proof tank. No wonder the building had quaked when she landed. A uniformed chauffeur stood on the edge of the building and stared out at the lit night.

Three minutes later the woman emerged and strode across the landing stage. The chauffeur hurried to open the door and the woman slipped inside.

The Zil fired its 'aft jets, and I experienced the sudden pang of physical pain and mental torture that always hit me whenever I forgot to close my eyes. Even the *sound* of burners filled me with nausea.

I was fifteen when I took a short cut through a rank of fliers and the sudden ignition of twin Mitsubishi 500s roasted me alive. Only the skill of the surgeons and my parents' life-savings had saved my life and financed the reconstruction of my face so that it was as pretty as the rest of my body was hideous. I'd been rushing to meet a young Arab I thought I loved. He'd dropped me not long after.

The Zil lifted ponderously and inched out over the boulevard; the jets fired again and it banked with sudden speed into an air-lane, heading north.

'Easy does it, Claude.'

He flipped switches and growled in Breton to his on-board computer, and we lifted. He steered barefoot and I was forced into the cushioned seat as we accelerated in pursuit.

Traffic was light, which had its advantages: although we had to keep our distance to remain inconspicuous, the Zil was easy to trace in the empty Paris sky. Lights spangled the city far below, but against the darkened dome our quarry's burners glowed red like devils' eyes.

Three minutes later the flier swooped from the air-lane and banked around the silvered bends of the Seine. Claude touched my hand and pointed to one o'clock. A small air-car flew alongside the Zil in a parallel lane. 'Been following her since we took off,' he told me.

The Zil decelerated and went down behind the high iron railings of a riverside mansion. 'Passy,' Claude commented. 'Expensive. What now?'

The one-man flier, having followed the woman to base, banked and fired off across Paris.

'Move in, Claude. And when you've dropped me, follow that flier. I want everything you can get on it, OK?'

The mansion was a large square building as old as the revolution. Antiquity, though, was not its most notable feature. Even from a distance of five hundred metres I recognized the colony world flora that was fast becoming the latest sensation with the hopelessly rich.

'Now cut the jets and take us in low. I'm going to jump.'

'Phuong—'

'Do as I say!'

He curled his lips and cut the flier across the corner of the extensive grounds at a height of ten metres. I swung the door open, picked my spot and jumped.

I landed bull's-eye in a fungoid growth like a giant marshmallow. I bounced, rolled to the edge and fell from a height of a couple of metres, landing on my backside and jarring my spine.

I was in a xeno-biological jungle. Through a lattice of vines and lianas I made out the lit windows of the mansion. I picked myself up and began hacking a path through the alien salad. It was hard to imagine I was on the banks of the Seine. I might have been an intrepid explorer trekking through the sweltering tropics of Delta Pavonis IV.

Then I came to the lawn before the mansion and saw the smallship, sitting inside a red-and-white striped, open-ended marquee. The ship was a rusty, ex-Indian Navy cargo ferry, a vintage antique at home in the alien environment of the garden. I recognized its type from the days of my childhood, when I'd skipped college and spent hours at the Orly star terminal; the reversed swastikas and hooked Hindi script brought back a flood of memories. I knew the structural schematics of the ferry inside out, and I was tempted to fulfil an old ambition by boarding the ship through the dorsal escape chute. But I resisted the urge.

Instead I sprinted across the lawn to a long veranda and climbed aboard. I crept along the wall of the mansion, came to a lit window and peered inside. The room was empty. I moved on to the next window and found the woman.

She stood with her back against the far wall, holding a drink in a long-stemmed glass. She'd changed her mac for a gown, cut low to reveal the scars of her fashionable mutilation. It struck me as sacrilege, like the desecration of a work of art.

She was discussing the merits of various restaurants with someone on a vidscreen. I sat with my back against the brickwork and listened in for, perhaps, ten minutes, at the end of which I was none the wiser as to the identity of the woman – though I did know which restaurants to patronize next time I had five hundred dollars to blow.

I was thinking about quitting the scene when I noticed a quick shadow beyond the light shed by the room. I thought I recognized the shape of the uniformed chauffeur. I jumped up and ran, but I was too slow. He hit me with a neural incapacitator. I jerked once and blacked out.

When I came to my senses I found myself staring at a moving strip of parquet tiling, and felt a strong arm encircling my waist. The chauffeur's jackboots marched at the periphery of my vision. I was being carried through the mansion.

I put up a feeble struggle, kicked out and yelled at him to put me down. We came to a large polished door and he used my head to push it open, then marched in with me under his arm like a prize.

'And . . . what *have* we got here?' the woman exclaimed.

'I found her on the veranda.'

He stood me upright and gripped my elbow, and I played the idiot. I babbled in Cambodian and made as if stuffing an invisible club sandwich into my mouth with both hands.

The woman glanced at the chauffeur. 'I do believe the girl is hungry.'

I nodded. '*Bouffe, merci, mademoiselle*'

Then I saw the pix on the wall behind her.

There were perhaps a hundred of them, all depicting the same woman, close-ups and stills from old films and others of her accepting awards – small, golden figures with bald heads – framed and displayed in a monomaniacal exhibition of vanity. I thought I recognized the woman in those shots, though the face was subtly different, the planes of her cheeks altered by cosmetics to conform to some bygone ideal of beauty. Also – but this was ridiculous – the woman on the wall seemed *older* than the woman who stood before me.

She saw the scars on my neck that the collar failed to hide. She reached out, and I pulled my head away. Her lips described a moue, as if to calm a frightened animal, and she unfastened the top three buttons of my *cheongsam*.

She stared at me. I felt the weight of pity in her eyes that I came to understand only later – at the time I hated her for it. The usual reaction to my deformity was horror or derision, and I could handle that. But pity was rare, and I could not take pity from someone so beautiful.

She said in a whisper, 'Take her away.' And, before I could dive at her, the chauffeur dragged me from the silent room and frogmarched me through the mansion. I was holding back my tears as we hurried outside and through the grounds. He opened a pair of wrought iron gates, pushed me to the sidewalk and kicked me in the midriff. I gasped for breath and closed my eyes as his footsteps receded and the gate squeaked shut. Then, painfully, I pulled myself to my feet, fumbled with the buttons at my chest and limped back to the main drag.

I knew the woman. I'd seen her many, many times before.

That same face . . .

Her poise, the way she had of making her every movement a unique performance.

Stephanie Etteridge.

But that was impossible, of course.

Dan was out when I got back. I left the lights off, swung the Batan II terminal from the ceiling and dialled the catalogue of classic Etteridge movies. I sent out for a meal, sat back in the flickering luminescence of the screen and tried not to feel sorry for myself.

For the next hour I ate dim sum and noodles and stared at a soporific succession of dated entertainments. Even in the better films the acting was stylized, the form limited. At the end of every scene I found myself reaching for the participation-bar on the keyboard, only to be flashed the message that I was watching a pre-modern film and that viewer participation was impossible. So I sat back and fumed and watched the story-line go its unalterable way.

There was no doubting that, despite the limitations of the form, Stephanie Etteridge had something special. If I could suspend comparison between her movies and the holographic, computerized participation dramas of today, I had to admit that Etteridge had a certain star quality, a charismatic presence.

When I'd seen enough, I returned to the main menu and called up *The Life of Stephanie Etteridge*, a eulogistic documentary made only two years ago.

It was the usual life of a movie star; there was the regular quota of marriages and affairs, drug addictions and suicide attempts; low points when her performances were below standard and the fickle public switched allegiance for a time to some parvenue starlet with good looks and better publicity – and high points when she fought back from cocaine addiction, the death of a husband and universal unpopularity to carry off three successive Oscars in films the critics came to hail as classics.

And then the final tragedy.

The film industry died a death, overnight – a Paris 'night', that is. In one month the studios in Hollywood, Bombay, Rio and Sydney shut up shop, and the stars found themselves redundant. In Geneva, a cartel of computer-wizards developed Inter-Active computer-simulated holo-graphics, and actors, directors, script-writers were a thing of the past, superseded by the all-powerful Programmer. A dozen or so mega-stars were paid retainers so that their personas could be used to give Joe public familiar, reassur-ing faces to see them through the period of transition – until a whole new pantheon of computer-generated screen Gods was invented for mass worship. Etteridge was one of these tide-over stars, which was how I recognized her face; I'd seen many 'Etteridge' Inter-Active dramas as a kid. But it didn't take a degree in psychology to read between the lines of the documentary and realize that lending your face to what was little more than a cartoon character was no compensation for the denial of stardom.

The documentary didn't dwell on the personal tragedy, of course; the last scene showed her marriage to an Italian surgeon, and while the credits rolled a voice-over reported that Stephanie Etteridge had made her last film in '30 and thereafter retired to a secluded villa in the South of France.

I was rerunning that last film when Dan came back.

He'd washed and changed; he wore a smart, side-fastening blue suit with a high collar. I preferred him in casuals – but perhaps that was because I knew where he was going.

'You dining with that woman, Dan?' I asked.

He nodded. 'The Gastrodome at twelve.'

'I wish you wouldn't,' I whispered, and I was unable to tell whether I was jealous, or scared at what the woman might want Dan to do.

'Like you said earlier, we need the dollars.' He mussed my hair. 'Did you find out who she is?'

I told him that I'd followed her to a mansion on the left bank, but I said nothing about my capture.

'There were tons of blown-up stills on the walls,' I said, 'all of the old film actress Stephanie Etteridge. I know you're going to call me dumb, but the resemblance is remarkable. Not only her face, but the way she moves. Look . . .'

I turned the screen to him while Etteridge played the spurned lover with a bravura performance of venom and spite. 'Recognize?'

He leaned close and whispered in my ear. 'You're dumb.'

'I know, I know. But you must admit, the resemblance . . .'

Dan nodded. 'OK, the woman does look like Etteridge. But that film's what . . .? Thirty years old? I'd say that Etteridge was about forty there. That'd make her seventy now . . . Are you trying to tell me that the woman we saw here today was that old?'

'But why all the pictures?'

He shrugged. 'Beats me. Perhaps she's the daughter of the actress. Or a fan. Or some fruit cake who thinks she's Etteridge. Have you accessed her? A hundred to one you'll find her dead.'

So I turned back to the Batan and called up the information on Stephanie Katerina Etteridge. We scanned her life story in cold, bureaucratic fact. Date of birth, education, professional status, the four marriages, her involvement with an American businessman jailed for an unspecified misdemeanour a matter of days before they were due to marry – though the documentary had said nothing about this. And her death . . .?

I threw the nearest thing to hand – a vid cartridge – at Dan. 'You owe me!'

He fielded the cartridge and waved it. 'OK, so she's still alive – a crotchety old dame somewhere living on caviare and memories. She's seventy, Phuong . . .'

I turned away in a huff.

Dan readied the tape on the desk. He slipped a small mic into his pocket so that I'd be able to monitor his conversation with the woman over dinner.

'I'll catch you later.'

I came out of my sulk. 'Dan, take care. OK?'

I ran to the door and tried to pull him to me, but he stiffened and kissed the top of my head as if I were a kid. Despite all the Zen he'd been pumping into his skull, he still could not accept me. From needing to show affection, my feelings polarized and I wanted suddenly to strike him, to hurt him as much as he hurt me. He murmured goodbye and took the downchute to the boulevard.

*

Two years ago Dan was an Engineman with the Javelin Line, a spacer who mind-pushed bigships through the *nada*-continuum. Then he got scared; the ineffable union with the infinite, with Nirvana, that all Enginemen attained when they fluxed, was draining reality of meaning and leaving him strung out and crazy and in need of constant flux oblivion. He knew that if he went on fluxing for much longer he'd end up dead. So he did the brave thing and got out and started a third-rate investigative agency in Montparnasse. He advertised for an assistant to do the legwork, and I got the job.

We got along fine for weeks, even though I was evasive and distant and didn't let him get too close. Then as I got to know him better I began to believe that we were both disabled, and that if I could accept the state of his head, then perhaps he could come to some acceptance of my body.

One night he asked me back to his place, and like a fool I nodded yes. The usual scene, as far as I could gather from the tapes I'd watched: soft light, music, wine . . . And after a bottle of Chianti I found myself close to him. His fingers mimed the shape of my face, centimetres away; it was as if he had difficulty believing my beauty and was afraid to let his fingertips discover a lie. But it was no lie, just reconstructed osseous underlay and synthi-flesh done with the touch of an artist. We kissed. He fumbled my buttons and I went for his zip, meaning to get him with my mouth before he discovered my secret. I didn't make it. He touched me where my right breast should have been, then ripped open my bodice. He gagged and tipped me to the floor, strode to the window and stared out while I gathered my stuff and ran.

I stayed away for weeks, until he came for me and apologized. I returned to the office and we began again from the beginning, and it was as if we were closer, having shared our secrets – though never, of course, close enough.

Soon after that night at his place he began experimenting. He claimed that he was doing it for me. By embracing illegal skull-tapes, second-hand Buddhism and the *Bardo Thodol* rewritten for the twenty-first century, he was attempting to come to some acceptance of my disfigurement. But he was also doing it for himself; he wanted the thrill of Nirvana without the threat of dependence.

Now I stared at the mystical junk that littered the desk and the chesterfield: the pamphlets, the mandalas, the meditation vids and bootleg tapes. In a rage I picked up a great drift of the stuff and threw it the length of the room. When the desk and chesterfield were cleared, and my anger was still not exhausted, I ran across the office, fell to my knees and pitched *tankas* and tapes, magazines and effigies of Gautama through the window. I leaned out and laughed like a fool, then rushed down into the street and stomped on the useless relics and idols of mysticism, ground them into the sidewalk and kicked the debris into the storm drain. Then, as the rain poured down around me, I sat on the kerb and cried.

Hell, *real* love rarely lasted; so what chance had our corrupted version of attraction, what chance had the relationship between a screwed up flux-junky attempting to rewire his head with bogus Buddhist tracts so that he could, in theory, ignore the physical, and someone whose body was no more than a puckered mass of raddled meat? It was unfair to both of us; it was unfair of myself to expect love and affection after so many years without hope, and it was unfair of me to keep Dan from other women who could offer him more than just companionship and a pretty face.

*

The tape was running when I returned to the office.

I lay on the chesterfield in the darkness and listened to the clink of glasses, the murmur of polite conversation. The Gastrodome was the decommissioned astrodome of an old French bigship, amputated and welded on to the Eiffel Tower. I'd been up there once, but the view had given me vertigo. Now I lay half asleep and listened to the dialogue that filled the room.

All I wanted was for Dan to refuse to work for the woman, so that he would be free from the danger of whatever it was she wanted him to do. Then, when he returned, I could tell him that I was leaving, and that this time there was nothing he could say to make me return.

'Tell me about when you worked for the Javelin Line,' the woman said. 'Is it true that in flux you experience Nirvana?'

'Some Enginemen claim that.'

'Did you?'

'Do we have to talk about this?' he said, and I knew that his hands would be trembling.

In my mind's eye I could see the woman giving an unconcerned shrug. 'Very well, but I hope you don't mind discussing your occipital implant.'

Dan: 'Why?' Suspicious.

'Because I'm interested.' Her tone was hard. 'What kind is it, Leferve?'

'Standard Sony neo-cortical implant—'

'With a dozen chips in the pre-frontal lobe, sub-cortex, cerebellum, etc?'

'You've done your homework,' Dan said. 'Why the interest?'

'When was the last time you fluxed?'

I cried out.

It took Dan aback, too. The silence stretched. Then: 'Almost two years ago . . .'

'Would you consider doing it just one more time,' she asked, 'for twenty-five thousand dollars?'

I could sense Dan's indecision.

I balled my fists and willed him to say no . . .

'I have a smallship I need taking on a short haul,' she said.

There was a brief moment of silence, then Dan spoke.

'Insystem or interstellar?'

And I yelled: 'Dan . . .'

'Neither,' the woman said. 'I want you to push the ship through the *nada*-continuum from here to Frankfurt.'

Dan laughed. 'You're mad.'

'I'm quite sane, I assure you. From A to B and back again. You'd be in the tank for about twenty, thirty minutes.'

'And the ship?'

'An ex-Indian Navy Hindustan-Tata with Rolls-Royce ion drive—'

'Crew?'

'None. Just you and me. The ship is pre-programmed with the co-ordinates. All it needs is someone to push it.'

'And I'd be wasting my time asking what all this is about?'

The woman assented. 'You'd be wasting your time. Can I take it that you want the job?'

Dan murmured something.

'Good,' she said. 'Here's my card. If you arrive at five, we'll phase out at six.'

They left the restaurant and took the downchute to the landing stage. I sat in the darkness and stared at the wall, wishing that Dan had had the strength of will to turn his back on that which had almost killed him.

I switched off the tape, then switched it on again. I couldn't face Dan and tell him that I was leaving – that way I'd end up screaming and shouting how much I hated him, which wasn't true. I'd leave a taped message to the effect that I needed a long break, and quit before he got back. I picked up the microphone.

Then the Batan chimed and Claude's big monkey face filled the screen. 'Phuong, I got the information on that flier.'

'Yeah?' My thoughts were elsewhere.

'Belongs to a guy called Lassolini – Sam Lassolini . . .'

I just shrugged.

Claude went on: 'He's a surgeon, a big noise in European bio-engineering.'

I remembered the documentary, and Etteridge's last marriage. 'Hey, wasn't he married to—?'

Claude nodded. 'That's the guy. He hit the headlines ten years ago when the film star Stephanie Etteridge left him.'

'You got his address, Claude?'

'Sure.'

'Then pick me up *tout-de-suite*.'

I thought about it.

Now why would Sam Lassolini follow the Stephanie Etteridge look-alike to her mansion in Passy . . .?

There was only one way to find out.

The de Gaulle building was the old city morgue, deserted and derelict but for the converted top floor, now a penthouse suite. Claude dropped me on the landing stage and I told him to wait. I took the downchute one floor and hiked along a corridor. I came to a pair of double doors and hit the chime. I felt suddenly conspicuous. I hadn't washed for two days, and I'd hardly had time to learn my lines.

A small Japanese butler opened the door.

'Lassolini residence?' I asked.

'The doctor sees no one without an appointment.'

'Then I'll make an appointment – for *now*.'

I tried to push past him. When he barred my way I showed him my pistol and said that if he didn't sit down and keep quiet I'd blow a hole in his head. He sat down quickly, hands in the air.

I tiptoed down a passage and came to a vast ballroom with a chequerboard floor of marble and onyx tiles, and a dozen chandeliers burning against the long Paris night outside. There was no sign of Lassolini; I would have called out, but the weight of the silence intimidated me.

I opened the first door on the right.

It took me about fifteen seconds to recognize the woman who this morning had visited the office, whom I had followed to the mansion, and who, less than thirty minutes ago, had been dining with Dan.

She was hanging by the neck and her torso had been opened with something sharp from sternum to stomach; the contents of her abdomen had spilled, and the weight of her entrails anchored her to the floor.

I heard a sound behind me and turned. A tall, Latin guy looked down on me. He wore a white suit and too much gold. I did mental arithmetic and decided that he looked good for sixty.

'Sam Lassolini?' I asked.

He didn't deny it. 'Who are you, and what do you want?'

I lifted my pistol and aimed at his chest. Next to it I hung my identification. 'Phuong Li Xian,' I said. 'I have the power of arrest.' I indicated the woman. 'Why did you do it, Lassolini?'

He looked past me at the the body and smiled. 'If I may answer a question with a question: why your interest?'

I hesitated. 'I was working on her case.'

He threw his head back and laughed.

My fist tightened on the pistol. 'I don't see what's so funny.'

He indicated another door along the hall. 'Follow me.'

He opened the door and entered the room. He turned to face me, his laughter mocking my shock.

Behind him, spread across the floor and the far wall, were the remains of what once might have been a human being. It was as if the wall and the floor had suddenly snapped shut to create a grotesque Rorschach blot of flesh and blood. The only part of the body that had survived the mutilation was the head. It sat beside Lassolini's right foot, staring at me.

It was the head of the same woman . . .

Lassolini left the room and strode to the next door. He paused on the threshold. 'My dear . . .' I stumbled after him, amenable with shock.

Another atrocity. This time the woman had been lasered into bloody chunks and arranged on plinths around the room after the fashion of Dali.

'You're mad!' I cried.

'That did occur to me, my dear. Though what you see here is not the cause or symptom of it, but an attempt to cure myself. A catharsis, if you like.'

'But . . . but which one is Stephanie Etteridge?'

'None of them is Stephanie,' he said. 'She is alive and well and living in Paris. And yet . . . all of them *were* Stephanie.'

I took control of my shock, levelled the pistol and said with determination: 'Look, Lassolini – I want answers. And if I don't get them . . .'

He bowed. 'Very well, my dear. This way – and I assure you, no more horrors.'

He strode down a long corridor. I had to run to keep up. We came to a pair of swing doors with circular portholes, and Lassolini pushed through. Another surprise: after the luxury of the ballroom, the stark and antiseptic utility of what looked like a hospital ward. Then I remembered that this place was once the city morgue.

We stopped at a line of horizontal silver tanks, and with an outstretched hand Lassolini invited me to inspect their contents.

I peered through the first frosted faceplate and made out the young, beautiful face of Stephanie Etteridge. In a daze I moved on to the next one, and the next: Etteridge, again, and again. Each tank contained a flawless replica of the actress.

I stared at him. He smiled.

'Clones . . .' I murmured, and I experienced a curious vacuum within my chest.

'Perspicacious of you, my dear.'

'But I thought the science was still in its experimental stages – I thought the Kilimanjiro Corporation had the rights . . .'

'The science *is* still in its experimental stages.' Lassolini smiled. 'And I *am* the Kilimanjiro Corporation.'

I gestured in the direction of the ritually slaughtered Etteridge clones. 'But you still murdered human beings,' I said. 'Even clones are—'

He was shaking his head. 'By no stretch of the imagination can they be considered human – as of yet. They are grown from DNA samples taken from the original Stephanie Etteridge, and their minds remain blank until the encoded identity of the subject is downloaded into them.'

'So those . . .?'

'Merely so much dead meat. But it pleased me to sacrifice Stephanie, if only in effigy. These bodies were the ones I kept in supply for the time when she aged and required her youth again.'

I looked into his youthful face. 'So both you *and* the Stephanie Etteridge out there are clones?' I was beginning to understand.

He regarded me, as if calculating how much to divulge.

'We were married for twenty years,' he said. 'When her career came to an end, and she began to show signs of age, I promised her a new lease of life – virtual immortality. Perhaps only this kept her with me for so long, until my scientists perfected the technique of cloning, and the more difficult procedure of recording and downloading individual identity from one brain to another.

'She was sixty, ten years ago, when we downloaded her into the body of her twenty-year-old clone. Then she left me, and nothing I could do or say would make her return. I had such plans! We could have toured the universe together in eternal youth . . .' He seemed to deflate at the recollection of her betrayal.

'I considered hiring an assassin to kill the man she left me for, but, as events transpired, that proved unnecessary. She divorced me, and a matter of days before she was due to marry her lover he was arrested by the German police and charged with conspiring to sabotage a European military satellite. He was jailed for life.'

He paused there and licked his lips. When he spoke next it was barely a whisper. 'You mentioned that you were on her "case"?'

'That's right.'

'Then . . . you're in contact with her?'

I was guarded. 'I might be.'

'*Then bring her to me!*' And I was shocked by the intensity of his emotion.

I glanced at the Etteridge clones, then back at the surgeon who had performed this miracle.

'I have a price,' I said.

'Name it!'

With trembling fingers I fumbled with the buttons of my *cheongsam* and revealed my body.

*

Claude was snoozing in his flier when I jumped aboard and yelled at him to take off. I checked my watch. It was five-forty. Etteridge and Dan were due to phase-out at six. We burned across Paris towards Passy.

Ten minutes later we sailed in over the Seine. Claude slowed and we cut across the corner of the Etteridge estate. I opened the hatch and prepared to jump. 'See you later, Claude.'

His reply was lost as I dived.

This time I missed the marshmallow and fell through a bush with leaves like sabres. I picked myself up, bleeding from a dozen cuts, and limped through the jungle. It was three minutes to six when I emerged from the trees, and the smallship was still berthed inside the marquee. I ducked back into the vegetation and ran along the side of the tent. Once behind it I left the cover and dodged guy ropes.

I lifted the tarpaulin wall of the tent, squirmed through the gap and ran over to the dorsal escape chute. I palmed the sensor and waited for the hatch to cycle – ten seconds, though it seemed like as many minutes. I checked my watch: one minute to go. Then the hatch slid open and I jumped inside and curled in the darkness. Above me, the computerized locking system of the interior hatch rumbled away to itself and finally opened. I pulled myself into the carpeted, semi-lit corridor. And I'd realized a childhood ambition: I was inside a smallship.

I could see along the corridor and into the bridge. Etteridge sat in a swivel-seat between the arms of a V-shaped instrument console, speaking to a soft-voiced computer. Beside her was the flux-tank, the hatch dogged and the alpha-numerics pulsing a countdown sequence. Dan was already in there.

I drew my pistol and started towards the bridge. If I could untank Dan before he fluxed . . .

Then the 'ship phased into the *nada*-continuum.

And I could not move. I was a fly in amber, a statue immobile in the gelid medium of null-space. My watch insisted that we were in there for less than ten minutes, but going by the biological clock in my head it was more like ten hours. Outside, the void of the *nada*-continuum was a featureless grey mist. I felt ill.

Then my stomach lurched, the nausea lifted, and through the viewscreen I could see the concrete expanse of a penitentiary exercise yard. We were there for less than ten seconds. I heard the hatch wheeze open, and Stephanie's cries as a prisoner ran towards the 'ship and scrambled aboard. Laser bolts ricocheted from the concrete and hissed across the skin of the 'ship. Then the hatch slammed shut and I readied myself for another dose of space sickness.

We converted, and I giggled like a lunatic. If only my younger self, the kid who'd haunted the Orly star terminal just to get a glimpse of phasing starships, could see me now: stowaway on the craziest jailbreak of all time.

Ten minutes became as many hours; time elasticated – then snapped back to normal as we re-emerged in the real world of the red-and-white striped marquee on the lawn of the riverbank mansion.

Through the viewscreen I could see Claude, waiting for me in his flier.

I ran up the corridor.

The Etteridge clone and the escapee were in each other's arms when I reached the bridge; they had time to look round and register surprise and shock before I raised my pistol and fired, sending them sprawling stunned across the deck.

When I delivered Stephanie Etteridge, Lassolini would take from me the DNA which in four years, when cloned, would be a fully grown nineteen-year-old replica of myself

– with the difference that whereas now my body was a ninety per cent mass of slurred flesh and scars, my new cloned body would be pristine, unflawed, and maybe even beautiful.

While Etteridge and her lover twitched on the deck, their motor neurone systems in temporary dysfunction, I untanked Dan. I hauled out the slide-bed, pulled the jacks from his spinal socket and occipital implant and helped him upright.

Of course, Lassolini had said nothing about what he intended to do with his ex-wife – and at the time I had hardly considered it; my mind was full of the thought that in four years I would be whole again, an attractive human being, and the shame and regret would be a thing of the past.

It never occurred to me that there would be a price to pay . . .

Now I thought of Stephanie Etteridge in the clutches of Lassolini. I imagined her dismembered corpse providing the sick surgeon with his final cathartic tableau, a sadistic arrangement of her parts exhibited beneath the chandeliers of the ballroom in the ultimate act of revenge.

Etteridge crawled across the deck to the man she had saved. She clung to him, and all I could do was stare as the tears coursed down my cheeks.

What some people will do for love . . .

I pulled Dan away from the tank. He was dazed and physically blitzed from his union with the infinite, his gaze still focused on some ineffable vision granted him in the *nada*-continuum.

'Phuong . . .?'

'Come on!' I cried, taking his weight as he stumbled legless across the bridge. I kicked open the hatch and we staggered from the smallship and out of the marquee. I had to be away from there, and fast, before I changed my mind.

Claude helped Dan into the flier. 'What about—?'

'I'm leaving her!' I sobbed. 'Just let's get out of here.'

I sat beside Dan on the back seat and closed my eyes as the burners caught and we lifted from the lawn. We banked over the Seine and Dan fell against me, his body warm and flux-spiced from the tank.

As we sped across Paris, I thought of Etteridge and her lover – and the fact that she would never realize the fate she had been spared. I wished them happiness, and gained a vicarious joy I often experience when considering people more fortunate than myself.

I assisted Dan into the darkened office and laid him out on the chesterfield. Then I sat on the edge of the cushion and stared at the tape on the desk, set up two hours ago to record my last farewell.

I picked up the microphone, switched it on and began in a whisper. 'I've enjoyed working for you, Dan. We've had some good times. But I'm getting tired of Paris – I need to see more of the world. They say Brazil's got a lot going for it. I might even take a look at Luna or Mars. They're always wanting colonists . . .' And I stopped there and thought about wiping it and just walking out. Even nothing seemed better than this bland goodbye.

Then Dan cried out and his arm snared my waist. I looked into his eyes and read his need, his fear after his confrontation with the infinite. And something more . . .

His lips moved in a whisper and, although I was unable to make out the words, I thought I knew what he wanted.

I reached out and wiped the tape, then lay on the chesterfield beside Dan and listened to his breathing and the rain falling in the boulevard outside.

The Disciples of Apollo

'I'm sorry . . .'

'How long?'

'At least six months, perhaps even as many as nine.'

'How will I know when—?'

'For two days beforehand you'll feel drowsy, lethargic.'

'And pain?'

'I can assure you that your condition is quite painless.'

'I suppose I should be thankful for small mercies.'

'There is a retreat for sufferers of the Syndrome. Because of the highly unusual nature of the disease, you are advised to spend your final weeks there. Of course, you can go before then, if you wish. Your family will be able to visit you—'

'I have no family.'

'In that case Farrow Island might be perfect.'

Between the time of diagnosis and the actual realization that he was going to die, Maitland passed through a period of disbelief. There is a difference between the intellectual knowledge of one's eventual end, and the sudden sentence of death. Grief came one morning when he awoke and knew that his awakenings were numbered, and as he watched the dawn he knew that soon the sun would rise without his continued presence to witness it; grief filled his chest with nausea and suffocated him, and he turned like a loner in a crowd for someone on whom he might unburden his anguish and regret. There was no one, and this compounded his pain. At times, in the past, Maitland had managed to convince himself that he could do without the usual human involvements that most people took for granted. Yet now, with the imminence of his extinction, he realized that no one could live – or die – without having shared in some experience of affection, even love. He cursed himself for so aloofly denying down the years the inner voice that had cried out for human contact, cursed the coward in him that had shied from the trauma of new experience with the excuse that he had existed for so long without it . . . It came to him with the intensity of a cerebral scream that now it was too late. He had no chance of finding in six months that which had eluded him for a lifetime. He would die alone, as he had lived, and whereas to live alone was easy, to die alone, with so much guilt and remorse, and yearning for a somehow *altered* past, he knew would be beyond endurance.

Then, however, he passed through this phase of anger and entered a period of passive resignation, and he saw his death as the inevitable consequence of a life lived as he had lived it. He would gain nothing from regret, he told himself; his former self was a stranger whose actions he had no way of changing. He could only accept his fate, and anticipate anything that might lie beyond. He recalled the doctor's recommendation, and made arrangements to leave.

In the following weeks Maitland said goodbye to his colleagues at the university, making the excuse that he was taking a short vacation. He sold his house and all his possessions, his books and his classical record collection. He felt a buoyant sense of relief when at last his house was empty. Since the diagnosis, he had been troubled at the thought of his material possessions remaining *in situ* after his death, mocking him; it was as if the acquisitions of a lifetime somehow circumscribed the parameters of his physical existence, and would bear mute testimony to his non-existence when he died.

Spring came and Maitland left the mainland on the ferry to Farrow Island. On the crossing he attempted to determine how many of his fellow passengers were also suffering from the Syndrome. As far as he knew there were no outward, physical symptoms of the disease – the physiological debilitation was taking place on a sequestered, cellular level. Nevertheless, Maitland convinced himself that at least a dozen other passengers, of the twenty or so aboard the ferry, were making their way to the hospice. Their despondent postures and sapped facial expressions spoke to him of moribund futures, bitter presents and only guilt and regret in retrospect. He realized, as the ferry approached the island, that they were mirror images of himself.

A car was awaiting him on the cobbled quayside of the small fishing village. He was greeted by Dr Masters, the woman with whom he'd corresponded.

'Aren't we waiting for the others?' he asked as he climbed into the rear of the car.

'Others?' Dr Masters regarded him with a smile. 'The other passengers are Islanders. You are my only new resident this week.'

The hospice was a sixteenth-century mansion set in wooded parkland on a clifftop overlooking the straits. Dr Masters conducted him around the workshops and recreation rooms, the library and dining hall. She told him that the residents could take their meals in their rooms, if they wished, and that the recreational facilities and group therapy sessions were optional.

Maitland was thus reassured. The thirty or so residents he had seen so far in the mansion had about them a collective air of apathy, as if the fact of their ends had reached back and retroactively killed them both in body and in mind.

By contrast, Maitland had briefly glimpsed a few lone individuals in the grounds, striding out resolutely across the greensward, or posed in isolation on the windy clifftop. Maitland fancied that he detected something heroic about their lonely defiance in the face of death, and ultimately sad and tragic also.

As the weeks passed and spring turned gradually to summer, Maitland imposed his own routine on the identical days that stretched ahead to the time of his death in the New Year.

He would rise early and breakfast alone in the hall before setting out on a walk around the island that would often take him three or four hours. He would speak to no one, not because he wished to be rude or uncivil, but because no one ever spoke to him. He was a stranger on the island and therefore an 'inmate' up at the mansion, and the locals viewed the victims of the Syndrome with suspicion, sometimes, even, hostility.

He would take lunch in his room and eat it slowly, sometimes taking an hour to finish. Then he would sit by the window and read, or listen to the radio, until the gong announced the evening meal at seven.

This meal he did take with the other residents in the main hall, though he rarely joined in the conversation, which he found inane and self-pitying. There were constant debates as to the reason for the disease, and the only conclusion ever arrived at by the residents was that they were the chosen ones of their God, Apollo. These people, in Maitland's opinion, were as irrational as the madmen who could no longer live with the thought of their deaths, and had to be removed to psychiatric units on the mainland.

One night, over coffee, Maitland decided that he had

heard enough. He threw down his napkin and cleared his throat. The dozen residents at the table, the people Maitland considered to be the hard-core of the hospice's strange religious movement, until now debating among themselves, fell silent and stared at him. They sensed his long-awaited contribution to the discussion.

'There is,' Maitland said, 'no *reason* for what we have. It's a freak, an accident, a cellular mutation. We are just as likely to be disciples of the Devil as we are to be the chosen ones of your God. In my opinion we are neither.'

Later, as he stood by the french windows and watched the sun fall behind the oaks across the river, he sensed someone beside him. 'But how can you continue, Mr Maitland? How do you manage to live from day to day if you believe in nothing?'

Maitland could not reply, and retired to his room. He often wondered the same thing himself.

Summer gave way to autumn, and the sunsets beyond the stand of oak turned the golden leaves molten. Maitland struck up an acquaintance with a fellow resident, a retired major who bored him with stories of his army life. The only reason Maitland tolerated his company was because he played a passable game of chess, and they would spend the long autumn afternoons in the library, intent on the chequered board between them. They rarely spoke; that is, they rarely *conversed*. Maitland tried to ignore the major's monologues, for he was contemplating – in contrast to the old soldier's full and eventful life – the arid years of his own brief existence to date, his time at university, both as a student and later as a lecturer, and the missed opportunities he told himself he did not regret, but which, of course, he did.

The major's going came about on the third week of

their acquaintance. The old man had been complaining of headaches and tiredness for two days, and his concentration had often wandered from the game. Maitland realized what this meant, and he was unable to say whether he was shocked by the fact of the Major's approaching death, or at the understanding, for the first time, that his own life, too, would end like this.

On the third day the major did not arrive, and Maitland sat alone by the window, his white pawn advanced to queen's four in futile anticipation of the challenge.

He took to playing chess against himself in the empty afternoons that followed the major's death. Winter came early that year, impinging on the territory that the calendar claimed still belonged to autumn. Maitland found it too cold to enjoy his walks; the wind from the sea was bitter, and it often rained.

He appeared a lonely figure in the library, bent over the chessboard, apparently rapt in concentration but often, in reality, devising for himself an alternative set of events with which he wished he had filled his life. He repulsed all offers to challenge him, not with harsh or impolite words, but with a silent stare that frightened away would-be opponents with its freight of tragedy and regret.

One afternoon, during a storm that lashed and rattled the windows, Dr Masters joined Maitland in the library and tried to persuade him to take up her offer of group therapy, or at least counselling. They had experts who could . . .

He wanted to ask her if they had experts who could revise his past, give him the happiness he should have had long ago, but which had passed him by. He stopped himself before asking this, however. He knew that he had only himself to blame for the emptiness of his life.

Dr Masters said that she thought he should mix more with the other residents. Didn't he know that, even now, nothing was so important or rewarding as human relationships?

And Maitland replied that he needed nothing, and never had, of *human relationships*.

One week later he met Caroline.

He noticed her first one Sunday at the evening meal. She was at the far table by the blazing fire, and it was more than just her youth that set her apart from the other diners; she was *alive* in a way that none of the others were. Something in her manner, her movements, told Maitland that she could *not* be dying. Then he experienced a sudden stab of grief as he realized that her dynamism might be just a façade, an act to disguise her despair.

Later it came to him – with a sweeping sense of relief – that she was related to one of the residents and down here on a visit. Relatives came so infrequently – like the Islanders they saw the victims of the Syndrome as bizarre and freakish, as if the disease were some kind of curse, or could be transmitted – that it hadn't occurred to him that this was what she was, the daughter or granddaughter of one of the afflicted.

She excused herself from the table and Maitland watched her leave the room. Seconds later he saw her again through the window. She crossed the patio and ran across the greensward towards the clifftop. She wore moonboots, tight denims and a chunky red parka, and he guessed that she could be no more than twenty-five. Maitland had almost forgotten what it was like to feel such yearning, and to experience it now served only to remind him of his wasted years and the fact of his premature death.

In the morning Maitland went for a long walk through the wind and the rain. He returned, showered and ate lunch in his room and, feeling refreshed and invigorated, went downstairs to the library and played himself at chess.

In the middle of the afternoon he sensed someone beside him. He turned and saw the young woman.

She smiled. She was dressed as she was last night, with the addition of a yellow ski-cap pulled down over her ears, and mittens. Evidently she too had just returned from a walk.

'Can I give you a game?' she asked, indicating the board. Despite himself, Maitland smiled and began setting up the pieces.

They played for an hour with only the occasional comment, and then she looked up, directly at him, and said: 'You're not like the others. You've not given in . . .'

He wanted to tell her that he had surrendered long ago, that his resolution now in the face of death was nothing more than the cynicism that had fossilized his emotions years before.

Instead he smiled.

'I mean it,' she said, as she toppled her king in defeat. 'There's something about you . . .' She gestured. 'The other fools have given in, one way or another – gone stark staring mad or joined that crackpot cult.'

She mistook his cynicism for valour, seeing him through eyes of youthful enthusiasm, and Maitland hated himself for the charlatan he knew himself to be.

He felt a sudden sympathy, then, with the residents who had taken to religion, or madness, as protection against the inevitable. At least they had had full and worthwhile lives against which to measure the futility and horror of their deaths.

'Perhaps if you were in the position of these people, facing death, you might give in too. Don't belittle them—'

Something in her eyes made him stop.

She began collecting the scattered pieces, placing them

in the wrong positions. 'But I am a resident here,' she said. 'Another game?'

They played all day, but Maitland gave little attention to the games. During the hours that followed he found himself intrigued by the young woman, who introduced herself as Caroline. He opened up, talked about himself for the first time in years. He wanted to turn the conversation around, to ask Caroline about herself, her life before the hospice but mainly her life since the diagnosis. Most of all Maitland wanted to know how she could remain so overtly optimistic with the knowledge of what was to come.

But she parried his questions and kept the conversation trivial, and Maitland was happy to join her in the exchange of banalities he would have found intolerable at any other time.

Over the next few weeks Maitland and Caroline sought each other's company as often as possible. They went on long walks around the island, and spoke guardedly of their respective pasts. Maitland was attracted to Caroline because of her courage, her optimism and disregard for the proximity of her death; she perhaps was attracted to Maitland for what she saw as similar qualities. It hurt him to deceive her – he often wanted to tell her that you could not fear death if you had never really lived – but as time went by he became too attached to her to tell her the truth.

Their liaison stopped short of physical intimacy, however, and it was as if this was a tacit agreement between them. For his part, Maitland could hardly conceive that intimacy might be possible, much less how he might react emotionally to something he was yet to experience. Perhaps fear prevented him acceding to the desires of his body, as if to consummate what he felt for Caroline would bring home to him the fact of how much he had come to delight in life of late, and consequently how much he had to lose.

As for Caroline . . . They talked all day, and often into

the early hours, but never about their relationship. Maitland was still in ignorance as to her almost blind, at times even childish optimism.

For days now the wind and the freezing rain had promised worse to come, and then one quiet night, with only two weeks to go before Maitland died, snow fell.

In the morning he awoke to find a pearly radiance filling the room. He dressed and drew aside the curtains and was dazzled by the brilliance of the white mantle.

He pulled on extra clothes with the enthusiasm of a child and met Caroline in the hall. They embraced, restricted by the bulkiness of their padding, and hurried outside hand in hand.

For as far as the eye could see, snow had covered the land with a perfect record of passage. They were the first residents abroad this morning, and they set off together away from the mansion. At one point, Maitland looked back at the building – its hard angles softened and upholstered in a thick, dazzling fleece – and he saw their footprints following them to their present position. He looked ahead at the virgin expanse of snow, and he shivered with what he told himself was nothing more than a sudden chill.

They walked through the woods and came out on the far side of the headland. They stood side by side and stared out across the shipping lanes, at the scimitar-shape of a tanker on the distant grey horizon. Then they moved towards the small pavilion where they often spent the afternoons, talking and staring out to sea.

As they made their way towards the open entrance of the small, stone building, Caroline pulled away from him, then bent double and screamed into her mittens. Maitland looked from her to the pavilion, and saw with revulsion that during the night a resident had chosen this place in which to die.

They returned to the mansion and for the rest of the day and all through the night they remained in bed and made love. This set the pattern for the following week. They would take a brisk morning walk and then seek the refuge of bed and the bliss of each other's body, as if making up for the weeks of wasted opportunity. Caroline said nothing about the obvious fear the sight of the corpse had instilled in her – instead it was as if she were trying to exorcize from her mind the fact of her death with the positive catharsis of sex.

Maitland, at last, found what he knew to be love, and he passed through the fear of the inevitable with the knowledge that he might never have found happiness were it not for the fact of his terminal illness. His only regret was that he had not found such happiness earlier.

One week later he felt himself going.

On the morning of the first day he felt too drowsy to accompany Caroline on their ritual stroll through the snow. He made the effort, though, but something about his lethargy as they walked side by side communicated itself to Caroline, and she was silent.

In the afternoon they went to bed, but Maitland fell asleep beside her within seconds. In the morning he felt vaguely ill, nauseous. He tried to hide this from Caroline, but it was impossible. She dressed him and assisted him downstairs to the library, where they played chess. Often Maitland slipped into sleep, and he would awake with a start to see Caroline crying quietly to herself at the far end of the room.

On the morning of his last day, Maitland awoke before Caroline and forced himself out of bed. He dressed with difficulty, then kissed Caroline on the cheek and slipped quietly from the room so as not to wake her.

He walked through the woods to the pavilion overlooking the sea. Already he was tired, as if the short walk had exhausted him, and he hoped he would be asleep when it happened.

Caroline joined him not long after, as he guessed, and secretly hoped, she would. 'You should go back,' he told her, but he knew it was a token protest. 'You still have months to live.'

She ignored him; he sensed that she wanted to speak, to say something, but could not bring herself to do so without tears.

Later, for the first time, she mentioned the Syndrome.

'Years ago we wouldn't have known we were ill,' she whispered, her breath visible in the air. 'We would have . . . *gone*, suddenly, without all these months of . . .' And Maitland realized, then, that she was crying. 'Why?' she said at last. 'Why did they have to tell us?'

Maitland held her, shocked at her sudden capitulation. 'Modern medicine,' he said. 'They can diagnose it now. They know when it's going to happen. Given that knowledge, they have to inform the sufferer. Otherwise we could go at any time, anywhere, endangering others besides ourselves. There are many more of us now. The Syndrome has reached almost epidemic proportions.' He drew her to him affectionately. 'I thought you were doing rather well,' he said, and recalled that first Sunday weeks ago when he had wondered briefly if her vivacity had been nothing but an act.

'I was so scared, the only way I could stay sane was to pretend I wasn't affected. Being seen as unafraid by others gave me strength, confidence. Can you understand that? Then I met you and found someone who wasn't afraid . . .'

Maitland stifled a cry of despair. He convinced himself

he could detect, in the frozen morning air, the odour of the resident who had died here before him. He felt grief constrict his chest, fill his throat and render him speechless.

Caroline laughed. 'Do you know . . . do you know what they call us? The Islanders? Everyone else out there? They call us the "Disciples of Apollo" . . .'

They held each other as the snow began to fall.

Then Maitland ignited and consumed her in his flame, uniting them forever in a mutual, carbonized embrace.

Elegy Perpetuum

It began one warm evening on the cantilevered, clover-leaf patio of the Oasis bar. Below us the artists' domes, hanging from great arching scimitar supports, glowed with the pale lustre of opals in the quick Saharan twilight. The oasis itself caught the sunset and turned it into a million coruscating scales, like silver lamé made liquid.

There were perhaps a dozen of us seated around the circular onyx table – fellow artists, agents and critics, enjoying wine and pleasant conversation. Beneath the polite chatter, however, there was the tacit understanding that this was the overture to the inevitable clash of opinions, not to say egos, of the two most distinguished artists present.

This was my first stay at Sapphire Oasis, and I was still somewhat out of my depth. I feared being seen as an artist of little originality, who had gained admittance to the exclusive colony through the patronage of the celebrated Primitivist Ralph Standish. I did not want to be known as an imitator – though admittedly my early work did show his influence – a novice riding on the coat-tails of genius.

I sat next to the white-haired, leonine figure of Standish, one of the last of the old romantics. As if to dissociate himself totally from the Modernists, he affected the aspect of a bohemian artist of old. He wore a shirt splashed with oils, though he rarely worked in that medium, and the beret by which he was known.

Seated across from him was Perry Bartholomew.

The Modernist – he struck me more as a businessman than an artist – was suave in an impeccably cut grey suit.

He lounged in his seat and twirled the stem of his wine glass. He seemed always to wear an expression of rather superior amusement, as if he found everything that everyone said fallacious but not worth his effort to correct.

I had lost interest in the conversation – two critics were airing their views on the forthcoming contest. I turned my attention to the spectacular oval, perhaps a kilometre in length, formed by the illuminated domes. I was wondering whether I might slip away unnoticed, before Ralph and Bartholomew began their sniping, when for the first time that night the latter spoke up.

He cleared his throat, and this seemed to be taken by all present as a signal for silence. 'In my experience,' Bartholomew said, 'contests and competitions to ascertain the merit of works of art can never be successful. Great art cannot be judged by consensus. Are you submitting anything, Standish?'

Ralph looked up, surprised that Bartholomew was addressing him. He suppressed a belch and stared into his tumbler of whisky. 'I can't. I'm ineligible. I'm on the contest's organizing committee.'

'Ah . . .' Bartholomew said. 'So *you* are responsible?' His eyes twinkled.

Ralph appeared irritated. 'The Sapphire Oasis Summer Contest is a long-standing event, Perry. I see nothing wrong in friendly competition. The publicity will help everyone. Anyway, if you're so against the idea, why have you submitted a piece?'

The crowd around the table, swelled now by a party that had drifted up from the lawns below, watched the two men with the hushed anticipation of spectators at a duel.

'Why not?' Bartholomew asked. 'Although I disagree in principle to the idea of the contest, I see no reason why I should not benefit by winning it.'

Ralph laughed. 'Your optimism amazes me, sir.'

Bartholomew inclined his head in gracious acknowledgement.

The resident physician, a man called Roberts, asked the artist if he would be willing to discuss his latest creation.

'By all means,' Bartholomew said. 'It is perhaps my finest accomplishment, and has also the distinction of being totally original in form.' Just when he was becoming interesting, if pompous, he damned himself by continuing, 'It should make me millions – which might just satisfy the demands of my wife.'

There was a round of polite laughter.

Ralph exchanged a glance with me and shook his head, despairing.

Perry Bartholomew's separation from his wife, also an artist of international repute, had made big news a couple of years ago. Their ten-year marriage had been a constant feature in the gossip columns, fraught as it was with acrimony and recriminations before the final split. The artist, it was reported, had taken it badly – even an arch-cynic like Bartholomew, I read, had a heart which could be hurt – unless it was his ego that had suffered. For a year he had lived the life of a recluse, emerging only when he moved to the oasis for an extended period of work.

Tonight Bartholomew looked far from well. He was a handsome man in his early fifties, with a tanned face and dark hair greying fashionably at the temples – but now he looked drawn, his dark eyes tired.

Someone asked, 'Original in form?' in a tone of incredulity which prompted a sharp response.

'Of course!' Bartholomew said. 'I am aware that this is a bold claim to make, but it is nevertheless true, as you will learn when I exhibit the piece. I have utilized a prototype continuum-frame to harness an electro-analogue of my psyche . . .'

There was an instant babble of comment. A critic said,

'Can we have that again?' and scribbled it down when Bartholomew patiently repeated himself.

'But what exactly is it?' someone asked.

Bartholomew held up both hands. 'You will find out tomorrow. I assure you that its originality of form will be more than matched by its content.'

Roberts, from where he was leaning against the balustrade, asked, 'I take it that this is an example of a work of art which you would contend is worth a human life?' He smiled to himself with the knowledge of what he was doing.

Bartholomew calculated his response. He was aware that all eyes were on him, aware that his reply would re-open the old argument between him and Ralph Standish – which was exactly what the onlookers were anticipating.

Bartholomew gave the slightest of nods. 'Yes, Doctor. In my opinion my latest piece is of sufficient merit to be worth the sacrifice.'

Ralph frowned into his whisky, his lips pursed grimly. Bartholomew had made a similar declaration in the pages of a respected arts journal a couple of years ago, and Ralph had responded with a series of angry letters.

I willed him not to reply now, convinced that he would only be playing Bartholomew's childish game if he did so. But all eyes were on him, and he could not let the comment pass.

'Your views sicken me, Perry – but you know that. We've had this out many times before. I see no need to cover old ground.'

'But why ever not, my friend? Surely you are able to defend your corner, or perhaps you fear losing the argument?'

Ralph made a sound that was part laugh, part grunt of indignation. 'Losing it? I thought I'd won it years ago!'

Bartholomew smiled. 'You merely stated your case with

precision and eloquence, if I may say so. But you signally failed to convince me. Therefore you cannot claim victory.'

Ralph was shaking his head. 'What will it take to convince you that your philosophy is morally objectionable?'

'My dear Ralph, I might ask you the very same question.' Perry Bartholomew smiled. He was enjoying himself. 'So far as I am concerned, I occupy the moral high ground.'

'I cannot accept that art is more important than humanity,' Ralph began.

'You,' Bartholomew cut in, 'are a traitor to your art.'

'And you, a traitor to humanity.'

'Ralph, Ralph,' Bartholomew laughed, condescending. 'I consider my view the height of humanity. I merely contend that a supreme work of art, which will bring insight and enlightenment to generations, is worth the life of some peasant in Asia or wherever. What was that old moral dilemma? 'Would you wish dead one Chinaman if by doing so you would gain unlimited wealth?' Well, in this case the unlimited wealth is in the form of a work of art for all humanity to appreciate in perpetuity.'

Ralph was shaking his head. 'I disagree,' he said. 'But why don't we throw the question open? What do you think? Anyone? Richard?'

I cleared my throat, nervous. I looked across at Bartholomew. 'I side with Ralph,' I said. 'I also think your example of "one Asian peasant" is spurious and misleading.'

Bartholomew threw back his head and laughed. 'Oh, you do, do you? But what should I expect from one of Ralph's disciples?'

'That's unfair, Perry,' Ralph cut in. 'Richard has a valid point.'

'Perhaps,' Roberts said, 'you might be less willing to expend a human life if that life was one closer to home. Your own, for instance?'

Bartholomew regarded the physician with startlingly blue eyes, unflinching. 'I state categorically that my life is worth *nothing* beside the existence of a truly fine work of art.'

'That,' Ralph said, taking over the argument, 'is letting Perry off the hook too easily.' He swirled the contents of his tumbler, regarding Bartholomew across the table. 'Would you be as willing to lay down the life of someone you loved?'

I was suddenly aware of a charged silence on the patio.

Everyone was watching Perry Bartholomew as he considered his wine glass, a slight smile of amusement playing on his lips. 'Perhaps we should first of all conduct a semantic analysis of what you mean by the word "love"?'

Ralph was red in the face by now. 'You know damn well what I mean. But to counter your cynicism, I'll rephrase the question: would you lay down the life of someone *close* to you for a work of art?'

Bartholomew thought about this, a consummate performer playing the cynosure. 'Would I?' he said at last. 'That is a very interesting question. If I were to be true to my ideals, then by all means I should. Perhaps though, in my weakness, I would not . . .' He paused there, and I thought we had him. Then he continued, 'But if I did not, if I chose the life of someone close to me over the existence of a work of art – *then I would be morally wrong in doing so*, prey to temporary and sentimental aberration.'

Ralph massaged his eyes with thumb and forefinger in a weary gesture of despair. He looked up suddenly. 'I pity you, Perry. I really do. Don't you realize, it's the thing that you call the "sentimental aberration" that is at the very heart of each of us – that thing called love, which you claim not to know?'

Bartholomew merely stared at him, that superior smile

on his lips. 'I think we should have that semantic debate, after all.'

'You can't apply your reductionist sciences to human emotion, damn you!'

'I think, perhaps, I could, and disprove for good the notion of love.'

Ralph said: 'You don't convince me, Perry – for all your cynicism.' He climbed to his feet. 'But I can see that I'm wasting my time. If you'll excuse me, I'll bid you good night.' He nodded at Bartholomew and left the patio with a quiet dignity that won the respect of everyone present.

Bartholomew gave a listless wave and watched him go, a twist of sardonic amusement in his expression. 'Romantics!' he said with venom when Ralph was out of earshot.

The party broke up soon after that and I retired to my dome.

I woke late the following morning, breakfasted on the balcony overlooking the lawns, and then strolled around the oasis towards Ralph's dome. A couple of days earlier I'd finished the sculpture I had been working on, and I was still in that phase of contented self-satisfaction which follows creation.

I was passing beneath the pendant globe of Perry Bartholomew's dome when I heard his summons.

'Ah, Richard ... Just the man. Do you think I might borrow your body for a minute or two?' He was leaning from an upper balcony, attired in a green silk dressing-gown. 'I require a little assistance in moving my exhibit.'

After his arrogance last night, I was tempted to ignore him. The oasis had attendants to do the manual labour, but at the moment they were busy with other artists' work on the concourse beside the water, ready for the judging of the competition tomorrow. I was about to call up to him that I was busy and that he'd have to wait until the attendants were free, when I recalled his overblown claims concerning his latest work of art. My curiosity was piqued.

'I'll be right up,' I said.

I passed beneath the globe and entered the escalator shaft which carried me up to the central lounge. The door slid open and I paused on the threshold. 'Enter,' Bartholomew called from another room. 'I'm dressing. I'll be with you in a minute.'

I stepped into a large, circular room covered with a luxurious, cream carpet more like a pelt, and dotted with sunken sofa-bunkers. Several of Bartholomew's abstract sculptures occupied prominent positions – hard, angular designs in grey metals, striking in their ugliness.

Bartholomew emerged on the far side of the room. 'Good of you to help me, dear boy. The attendants are never around when one needs them.'

He wore a white suit with a pink cravat, and seen at close quarters I was struck by how seedy, how ill the man appeared. He liked to project an image of foppish sophistication, but such a display from someone so evidently unwell seemed merely pathetic.

'I hope Ralph hasn't taken the huff over our disagreement last night?'

'I don't know,' I said. 'I haven't seen him today.'

Bartholomew chuckled. 'The man is a silly old goat,' he said. 'When will he learn?'

I was about to respond that Ralph was a fine artist and a good man, then paused. 'Learn what?' I asked, suspicious.

Bartholomew crossed to a pedestal arrayed with bottles and glasses. 'Would you care for a drink, Richard?'

I told him that it was a little too early for me, frustrated by his calculated reticence. He was clearly playing another of his infuriating mind games. He poured himself a large brandy, turned and considered me.

'Learn,' he said, 'not to take so seriously my little digs. Our differences of opinion hardly matter.'

'They matter to Ralph,' I said. 'He objects strongly to your philosophy. What should he do? Sit back and let your comments go unopposed?'

'But, my dear boy, don't you think that *I* object to *his* philosophy? I assure you, I find his sentimentality just as sickening as he evidently finds my . . . my *realism*.' He sighed.

'It's a pity we can't still be friends. We were once very close, you know?'

I hesitated. Ralph rarely spoke of his friendship with Bartholomew. 'What happened?'

'Oh, we encountered different circumstances, experienced divergent phenomena, and adopted our own philosophies to deal with them. Ralph was always an idealist, a romantic at heart. I was a realist, and the more I experienced, the more I came to see that my view of the world was the right one. Ralph has always had it too easy.' He shrugged. 'We've reached the stage now where our respective views are irreconcilable. I think he's a woolly-minded bleeding heart, and he no doubt thinks me a hard-nosed neo-fascist. But you know this – you probably think of me in the same way.' He smiled, challengingly, across at me.

I murmured something to the contrary and avoided his gaze, wishing I had the strength to tell him what I really thought.

While he was speaking, I noticed a holo-cube on a polished wooden table in the centre of the room. It was large, perhaps half a metre square, and depicted a brown-limbed little girl in a bright blue dress, with masses of black hair and big eyes of lustrous obsidian. The contradiction between Bartholomew's ideals, and the display of such a romantic work of art, was not lost on me.

I crossed the room and paused beside the table. 'It's quite beautiful,' I said.

'I'm glad you like it. She is my daughter Elegy.'

'Your daughter?' I was taken aback, surprised first of all that he had a daughter, and then that he should choose to display her image in a holo-cube for all to see.

'The child,' he said, 'is incredibly intelligent. Precocious, in fact. She will go far.' And, with that, any notion that Bartholomew had succumbed to paternal sentiment was erased. For him, the holo-cube of his daughter was merely a reminder of her intelligence quotient.

'She celebrates her eighth birthday tomorrow,' he went on. 'She is visiting me directly from her boarding school in Rome. You'll be able to debate world affairs with her, Richard.'

I ignored the sarcasm. 'I look forward to meeting her.'

Bartholomew smiled. 'But come, I'm keeping you. Please, this way.'

We took a spiral staircase down to his studio. I recalled that he had described his work last night as utilizing a prototype continuum-frame, and I wondered what to expect. The large, circular chamber was filled with sunlight and the machinery of his art: large power tools, computers, slabs of steel and other raw materials.

He gestured across the room to his latest creation, standing against the far wall. It was a heavy, industrial-looking metal frame, hexagonal and perhaps three metres high – for all the world like the nut of a giant nut and bolt. It was not the dull, rusting frame, however, that was the work of art, but what the frame contained: an eerie, cobalt glow, shot through with white light, like fireworks exploding in slow motion. As I stared at it I convinced myself that I could make out vague shapes and forms, human figures and faces, surfacing from within the glow. But the images never remained long enough, or appeared with sufficient definition, for me to be sure. I might merely have been imagining the forms. The piece did, however, fill me with unease.

'The frame is an early prototype of the telemass portal,' Bartholomew said. 'It's about fifty years old – there are still a few of them about in the odd spaceyard. I bought it for an absolute fortune when I realized it could be put to artistic use. What you see at its centre is a section of the ur-continuum, the timeless, spaceless form that underpins reality. It was once known as the *nada*-continuum, in the time of the bigships, and Enginemen tell tales of it as being Nirvana, and filled with wonder. Of course, we now know that it was filled with nothing but the creations of their own psyches – which gave me the idea for this piece.'

He indicated a computer keyboard set into the frame. 'I programmed it directly from here' – tapping his head – 'and it was the gruelling work of almost a year. It is totally original in form and content, and well worth the agony of creation.'

'Is it titled?' I asked.

Bartholomew nodded. '*Experience.*' he said.

I looked from what might have been a woman's face, screaming in terror, to the artist. 'I'm impressed,' I said.

He barked a laugh. 'You romantics! Unlike your work, this is not merely visual. It was created with the express intention of being participated in. Go ahead, pass through.'

I stared again into its pulsing cobalt depths, veined with coruscating light, and stepped on to the plinth.

I glanced back at Bartholomew. 'Are you quite sure?'

'Of course, my dear boy! Don't be afraid. I'll follow in, if you wish.'

I nodded uncertainly, wondering if I was doing the right thing. With reluctance, and not a little fear, I took one hesitant pace into the blue light. I was immediately enveloped in the glow, and without points of reference to guide my senses I experienced instant disorientation and nausea. I felt as though I were weightless and spinning out of control, head over heels.

More disconcerting than the physical discomfort, however, was the psychological. Whereas seen from outside the images in the glow were fleeting, nebulous, now they assailed me, or rather appeared in my mind's eye, full-blown and frightening. I beheld human forms bent and twisted in horrifying torques of torture – limbs elasticating to breaking-point, torsos wound like springs of flesh, faces stretched into caricatures of agony. These depredations were merely the physical counterpart of a prevailing mental anguish which permeated, at Bartholomew's perverted behest, this nightmare continuum. And beyond this, as the intellectual sub-text to the work of art, there invaded my head the ethos that humanity is driven by the subconscious devil of rapacity, power and reward – to the total exclusion of the attributes of selflessness, altruism and love.

Then, one pace later – though I seemed to have suffered the ur-reality for hours – I was out of the frame and in the blessed sanity of the real world. As the horror of the experience gradually diminished, I took in my surroundings. I had assumed I would come out in the narrow gap between the frame and the wall – but to my amazement I found myself in the adjacent room. I turned and stared. Projecting from the wall – through which I had passed – was a horizontal column of blue light, extending perhaps half-way into the room. As I watched, Bartholomew stepped from the glowing bar of light – the artist *emerging* from his work – and smiled at me. 'Well, Richard, what do you think?' He regarded me intently, a torturer's gleam in his eye.

To my shame I said, 'It's incredible,' when I should have had the courage to say, 'If that's the state of your psyche, then I pity you.' I only hoped that the agony I had experienced within the frame was a partial, or exaggerated, reflection of Bartholomew's state of mind.

'The depth of the beam can be increased from one metre to around fifteen. The devices are still used in shipyards and factories to transport heavy goods over short distances. I'll show you.' He stepped into the next room, and while he was gone I marvelled at how he could prattle on so matter-of-factly about the mechanics of something so monstrous.

Before me, the beam extended even further into the room, almost touching the far viewscreen. Then it decreased in length to just one metre. He shortened it even further and, as if by magic, the wall suddenly appeared.

I returned to the studio. The blue glow pulsed malignantly in the frame, giving off subtle images of agony and waves of despair.

'We'll leave it at its original setting,' Bartholomew said. 'It's easier to move that way.'

For the next thirty minutes we edged the frame on to a wheeled trolley and rolled it into the elevator. 'We must handle it with the utmost care!' Bartholomew warned. 'I know through bitter experience that the slightest jolt might eliminate the analogues imprinted upon the ur-reality. The aspects of my psyche programmed within it exist tremulously. If we should drop it now . . .'

We emerged into the sunlight, and I had never been so thankful to experience fresh air as I was then. We gingerly trolleyed the great frame along a tiled path to the concourse, Bartholomew flinching at the slightest jolt or wobble on the way. Part of me wanted nothing more than to topple the frame, but the moralist in me – or the coward – overruled the urge. At journey's end a couple of attendants helped us ease the frame to the ground. 'Careful!' Bartholomew shouted. 'It should be treated with the greatest respect. The slightest mishandling . . .'

By now, word was out that Perry Bartholomew was

exhibiting his *magnum opus*, and a crowd had gathered before the frame like suppliants at the portals of a cathedral.

I took the opportunity, as Bartholomew prepared to make a speech, to slip away. Filled with a residuum of unease from my experience of *Experience*. I made my way around the oasis to Ralph Standish's dome.

I entered without knocking and made my way to the studio. I paused on the gallery that encircled the sunken working area. Ralph was standing in the centre of the room, holding his chin and contemplating the small figures playing out a drama of his own devising below me. The figures were perhaps half life-sized, at this distance very realistic, though seen at close quarters, as I had on earlier occasions, they were slightly blurred and ill-defined. I had been surprised to find Ralph dabbling in graphics when I joined him here last year – he usually spurned computer-generated art forms – but he had reassured me that though the method might be modern, the resultant work would be traditional.

He looked up and saw me. 'Rich, come on down.' He pressed a foot-pedal to kill the projectors hidden in the walls. The strutting figures flickered briefly and winked out of existence.

I descended the steps. 'How are you this morning?' I asked. I was a little concerned about him after last night's run-in with Bartholomew.

'Never better!' He beamed at me. He wore his old paint-stained shirt, splashed with the wine he squirted from a goat-skin at frequent intervals. 'Last night did me the world of good.'

'It did? I must admit, I was surprised when you invited Bartholomew to join us.'

'I'd been avoiding him for the better part of the year,' Ralph said. 'Last night I thought I'd give him the benefit of the doubt – see if he was still as eager to expound his odious views.'

'Well, you certainly found out.'

'It made me feel wonderful, Rich. Made me even more convinced that my ideas are right – not that I was ever in any doubt.' He peered closely at me. 'Talking about feeling wonderful, you're looking terrible.'

I was surprised that it showed. 'Well . . . Bartholomew just called me in to help him move his latest work of genius.'

'You didn't actually *enter* the thing?'

'So you know about it?'

'He invited me across earlier this year, before you arrived. I stepped into it then, though at the time it was still in its early stages.'

'What did you think?'

'I was appalled, of course. The thing's an abomination. I dread to think what it's like now he's completed it.' He directed a line of vino expertly into his mouth, pursed his lips around it and nodded. 'To be honest, the whole episode's a tragedy. Quite apart from poisoning the minds of all who enter it, its creation has made him quite ill both physically and mentally. Did you notice, Rich, that the figures within the ur-reality were female?'

I recalled the twisted travesties of the human form I had experienced in the blue light. 'Now you come to mention it . . .' I said. 'Yes, I think they were.'

Ralph nodded. 'Did you also notice that they were all aspects of the same person – Electra Perpetuum, his wife?'

'They were? Christ, how he must hate her!'

Ralph perched himself on the arm of a chesterfield, watching me closely. 'Do you want my honest opinion,

Richard?' There was a light in his eyes, an enthusiasm in his attitude.

I smiled. 'Do I have any choice?'

Ralph was too occupied with his own thoughts to notice my affectionate sarcasm. 'I think that although Perry might want to hate her, in fact he still loves her.'

I grunted. 'I'm not sure he knows the meaning of the word.'

'Of course he does! He's human, dammit! He might have experienced tragedy and hardship over the years, which have no doubt hardened him, but in here . . .' Ralph thumped his chest ' . . . in here, he's like all the rest of us. He's a fallible human being.'

'What makes you think he still loves Perpetuum?'

Ralph hesitated. 'I was with him when he first met Electra,' he told me. 'That was ten years ago – at the time he was just getting over his disastrous relationship with the vid-star Bo Ventura. We were still quite close friends. He was not quite the cynic he is now, but he was getting that way – I could see that from his criticism of my work, his views on art and life in general. When he started seeing Electra, I thought perhaps she might be good for him. She was – still is – his total opposite: warm, loving, generous to a fault. She lived life at a pace which honestly frightened me. I thought that Perry might be good for her, too – might slow her down a little, provide a calming influence . . . I saw them at intervals of perhaps a year over the next six or seven years. I was still on socializing terms with Perry, though things were getting pretty heated between us by the end. For the first few years, everything was fine between him and Electra . . .'

'And then?'

'Perry became ever more distant, withdrawn into himself and his thoughts. He alienated her with his philosophy, reducing everything to basic animal responses, where emotions like love had no place. Life to him became a vast, meaningless farce. When he published the articles attacking me and my work, Electra could stand no more.'

Ralph paused there, then went on, 'Anyway, she met someone else. I know it wasn't serious. She used this man as a means to escape from Perry. That was two years ago. I saw him shortly after the separation, and on the surface it was as if nothing at all had happened. He was still working hard, turning out his empty, minimalist sculptures. But about a month after Electra left, Perry went into hiding, became a recluse for a year. He saw no one, and I guessed that he didn't want to admit to the people who knew him that he'd been affected. He turned up here a year ago, and that . . . that *thing* is his first response to the end of his relationship with Electra.'

'But it's a monument of his hate for Perpetuum,' I said. 'How can you possibly claim he still loves her?'

Ralph shook his head, emphatic. 'I know the man, Richard. He's torn apart by a great contradiction at the heart of his life. He intellectually believes that such things as love, friendship, altruism do not exist – he thinks they're how we rationalize our animal instincts. And yet he loves Electra, he loves his daughter, even though these feelings don't fit in with his reductionism. That work he calls *Experience* is, in my opinion, a response to the anguish of his separation from his wife. The only way he can overcome what he sees as the aberration of his feelings for Electra is by creating a work which he hopes will at once validate his cynicism and exorcize her from his mind.'

'You almost sound sorry for him,' I commented.

'Oh, I am, Richard. The man needs saving from himself.'

I recalled the holo-cube of his daughter. As much as I found it hard to believe that Perry Bartholomew did indeed, as Ralph suggested, harbour human feelings in his heart, there was the memento of Elegy he kept on display in his lounge. I mentioned this. 'I assumed it was merely to remind him of her intellect,' I said.

'He purposefully gives that impression,' Ralph said. 'But believe me, he loves her. Why else would he agree to having her stay with him over her birthday?'

I was not totally convinced. 'Because he wants to impress everyone with her genius?' I suggested.

Ralph smiled to himself. 'We'll see,' he said. 'It should be quite an interesting few days.'

He climbed from the chesterfield and moved to the balcony. I joined him. Across the sparkling expanse of the water, the concourse was thronged with a crowd of artists. Bartholomew's continuum-frame was the centre of attention. Ralph smiled to himself. 'Will they ever learn?' he said.

I glanced at my watch. The sight of all the work arranged on the concourse reminded me that I had yet to exhibit my own piece. I would put the finishing touches to it that afternoon. 'What are you doing this evening, Ralph?'

'Working, unfortunately. I have a few things I want to get ready for tomorrow.'

We made arrangements to meet for breakfast and I left for my dome. I took the long way around the oasis, so as to avoid the crowd and the malign aura that surrounded Perry Bartholomew's latest work of art.

Ralph was in good humour the following morning as we breakfasted on the patio overlooking the oasis. He buttered his toast lavishly, as if it were a palette, and gestured with it as he told me about a group of new artists whose work he admired. He was prone to mood swings, depending on how his work was progressing, and I could only assume that it was going well now.

Below us, on the concourse, a cover had been erected to

protect the exhibits from the effects of the sun. People strolled down the aisles formed by the works, pausing occasionally to admire a piece more closely. Bartholomew's continuum-frame, huge and ungainly, looked out of place among the smaller crystals, sculptures and paintings.

I was about to comment that the piece would be more at home in a breaker's yard when the artist himself rode up the escalator and crossed the patio. As he passed our table he inclined his head. 'Gentlemen.' He appeared rather frail this morning, his white suit hanging on his tall frame.

Ralph gestured, swallowed a bite of toast. 'Perry, why not join us?'

Bartholomew paused, raised an eyebrow. 'I think perhaps I might,' he said. 'Very kind of you.'

He seated himself at the table and ordered breakfast – a single cup of black coffee. I felt uneasy in his presence. I recalled what Ralph had said yesterday about saving Bartholomew from himself, but wished that Ralph had waited until I was elsewhere to indulge his missionary streak.

Bartholomew nodded towards the exhibition. 'When does the fun begin, Ralph?'

'This afternoon, when the judges arrive.'

Bartholomew nodded. He had the ability to make his every gesture regal. 'And who might they be?'

'Ah . . . can't tell you that. Utmost secrecy. Competition rules . . .'

Bartholomew smiled, and sipped his coffee. His attitude suggested that he thought the result of the contest a forgone conclusion. 'I see Delgardo's showing a crystal. I rather like his work.'

Ralph didn't, and was usually vocal about the fact. 'He has a certain technical expertise,' he said.

They continued with this vein of light banter, and I

ceased to listen. I moved my chair back and propped my feet on the balustrade, enjoying the sun.

I was the first to notice them – two small figures hurrying around the oasis towards the patio. They almost ran up the escalator, and this exertion, in an environment where a leisurely stroll was *de rigueur*, caused me to sit up. The two men stepped from the escalator and crossed the patio. I recognized Roberts, the resident physician, and with him was a man in the uniform of a chauffeur: he walked with a limp and his jacket was scuffed and ripped.

They paused at our table.

Roberts cleared his throat. 'Mr Bartholomew . . .'

The artist looked up, irritated at the interruption. 'Yes? What is it?' His gaze took in the unlikely pair without any sign of consternation. At the sight of Roberts' diffidence and the chauffeur's bruised face, my stomach turned sickeningly.

'Mr Bartholomew . . . I'm afraid there's been an accident—'

'Elegy?' Bartholomew's face was expressionless. 'Where is she?'

'If you'd care to come with me,' Roberts said.

Ralph took Bartholomew's elbow and we followed the doctor down the descending escalator, across the concourse and through the main gates of the oasis.

'What happened?' Bartholomew demanded.

Beside us, the chauffeur was tearful, shaking from the delayed effects of shock. 'I took the bend too fast . . . There was nothing I could do. I tried to . . .'

Outside the gates stood the open-top two-seater Mercedes, its flanks buckled and scraped, the windshield mangled as if it had taken a roll. The hairs on the nape of my neck stood on end. I expected to find Elegy – the small, sun-browned girl I'd first seen yesterday in the holo-cube – lying dead or injured on the front seat.

To my relief the Mercedes was empty.

Bartholomew cleared his throat. 'Where is she?' he asked.

'I'll drive this car back to the scene of the accident,' Roberts said. He beckoned the chauffeur. 'You'll have to direct me. Standish, you bring Perry in my pick-up.' He indicated a small truck in the parking lot.

While Roberts and the chauffeur climbed into the Mercedes, we shepherded Bartholomew across the tarmac towards the truck. Outside the air-conditioned confines of the complex, the heat was merciless.

Ralph took the wheel and Bartholomew sat between us. We lurched from the car park and along the straight, raised road after the battered Mercedes.

Bartholomew sat with his hands on his knees, staring into the shimmering heat haze ahead of us. I wanted to yell at him that he could show some sign of emotion, that we would fully understand.

'Why didn't the driver bring her back?' he said at last, as we bucketed over the uneven surface. 'Even if she were dead, he should have returned with her body . . .'

In the driver's seat, Ralph gripped the wheel and stared grimly ahead.

'Roberts wouldn't be coming out here if she'd died,' I said. 'She probably can't be moved.' I felt faint at the thought of what injuries Elegy might have sustained.

Ten minutes later the road began to climb into a range of low hills, no more than an outcropping of rocks and boulders, the only feature on the face of the flat, wind-sculpted desert. The surface of the road deteriorated and the truck lurched drunkenly from rut to pothole and back again.

We rounded a bend. Ahead, the Mercedes had pulled into the side of the road. As Ralph eased the truck to a halt behind it, Roberts and the chauffeur climbed out, crossed the road and walked out on to a flat slab of rock. The chauffeur pointed to something below him.

'Christ,' I said, unable to stop myself. 'She's down there.'

I jumped from the cab and ran across the road. The result of the Mercedes' prolonged skid was imprinted on the tarmac like double exclamation marks. Crystallized glass and flakes of paint littered the great anvil of rock across which the car had rolled.

Roberts was kneeling over a narrow fissure. The rock, perhaps the size of an oasis dome, had split into two uneven sections. One section comprised the greater part, while the other was no more than a sliver, perhaps a metre thick.

I joined Roberts and the chauffeur and stared into the crevice. Ten metres down, wedged upright and illuminated by a bright shaft of sunlight, was Elegy Perpetuum. Her head was turned at an unnatural angle, clamped between the two great slabs. She was staring up at us with an expression that combined both terror and entreaty.

Ralph and Bartholomew joined us.

Ralph, in a gesture of support, was gripping Bartholomew's arm just above the elbow. The latter stared into the fissure and, at the sight of his daughter, winced. It was his only concession to anguish, and seemed suitably in character.

Roberts was attempting to squirm down after the girl, and there was something faintly ludicrous, and at the same time terribly touching, about his futile efforts. He gave up at last and knelt, panting and staring down helplessly.

As my gaze adjusted to the sunlight and shadow in the well of the crevice, I made out greater detail. Elegy was wearing a red dress, and I saw that what I had at first taken to be torn strips of material hanging down her arms were in fact rivulets of blood. There was more blood on the slab of rock near the surface, splashed like patches of alien lichen.

'Elegy,' Roberts called. 'Can you hear me? Take deep breaths and try not to panic. We'll have you out in no time.'

The girl stared up at us, blinked. If she'd heard, she gave no sign. She began to cry, a thin, pitiful whimpering reaching us from the depths.

Bartholomew knelt and peered down. He looked at Roberts. 'Is there nothing you can do?' To his credit, there was a tremor in his voice.

'I contacted Timbuktu as soon as I found out what had happened. They won't be here for another two, three hours.' Roberts shook his head, went on under his breath, 'But she might not last that long. She's bleeding badly and God knows what internal injuries she's received.'

Bartholomew, down on one hand and knee like a dishevelled, ageing sprinter, just closed his eyes and kept them closed, in a gesture more demonstrative of despair than any amount of vocal bewailing.

Suddenly I could no longer bear to watch – either the little girl in agony, or Bartholomew in his own mental anguish. My redundancy, my utter inability to do a thing to help, only emphasized my fear that Bartholomew might resent my presence.

I strode over to the edge of the rock, taking measured breaths and trying to quell my shaking. Elegy's continual, plaintive whimpering, echoing eerily in the chasm, cut its way through the hot air and into our hearts.

There was a drop of perhaps ten metres to the shale-covered slope of the hillside. Elegy, pinned between the two planes, was positioned a little way above the surface of the hill. It occurred to me that if only we had the right tools to cut through the flake of rock . . .

I returned to the small group gathered around the dark

crevice. 'Are you sure there's nothing back at the oasis? Drills, cutting tools – even a sledge hammer? The rock down there can't be more than a metre thick.'

Roberts shook his head. 'Don't you think I've considered that? We might have hammers, but we'd never smash through the rock before the emergency team arrives.'

From down below, a pathetic voice called out, 'Daddy!'

'Elegy, I'm here. We'll get you out soon. Try not to cry.'

'I'm all bleeding!' she wailed. 'My leg hurts.'

As we watched, she choked, coughed, and blood bubbled over her lips and down her chin.

'Elegy . . .' Bartholomew pleaded, tears appearing in his eyes.

'We've got to do something,' I said. 'We can't just . . .'

Ralph was squatting beside Bartholomew, holding him. He looked up at me then and stared, and it was as if the idea occurred to both of us at the same time.

'Christ,' Ralph said, 'the continuum-frame . . .'

I felt suddenly dizzy at the thought.

Ralph looked from me to Bartholomew. 'It might just work, Perry.'

'We could position it down there on the hillside,' I said. 'If we took the truck we could have it back here in twenty minutes.'

I knelt beside Bartholomew, who was staring down at his daughter, his expression frozen as if he had heard not a word we had said. 'It's the only way to save her – we need the frame!'

He slowly turned his head and stared at me, stricken. Some subconscious part of me might have been aware of the incredible irony of what I was asking Bartholomew to sanction, but all I could think of at the time was the salvation of Elegy Perpetuum.

'It would never survive the journey,' he said in almost a whisper. 'Everything would be lost.'

Roberts exploded. 'Jesus! That's your daughter down there! If we don't get her out of that bloody hole she won't survive much longer!'

Bartholomew peered down the crevice at Elegy, who stared up at him mutely with massive, beseeching eyes. 'You don't know what it cost me to create the piece,' he said. 'It's unique, irreplaceable. I could never do another like it—'

In rage I gripped his arm and shook him. 'Elegy's unique, for chrissake! She's irreplaceable. Are you going to let her bleed to death?'

Something snapped within him, and his face registered a terrible capitulation. He closed his eyes and nodded. 'Very well . . .' he said. 'Very well, use the frame.'

I hauled him to his feet and we hurried across the road. With Ralph's help I assisted Bartholomew into the back of the truck, where we stood side by side clutching the bulkhead. Roberts and the chauffeur climbed into the cab and started the vehicle, and we rumbled off down the road at breakneck speed, Bartholomew rocking impassively from side to side between us. He stared into the never-ending sky and said not a word as the desert sped by.

Ten minutes later we roared through the gates of the oasis, manoeuvred through the concourse and backed up to the continuum-frame. We enlisted the aid of two attendants and for the next five minutes, with Bartholomew looking on and pleading with us to be careful, jacked the frame level with the back of the truck and dragged it aboard. Bartholomew insisted on travelling with it, as if his presence might ease its passage, and Ralph and I joined him in the back. We accelerated from the concourse and through the gates, leaving a posse of onlookers gaping in amazement.

As the truck raced along the desert road and into the hills, Bartholomew clung to the great rusting frame and gazed into the radiance at its centre, its veined depths reflected in his bright blue eyes. We lurched over potholes and the frame rocked back and forth. Bartholomew stared at me, mute appeal in his expression. 'It's going!' he called out. 'I'm losing it!'

I stared into the swirling cobalt glow. As I watched, the marmoreal threads of white luminance began to fade. I could only assume that these threads were the physical manifestation of Bartholomew's sick, psychic contribution to the piece, the phenomena I had experienced as tortured flesh and acute mental anguish. Over a period of minutes the white light dissolved and the bright glow waned to sky blue, and Bartholomew simply closed his eyes as he had at the plight of his daughter.

Before we arrived at the scene of the accident, the truck turned off the road and backed up to the great slab in which Elegy was imprisoned. We halted a metre from the face of the rock and Bartholomew, like a man in a trance, extended the blue beam into the boulder.

Then we jumped from the truck and climbed up the hillside. We gathered around the crevice, peering down to judge how near the beam was to the girl. I stood beside Bartholomew as he stared at his daughter and, at his expression of compassion tempered by terrible regret, I felt inexpressible pity for the man.

'We'll have you out in no time!' I called down to her.

She was staring up at us, blinking bravely. We were not so far off with the beam. It penetrated the rock one metre beyond her; all that was required was for someone to shift the frame a little closer to the girl.

When I looked up, Ralph, Roberts and the chauffeur were no longer with us. I assumed they had returned to the truck. I took Bartholomew's arm in reassurance and turned my attention to the girl.

I stared down into the crevice, expecting to see the beam move closer to the girl and encompass her in its radiance. Instead, the beam remained where it was . . .

I thought at first that my eyesight was at fault: I seemed to be looking *through* Elegy's crimson dress, through her round brown face and appealing eyes. As I watched, the girl became ever more indistinct, insubstantial – she seemed to be dematerializing before our very eyes. And then, along with all the blood, her image flickered briefly like a defective fluorescent and winked out of existence.

I had seen an identical vanishing act somewhere before – in Ralph's studio, just yesterday . . .

I looked at Bartholomew, and saw his face register at first shock, and then sudden understanding.

He stood and turned. 'Standish . . .' he cried, more in despair than rage at the deception. '*Standish!*'

But by this time Ralph, along with the other flesh-and-blood actors in his little drama, had taken the Mercedes and was speeding along the road towards Sapphire Oasis.

Which was not *quite* the end of the affair.

I drove Bartholomew back in the truck, and we unloaded the continuum-frame and set it among the other works of art on the concourse. Evidently word had got back that something had happened in the desert: a crowd had gathered, and artists watched from the balconies of the domes overlooking the concourse.

Bartholomew noticed nothing. He busied himself with the keyboard set into the frame. 'There still might be something in there I can salvage,' he told me. 'Something I can build on . . .'

I just smiled at him and began to walk away.

I was stopped in my tracks by a cry from a nearby dome. 'Daddy!'

Bartholomew turned and stared. Elegy Perpetuum, radiant in a bright blue dress and ribbons, walked quickly across the concourse towards her father, as upright as a little soldier. She ran the rest of the way and launched herself into his arms, and Bartholomew lifted her off the ground and hugged her to his chest.

She was followed by a tall, olive-skinned woman in a red trouser-suit. I recognized her face from a hundred art programmes and magazines – the burning eyes, the strong Berber features: Electra Perpetuum.

I was aware of someone at my side.

'Ralph!' I hissed. 'How the hell did she get here?'

'I invited her, of course – to judge the contest.' He smiled at me. 'I've told her about everything that happened out there.'

Electra paused at the centre of the concourse, an arm's length from Bartholomew. He lowered his daughter to the ground and stared at his wife.

'I know what you did, Perry,' Electra said in a voice choked with emotion. 'But what I want to know is, do you think you made the right decision?'

I realized, as I watched Perry Bartholomew regard Electra and his daughter for what seemed like minutes, that what Ralph Standish had created before us was either the last act of a drama in the finest of romantic traditions – or a tragedy.

It seemed that everyone in the oasis was willing Bartholomew to give the right reply. Beside me, Ralph clenched his fists and cursed him under his breath.

Bartholomew stared at Electra, seemingly seeing *through* her, as he considered his past and contemplated his future.

And then, with a dignity and courage I never expect to

witness again, Perry Bartholomew stepped forward, took the hands of his wife and daughter and, between Electra and Elegy, moved from the concourse and left behind him the destitute monument of his continuum-frame.

Song of Summer

It was long ago and far away, that last summer by the coast, and it seemed impossible that I might ever return. As I packed an overnight bag and drove from the city, I wondered if it was the ghost of Philomena in my memory, calling me back from down the years.

Philomena was my first love, though I did not call it love at the time. Love was the word that adults used to codify and categorize something magical, and so make manageable that wild, abandoned impulse of the heart. I had not been in love with the small, sun-browned girl in the red dress. I had been enchanted by her, possessed by her; I had been infected with a strange *malaise* that made me physically sick when she was not by my side, and then ecstatically light-headed when we were together.

As I turned down the empty coast road, heading south, I did not know what strange compulsion was compelling my return. The poets say never go back, but my present was a time of pain, my future uncertain, and it seemed that back was the only way to go.

I stopped for the night in the township situated a hundred miles north of my childhood home. I felt that I needed to pause before I immersed myself in the deep waters of the past, a diver on the brink of a turbulent ocean. The metaphor was not inappropriate. As I was repacking my bag the following morning I was surprised, but not shocked, to find that I had brought along a pistol, sufficient tablets to have me sleeping for all eternity, and a rope – as if my subconscious doubted my capacity to carry out what my conscious self had threatened more than once.

At dawn I set out on the last leg of the journey. This section of the road was a loop that followed the long curve of the cape. At a sequestered location along the coast, my father and mother had built a ten-roomed, weatherboard hotel, closed in winter but open for the long summer months, to cater for the halt and lame who came to worship, in hope of miracles, at the cave on the promontory.

I had quite forgotten the existence of the natural shrine until I saw the dilapidated signpost pointing to the beach. I slowed down and leaned from the car, the summer wind warm in my face. 'St Genevieve's Grotto' read the sign, and the memories came flooding back. I considered it some indication of the power of the mind that already my heart was racing at the recollection, forgotten or suppressed, of Philomena and her parents' daily pilgrimage to the cave.

I continued along the coast road. There were no tourists now, even though it was mid-summer. The road had the frayed and patched appearance of state neglect, and the condition of the sign had indicated that the shrine was hardly visited these days. In the naïvety of my youth, before I came to realize that human beings are weak and the need of an opiate is legitimate, I had often scorned the believers who sought solace in the cathedral of rock. Now I found it sad that time had passed it by, as if the stamping ground of my childhood, once so vital, had ceased to be of interest to anyone.

I came to the turning, the track along which stood the hotel, hidden now behind square fields of sunflower, linseed and rape. I pulled into the side of the road and climbed out to stretch my legs, or rather to delay my confrontation with the past. I was aware of my heartbeat, ticking away the seconds to the inevitable. On the other side of the road, the sea seemed to climb, flashing sunlight, to the horizon. As I stood, the morning telemass vector streaked across the horizon like marshalled lightning – five hundred-plus demolecularized passengers riding the beam to Earth.

I climbed back into the car and took the turning, the phalanx of sunflowers on my right slashing a margin of shadow along the track before me.

The track became a gravelled drive and opened out, and the gaunt, three-storey timber hotel came into view, its gothic gables austere against the blue sky. I had intended to book into the hotel if it still functioned as one, but the place had long since closed down and gone the way of the road and the signpost. Shutters hung awry and the windows were smashed; the paintwork had peeled and hung in scrolls. I climbed from the car and walked towards the broken front porch, retracing the steps I had taken thousands of times before.

A rocking-chair occupied one corner of the porch. In panic, I half expected my father to be seated in it, rocking back and forth with that deliberate steady motion that presaged a bout of rage. Then I saw that the chair was not my father's at all, but one much smaller and frailer, incapable of bearing his weight. I reached for the door handle, and it disintegrated in my grip. I pushed the peeling paintwork with my fingertips, and the door swung slowly open. After the heat of the day, the hall was cool, shadowed and inimical. Although subsequent owners had decorated it to their taste, the cavernous design of the hall and corridor imposed a funereal atmosphere I recalled so well.

I climbed the stairs to the first floor and turned right along the landing. Before me was the door to the bedroom my father and mother had shared. To the left ran the corridor to the west wing, at the end of which stood the single room my father had taken after my mother's death. The other rooms on this floor had been for the guests, not that they were ever full at any one time. My own room was on the second floor.

I climbed the narrow, twisting stairs. A large section of the roof was missing, and sunlight poured into the attic room. I stood in the middle of the floor and tried to discern one thread of emotion from the many that wove through my head. This was my sanctuary after beatings, the place where for days I hibernated after my mother's funeral, the base from which I struck out on many adventures via the sensorama deck that made those lonely years almost bearable.

But chief among the many thoughts and feelings that flooded through me then was the knowledge that it was from this room, from the very window to my right, that I first saw Philomena.

Now I moved to the window, and I was fifteen once again.

She swept into my life aboard a big open-top roadster as bright red as the dress she always wore. At first I noticed only her parents as they climbed from the car, pale, nondescript off-worlders who seemed ancient to me but were probably in their fifties. They collected their luggage from the boot and met my father before the porch. He was, as always in the company of paying guests, an actor playing a role at odds with reality: charming, courteous, even witty. As he ushered them inside, I could see him calculating the woman and her disability – she looked ill, and limped as she climbed the steps: would she be a long-term guest with faith in St Genevieve's reputed healing powers, or would she lack conviction when miracles failed to happen in the first week, and leave soon after?

Only then did I notice the girl. She bounded from the

back seat of the roadster, a hyperactive twist of colour, and then stood quite still – the transition from movement to rest suggestive of some bright, darting bird. She was small and slim, her tanned limbs and short, jet hair contrasting with her scarlet dress. I calculated that she was perhaps thirteen or fourteen. With her legs planted apart and her hands on her hips, she seemed confident and proud, even imperious.

Then, as I watched, she did a very unusual thing. She looked up and saw me, raised a hand and wiped a casual wave in the air.

I was not accustomed to being noticed by people – other than by my father whose attention was often belligerent, at best brusque. I was taught via interactive satellite by teachers whose classes numbered in their thousands. The world of sensorama was a programmed fantasy for inadequate adolescents like myself, and had taught me nothing about the protocol of social interaction. The guests were always elderly or middle-aged – I had never before known a child to stay – and for the most part I was ignored, or briefly patronized, and instructed by my father to be neither seen nor heard.

For a second or two I was taken aback by her effrontery. She was staring up at me, and I chose to interpret the quizzical expression on her face as one of challenge. To my surprise, I found myself lifting my arm and returning her wave.

Then her father called her inside and in an instant she was gone.

That night, as I lay in bed and stared out at the full moon, I was disturbed by my reaction; it was an aberration for which I felt ashamed. I resolved to keep to myself for the duration of their stay, and to avoid the girl at all costs. I did not analyse my motives at the time, and only later came to realize that I feared having my failings revealed to someone other than myself.

In the morning I heard their car sweep away from the hotel, and reached the window in time to see the girl seated primly in the back of the roadster as it carried her down the track between the fields of sunflowers. I dressed and went downstairs to help my father with the chores around the place.

The morning went well; that is, I achieved noon and lunch-time without a reprimand. He was silent all the while we fixed the garden fence, withdrawn, as if deep in thought. My mood took wing at this. I always knew I was in for a bad day if he initiated conversation: it would end in questions I could not answer, and then chastisement for duties done with insufficient expertise or care. From the vantage point of middle age I can see that my father resented me and picked fault with whatever I did, but at the time I began to believe that truly, in every respect, I was incompetent.

I escaped after lunch and decided to reward myself with an exploration of the rocky northern headland. As if to compensate for my austere life at home, I had an imagination as vivid as any sensorama programme. I was reading the romantic poets at the time, and I delighted in reliving plots, romantic assignations, and duels on the ancient promontory of the cove.

The red roadster braked before the porch just as I emerged. I ran past it, eyes averted, and took a secret short cut to the coast through the rearing sunflowers.

I fashioned a laser from a length of broken fence-post and I was Commander Kirkpatrick, starship captain, the winner of worlds, poet and dashing paramour. By the time I reached the dunes overlooking the beach, I had fought my way through hordes of hostile aliens. I stood in the warm wind, raised my laser to the heavens and proclaimed to the world at large: 'I've seen the Rings of Lyra / The

Aurora on Deneb Five / But none compare / None are so . . .' I stopped, then. I had the peculiar sense, honed from spending so much time alone, of being watched.

From the corner of my eye I glimpsed a flash of scarlet. The girl darted from her place of concealment among the sunflowers and stopped, regarding me. The way she braced her slim legs in the sliding sand of the dune gave her body a defiant twist, the torque of a turned brushstroke in Japanese art – still, yet containing enormous, bound vitality.

She was squinting at me. 'You like the romantics?'

I felt a rage building within me. Not only had she violated my secret pathway through the crop, but she had eavesdropped on my daydreams.

Unable to think of a suitable verbal riposte, I turned and stormed off through the dunes. I was sweating and trembling and my face, I know, was burning red.

She gave chase, as quick as the tropical bird her movements most resembled. As I descended into the trough of a dune, she emerged upon the summit behind me. I looked over my shoulder to see her slim silhouette against the skyline, the summer wind tugging at her dress. I climbed the avalanching side of the next dune and already she was sliding, crouched, down the one behind. At last I gave up. I stopped atop the knoll of a dune overlooking the coast road and turned as she approached.

'What do you want?' I yelled.

She flinched, as if my words were blows. 'I heard you reciting. Kirkpatrick, wasn't it?' She smiled, taking heart from the fact that I had not continued my ranting. 'I liked the romantics once, but I prefer the Modernists now.'

I, too, have come to cherish the harsh insights of the Modernists, the Bards of Despair as they are known. But then I had never heard of them, not that I was able, or willing, to tell her that.

'You know – Kaminski, Marley, Ostergaart?' Head on one side, one eye closed against the sun, she regarded me.

She emanated an almost palpable aura of being, of *presence*. Adults, too, gave off a similar personal charge – unlike the ghosts of sensorama that masqueraded as real people – but I had never experienced a presence as strong as hers.

I felt that if I moved too close I might burn up in her fire.

I wanted to tell her that, although I liked Kirkpatrick, his work was not my favourite. I opened my mouth, but the words would not pass the swollen stopper of my tongue.

In frustration at myself, and rage at her for making me confront my inadequacies, I turned and slid down the dune. I ran across the road and stopped when I came to the beach.

I hoped that she would see that I needed to be alone, and return to the hotel.

She was at my side again in seconds.

'Do you live here with no one but your father?'

I set off at a furious pace. She skipped to match my strides. 'You must be lonely.'

The remarkable thing was that, until she said those words, I had not realized that I was, indeed, lonely.

Her accent was strange – clipped, quick and confident. A part of me wanted to ask from which colony world she came.

I realized that I had been walking along by myself for some time. When I turned she was a tiny figure, waving. 'We'll talk again tomorrow, OK?'

I marched on, shoulders hunched in defiance.

That evening it was dark by the time I returned home. My father and his guests were eating in the dining-room. I grabbed food from the kitchen, pausing to peer through the door. The girl was sitting with her back to me. Her sandalled feet hung inches shy of the carpet. I found it hard to accept that someone so young was familiar with a movement of poets of whom I had never even heard.

The woman, ill and old-looking in her dowdy, flowered dress, smiled a ghastly smile across at my father. 'Philomena tells me she was speaking to your son today. He doesn't join you for meals?'

'Madame Duval . . .' My father refilled his brandy glass. His eyes were glazed with inebriation. 'My son,' he said, very deliberately, 'prefers to eat in his room.'

Philomena Duval, I thought as I carried my tray upstairs.

In the morning my father was standing by the window in the front room, watching Philomena as she climbed into the roadster. There were times when I caught him staring wistfully, clearly in some secret psychological pain, though if I was aware of his anguish I chose to shut my mind to the fact that others, and especially my father, had their worries also. Only now, having reached the age he was then, can I look back and apprehend the events and incidents that made my father what he was. At the time I hated him.

'The mower's ready,' I said.

He turned and stared at me. His silences could be as soul-destroying as his blows.

We mowed the vast lawn at the rear of the hotel until noon, and then he set me to painting the fence we had repaired the day before. I wondered if the task was in punishment for some misdemeanour on my part – the afternoons were usually my own – or merely the result of one of his moods.

I was still painting, hours later, when a shadow fell across the gloss-white finish of the picket fence. One second I was alone, and then she was standing beneath the apple tree, watching me. I stood and made a performance of straightening my back. The colour of my face was not due wholly to the sun.

'We could go for a walk when you're finished,' she said, one eye closed against the glare.

Her audacity left me breathless.

'I . . . I've all this to do,' I stuttered, indicating the fence. 'It'll take . . . take for ever. I'll still be at it come dark.'

'I could give you a hand.'

'I've only one spray-gun,' I said. I glanced, quickly, towards the hotel.

'Don't worry. Your father's drinking beer with Daddy on the front porch.'

I muttered something under my breath.

She said, 'You two don't get on, do you?'

I looked at her. 'What makes you think . . . ?' I began, grudgingly impressed by her insight.

'It's obvious. The way you act when you're together. You never speak to each other.'

I shrugged, unable to find a suitable reply. I continued spraying the fence. Philomena leaned against the tree and watched me.

At last she said, 'He's a strange man, your father.' She paused, as if awaiting my reply. 'The way he looks at people . . . I've noticed him looking at me. Why do you think he looks at me like that?'

'Like what?' I said. I was uneasy.

'Oh . . . like he wishes I wasn't here.'

'I don't know. We don't get many kids here. I think he doesn't like kids.'

She nodded, biting her lip. She watched me patiently as I sprayed one picket after another.

The silence stretched, and I felt the need to say something. In desperation, I pointed to a huge, red apple hanging above her head. 'Would . . . would you like an apple?' I asked.

She squinted up at the swollen fruit. In an instant she had shinned up the tree and was sitting on a bough, crunching into the apple.

She smiled down at me, swinging her legs. 'Beautiful tree,' she said.

'It's special. I . . . we planted it when I was young, my mother and I.'

She thrust out the half-eaten apple. 'Like a bite?'

I shook my head, trying to think of something else to say.

'Is this . . .' I began. 'I mean – have you been to Brimscombe before?'

She took a huge bite from the apple and shook her head. 'First time.'

'Where . . . I mean' – Rivulets of sweat trickled down my back – 'where's your homeplanet? Which colony world?' I was embarrassed that I did not possess her way with words. I wanted to explain to her that I was fascinated with the Expansion, the history of colonization, but there was no way I could embrace so complex a statement in simple words without making a stammering fool of myself.

She had no chance to reply. Her father appeared around the side of the hotel. 'Philomena! Dinner!'

She gave a pretty grimace. 'Damn! Look, can you sneak out tonight?'

'What do you mean?'

'I mean,' she said, as if explaining to a simpleton, 'can you leave your room at midnight and meet me out here?'

I must have given a fair imitation of a frightened rabbit. She raised her eyes to the sky.

'I just want to show you where my home star is, OK? I'll tell you about my planet.' She leaned from her perch and stared at me with exaggeratedly wide eyes. '*Comprendez-vous?*'

My face afire with embarrassment, I nodded, unable to respond with words.

'Good. Midnight. See you then.'

She launched herself from the bough and ran back to the hotel.

It was dark by the time I finished painting the fence. I took a tray of food to my room and ate slowly, thinking about Philomena. I set my alarm and woke up five minutes before midnight, then lay and contemplated whether I should remain in bed. But I wanted to hear about where she was from, despite my apprehension and feelings of inferiority.

She was waiting at the end of the garden, beneath the apple tree. She turned at my approach. 'So . . . here you are. I didn't think you would come.'

I shuffled, ill at ease with the new emotions personal contact stirred in me. 'Oh,' I said. 'Why's that?'

She hugged herself, one foot wrapped around her standing leg, and smiled at me. 'Just because you're you,' she said.

'But you don't know me,' I countered.

'No, perhaps I don't.'

I looked back at the house, suddenly uneasy that my father might overhear our whispered exchange.

'I'll show you where . . . where I sometimes spend the summer nights.'

I led the way through the gate and into the field that backed on to my father's property. In the dead of night, over a period of weeks, I had constructed an intricate maze through the tall grass. At its centre was a flattened clearing, perhaps twenty feet square. I sometimes brought a blanket and slept beneath the stars.

Moonlight silvered the layered grass. A warm wind soughed through the seed-heads swaying around us.

Philomena dropped to the ground, cross-legged. I sprawled beside her.

'I come from a city,' she said. 'I've never been anywhere so absolutely . . .' she struggled for the word, 'so *open*. And there are no people, also. Today as we drove, I saw only . . . oh, five people. It makes me feel uneasy.'

I shrugged. I had lived in the hotel all my life. I told her that I could not imagine what life must be like in a city.

'Oh! But it's so alive! Everywhere, night and day, something is happening!'

I smiled, feeling inadequate. Her words meant nothing to me.

'Don't you have friends out here?' she asked me. 'Kids your own age.'

I could feel my face burning in the half-light. 'You're the first person I've ever met who's the same age as me.'

She exclaimed something in French. 'You have not even brothers or sisters?'

'No,' I said. 'I mean, I had a sister. She died when I was two.'

She was still shaking her head in cosmopolitan wonder at my isolation. 'On Lascaux it is so different,' she began.

She patted the grass beside her. We lay on our backs and stared into the night sky. 'See there, that constellation . . .? The second star from the top is Vega. Its only habitable planet is Lascaux. I was born in the city of Apollonaire, the largest on the planet. For all its size, it is the most beautiful in all the Expansion, or, at least, its citizens think so.'

I propped myself on one elbow and listened to her for what seemed like hours. She told me of her city, her friends, her strange life on a world I could only ever dream of visiting. She did not mention her mother or her mother's illness. Perhaps she spoke so much in order to forget.

After a while I think I did not even hear her words. It

was enough just to watch her as she spoke rapidly in her lilting, sometimes ill-structured English.

'But listen to me,' she finished. 'And you've told me nothing of yourself. You are the quiet one! Tomorrow, OK? Tomorrow you will tell me all about yourself.'

Then she said she was tired, jumped to her feet and pulled me through the maze. I was surprised by the warmth and softness of her small hand. By the time we reached the house my pulse was racing. On the veranda she reached up on tiptoe and kissed me quickly, once on each cheek, and I think it was then, with that casual intimacy, that my infatuation began.

Twenty-five years later I stood in the remains of my bedroom and listened to the phantom whispers of the children we had been. It was all I could do to hold back my tears as visions of Philomena filled my head. I stared around at the decrepit room and the whispers receded into the past.

I climbed carefully down the stairs to the ground floor, then made my way to the rear of the house. I paused in the kitchen, reviewing old and faded memories. The dining-room was bright with afternoon sunlight. I opened the sliding glass door and stepped onto the veranda. To one side was the corner where my father had kept his canes, ostensibly for training tomato plants and runner beans.

The lawn was overgrown, the apple tree tall and gnarled through lack of attention. Beyond the garden fence, much of it torn down and rotting where it lay, a field of tall elephant grass undulated in the breeze – as if to reassure me that not everything had changed.

I stepped from the veranda and slowly walked the length of the garden. The maze would not have lasted, I knew, nor the flattened area where we had kept our nightly rendezvous, but nevertheless I felt compelled to step through the curtain of tall grass, move in some half-remembered approximation of the maze I had made all those years ago.

I discovered then that the flattened area was flattened still – not, of course, the same area that I had created, but the result of more recent storm damage. The notion that our trysting place had survived for a quarter of a century appealed to my conceit, and anyway its position in the field *felt* right. I sat down, overcome with emotion.

Every day for a week after our first midnight meeting, we kept our afternoons free for each other. We explored the coastline, the beach and the caves. Every morning, either working for my father or studying via the satellite link-up – while Philomena accompanied her mother and father to the shrine of St Genevieve – I had thoughts only for the girl and the time when we would be together.

We were friends. At first it was enough for me that we meant this much to each other – after all, I had never had a real, flesh-and-blood friend before. Perhaps it was amazing that it took a week for our friendship to develop into something more, but if so then the fault was wholly mine.

I knew my body wanted something, but it seemed that what it wanted was too great a prize ever to be achieved.

That afternoon we sat on the grass of the headland that dipped towards the sea and terminated in a tumble of rocks and grottoes. Far below us was the concrete walkway that serviced St Genevieve's cave. The shrine was busy today. I had counted four tiny figures traversing the walkway.

Philomena lay on her back, her legs crossed at the ankles, hands behind her head. We had progressed to holding hands on our walk to the beach, and I tried to find some excuse now to reach out and take her fingers. I wanted to experience again that stomach-churning sensation of being connected to another human being.

Dreamily, Philomena had recited a few lines of her favourite poem, and then lapsed into silence.

I shook my head. 'But it's so bleak,' I said. 'How can you like that?'

Her reply shocked me. 'But life is bleak,' she said, 'on the whole.'

I don't know, now, whether I was shocked that so young a girl could hold such views, or that her words indicated that she did not feel the same elation at being *alive* when in my company as I did in hers.

'Give me the romantics any day.'

She smiled at me, such an adult smile of indulgence on her little girl's face. 'We like what is right for us at the time,' she said, but deigned not to explain.

I changed the subject. 'Let's go to the shrine,' I said. 'I haven't seen it for ages.'

Such a crass suggestion in the circumstances! Yet I was new at the game of relationships, had yet to attune myself to the mysterious wavelength of another person's feelings.

She sat up and gave scrupulous attention to a graze on her knee.

'Philomena?'

She flashed a look at me. 'Don't you think I see enough of the place?'

Her censure was enough to earn my instant apology. 'I'm sorry. I didn't think . . .'

Over the past few days I had taken to closely observing her mother, trying to discern some sign of improvement, or otherwise, in her condition. I feared the day she decided that her obeisance had worked the hoped-for miracle, or conversely that her condition was deteriorating, and elected to leave the planet, taking her daughter with her.

So far, she seemed just as frail and ill as when she had arrived.

Philomena was sucking a graze on her knee. Her eyes regarded me above the process. Her gaze lingered without so much as a blink to break the intensity.

'What?' I said at last, uncomfortable.

She blinked, as if in reply, and kept on staring.

I felt myself redden, and looked away. When I glanced back, her eyes were laughing. Without a word she lodged her chin where her lips had been and hugged her shins. If anything, her stare intensified. She could not keep a smile from her pursed lips. Her timed blinks seemed at once innocent and coquettish.

In desperation, out of my depth, I turned my back to her. Perhaps I knew, or guessed, what was happening, and feared the consequences.

I heard movement behind me. My heartbeat thundered. She put an arm around my neck and hooked her chin over my shoulder. Cheek to cheek, she whispered my name.

Then she sat herself in my lap and kissed me, the intrusion of her tongue between my teeth a shocking but pleasurable sensation.

I held her to me so that my face was hidden from her eyes. I felt sick, and elated, and I wanted the moment never to end.

She drew back and regarded me. 'Where?' she asked.

'Not here.' I baulked at the thought of being seen by the pilgrims. 'The dunes?'

'Too sandy.'

Our eyes locked. 'The maze,' we said in unison.

We ran from the greensward, and across the coast road, and hand in hand hauled each other through the dunes. I had never been as desperate to reach a destination. We came to the field of sunflowers and took the short cut. A sensation comprised of equal parts elation and fear bubbled within me like silent laughter.

Before we reached the hotel I led Philomena on a circuitous route around the building. It seemed to me that my desire for Philomena was a physical manifestation, glaringly obvious to any casual observer. One glimpse of us and my father would have known what we intended.

We came to the field of grass and followed the maze, cutting corners in our haste. The heat, the sounds of skylarks in the adjoining meadows, a harvester far off, all these were peripheral sensations secondary to the feel of Philomena's hand in mine, the dance of her red dress against her legs as she tugged me along in her wake.

When it seemed that we might never reach the heart of the maze, we burst into the clearing and stood facing each other, exhausted. Now that the time conjoined with the place, and the universe sanctioned that the here and now was *right*, I was overcome with a debilitating paralysis.

As ever, Philomena took the lead. She lifted my shirt over my head, and then started on my belt buckle. While I took over and removed my trousers, she unbuttoned her dress and stepped from it, then pulled down her white knickers. They snagged on her sandals, and she was forced to sit down unceremoniously and tug them off. I could only stand, naked myself now, and stare. I had seen her bare brown arms and legs every day for a week, and I had thought that the sight of the rest of her body would provide just an incremental increase of pleasure. But I had never seen a girl naked before, never seen tiny breasts above well-defined ribs, or a flat stomach stretched taut as a drumhead, I had never before looked upon the split fruit of a girl's hidden place, and the sensation was exponential.

My reaction was suitably ridiculous.

I pointed to a pendant between her breasts. 'What's that?' I stammered.

She smiled up at me as she lay there on her back. She took the small, oval pendant and peered down at it. 'It can do many magical things,' she said. 'Come here and I'll show you.'

I cannot recall the details, the mechanics, of our first time together – they are a *mélange* of images and half-remembered sensations that merge with the memories of the many other times we made love over the following week. But I can recall the aftermath. I lay on my back with Philomena pressed against me and stared into the flawless sky. I was happy beyond words and it seemed that the world was a wonderful place.

Every afternoon after that, and also at midnight, we rendezvoused in the centre of the maze and spent hours in each other's arms beneath the falling sun and the illuminating stars. At times I had to convince myself that this was really happening. I contrasted what I had now with my life before Philomena, and it was as if I had been delivered into Paradise.

Then, one afternoon a week later, my father discovered us.

At noon each day, my chores or lessons completed, I would head through the field of sunflowers towards the beach, and then double back and make my way to the centre of the maze. So great was my fear of discovery, my dread of having my relationship with Philomena proscribed, that I felt such duplicity necessary. I almost always arrived before her, and that period of waiting, sometimes as long as thirty minutes, was an exquisite torture of passion deferred. Sometimes I would wait in mounting dread, sick with the thought that she might not arrive.

On this particular afternoon, however, she had returned early from the shrine. She had removed her dress and lay naked on her back, sun-bathing with her arms out-stretched.

I crept into the centre of the maze and knelt silently beside her. For a long time I merely gazed at her perfection. My eyes returned again and again to her face, and I think that it was then, in that profound moment of silence, that I realized that Philomena was the first person whose welfare I cherished above my own. It came to me that to lose her would be more than I could bear.

To banish the melancholy that came upon me, I plucked a stalk of grass and drew it lightly across her abdomen. She spasmed and sat up with a squeal, then launched herself at me and wrestled me to the ground. We rolled across the grass, Philomena exhibiting a determination at odds with her diminutive stature. She came out on top, pinioning my arms with her knees. She reached down and pushed my hair back off my forehead.

'Do you love me?' she asked in a whisper.

A dark cloud seemed to eclipse my thoughts. I had never told Philomena that I loved her, even though my feelings for her could be described as love.

I recalled an incident shortly after the death of my mother. I was returning with my father from the funeral in the township a hundred miles to the north. He sat at the wheel of his roadster, silent and admitting no sign of emotion. Likewise, as if it were a contest in which whoever broke down first was the weakest, I kept tight within me the grief I had felt for days.

When it seemed that the atmosphere in the car might explode with the tension, my father turned to me and said, 'I loved your mother, son. You'll never understand how much I loved her.' That was all, just that simple declaration, and then he turned his attention to the road and never again spoke to me of his wife of twenty years.

But I wanted to shout at him that he could not have

loved her, that if he'd loved her he would not have treated her as he had. Over the years I had watched my mother retreat into a defensive shell to protect herself from my father's barbed comments, his drunken rages in which he would not limit his attack to words alone. I wanted to accuse my father of driving mother to her death, but, of course, I said nothing and allowed the hatred to corrode within me.

Now, with Philomena seated upon my chest, I could not bring myself to speak. Perhaps I was loath to admit that my father, once upon a time many years ago, had felt as passionately about my mother as I did about Philomena; perhaps I did not want to admit to myself that what I felt for Philomena could be corrupted with the years.

Tears came to my eyes. I reached up and turned her over, reversing our positions, so that now she was beneath me. I straddled her chest and held my face inches from hers.

'Tell me you'll never leave me!' I said. 'Tell me that you'll stay here for ever!'

I assumed that her wide-eyed expression was in reaction to my vehemence. Even when the shadow fell across our bodies, I thought that a cloud had passed before the sun.

It was not until she cried my name and struggled that I knew we were not alone. I looked up. My father stood above us, boots planted astride. My first reaction was outrage that he had violated our special place, and then fear when I saw the cane braced into a bow between his clenched fists.

Philomena scrambled from beneath me and gathered her dress.

'You go back to the hotel,' my father told her. 'I'll deal with you later.' He looked from the girl to me as I cowered beneath him.

Philomena, her expression terrified, backed away step

by step, her eyes beseeching me to run. With her dress grasped to her chest, she moved to the exit and disappeared.

My father reached down and picked me up by the front of my shirt. The material cut my arm-pits, causing me to yell like a coward. When I was on my feet he pushed his face close to mine and whispered, 'You will not see that girl again, do you understand?'

Then he threw me to the ground and attacked me. He beat me and, as if to reinforce his command, timed each blow to coincide with a word. 'You – will – not – see – that – girl – again!'

I raised my hands to protect my face, and he struck my ribs and back repeatedly as I squirmed and tried to roll away. Each whistling *thwack* stung instantly like the blow of a red-hot iron bar. I was sure that he intended to kill me, and a part of me was shocked. On other occasions he had limited punishment to half-a-dozen counted strokes. This time he seemed possessed by a rage that would cease only when I was dead. I could not hold back the tears of pain that stung my eyes, but I was determined not to cry out or beg for mercy.

I rolled to the edge of the clearing, then lay on my back and stared up at him as he approached. It came to me that if he intended to kill me for loving Philomena, then I was quite prepared to die. I lowered my arms and looked up at him, inviting the *coup de grâce*.

He ceased his attack, rearing over me, the cane raised. I saw the expression on his face and I was shocked. He wiped spittle from his lips. 'Just keep away from her,' he panted. 'Just keep away . . .'

Then he hurried from the clearing, ignoring the route of the maze and barging down the grass in his haste to be away.

Almost the instant he was gone, Philomena appeared

from nowhere, that darting, bright red bird again. She knelt beside me, comforting me with soothing words and a gentle embrace.

'But, look . . . he cut you!' She unbuttoned my bloody shirt, peeling it gently from my flesh.

As I stared in the direction my father had taken, she leaned forwards and traced my wounds with her tongue.

I was still in shock. I could not forget the expression on my father's face, as he told me to keep away from Philomena. It was the first time I had ever seen him crying.

That night, at twelve, when I left my room and made my way in silence to the maze, Philomena was not there – nor did she appear in the long hours that followed. I curled on the ground and sobbed until my throat was sore and my cheeks stung with salt tears. My father had no doubt told her parents and they had ensured her captivity by locking the door of her bedroom. I cursed him with words I had never used before. I wanted to kill him, then. I wanted to go to his room armed with a kitchen knife and plunge it through his heart as he slept. For fifteen years he had kept me isolated from the world, and then, when I did find someone good and true and beautiful, he exacted the exquisite torture of denying me the right to see her. At dawn, the thought that I might never again hold Philomena made me physically sick.

All the following day my father had me making window frames in the cellar of the hotel. I did not even see Philomena as she set out to the shrine with her parents. By the time I was allowed up from the cellar, it was dark and the evening meal had been taken. My father escorted me in silence to my room, and there was no way I could check if the light was showing beneath Philomena's door. From the window of my room I was unable to see if the Duvals' roadster still stood in the drive.

For two days my father made me do my lessons on the computer-link in his study, and in the afternoons he would find me tasks to complete in the cellar. He made it impossible for me to catch even a glimpse of Philomena, much less find the time to speak to her, arrange a secret meeting. On the first night, I hurried to the maze, and then returned in tears when Philomena failed to show. The second night, at twelve, I crept along the corridor and paused outside her door. I knocked and called her name, fearful lest my father discover me. There was no reply. I tried the handle, but the door was locked. I imagined only the most dire possibilities to account for her silence.

Silently, I made my way downstairs and pulled open the drawer where the spare pass-cards were kept. I found the card to Philomena's room and returned upstairs. I could hardly imagine what punishment my father might serve on me if he discovered my deceit. I inserted the card, slipped quickly inside, and closed the door behind me. Standing there in the darkness, my heart hammering at the thought of what I might discover, I reached for the light-panel. The room was empty.

I fled to my own room, numbed with shock. All that night I lay awake, sick with the conviction that my father had evicted Philomena and her family, that she had returned to Lascaux and I would never see her again.

I was dozing off, towards dawn, when I heard the small knock upon my bedroom door. I jerked awake, sure even then that it was not my father's summons – that it could, against all logic, be only one person. I ran to the door and pulled it open. There was no one there, and I thought that I had imagined the summons until I heard another sound. A high, regular note, like bird song, sounded from the carpet at my feet. I looked down and saw Philomena's pendant. Elation swelling within me, I snatched it up. The thin sliver of metal warmed to my touch, tingling. Then, in the air before me, an apparition materialized – a projection of Philomena.

She was staring intently ahead. 'Don't be frightened – it isn't a ghost. It's me . . . I told you the pendant was magical. I coded it to your presence the other night in the maze. I . . . I thought it would come in useful.' She paused there, staring past me, then went on, 'Your father told my parents about us. They moved me to a new room and locked me in. They threatened that if I see you again, then we'll leave the hotel . . . But I'll take the risk. I'm in room ten.' She paused. Then, 'See you tonight, OK? I'll be waiting.' And with a smile and a wave, she was gone.

My father locked me in his study that morning, and in the afternoon banished me to the cellar. I accepted his cruelty with the secret knowledge that nothing he could do would ever keep us apart. That night I could not wait until twelve – as soon as I heard my father retire to his room, I crept downstairs and found the pass-card to room ten.

The card clicked home, the door opened, and Philomena was in my arms. Without a word we hurried from the hotel. The stars were out. The night was warm. Hand in hand we ran like the wind. In the maze at last we stood, panting, face to face. We undressed each other and, like a dignitary awarding an athlete a medal, I looped Philomena's pendant around her neck. Then we made love beneath the stars, and of all the times we had been together, this one was the sweetest.

. For the next ten days we rendezvoused at midnight and made up for the lost hours of the afternoons. Our feelings for each other increased with the time we were forced to spend apart; certainly my need for Philomena became insatiable. The long days without her were unbearable, reducing me to bouts of sickness and nausea. When at last we met at midnight there were not sufficient hours until dawn; between making love and trading intimacies, there was time for nothing else.

If anything, I was even happier during these periods of stolen, clandestine passion than at any other time. When ecstasy reaches a certain pitch, it seems that it might last for ever.

On the very last occasion that I saw Philomena I left my room well before midnight, my heart beating like a trip-hammer. At noon that day I had seen Madame Duval climb from the roadster on returning from the shrine. Supported by her husband, she seemed in great pain. She held herself stiffly erect, her eyes red with tears – a grief-stricken mourner attending her own funeral. Philomena had followed in her wake. She did not so much as glance up as she passed me in the hall.

When I arrived at the centre of the maze that night, I paced back and forth and rehearsed the declaration I had thought out all afternoon.

Philomena was late. She seemed subdued as she came into my arms, and she pressed her head against my chest for longer than was usual. I wanted to speak, to tell her what I had decided, but my plan was so momentous that I feared she might demur. I would tell her later.

My hands went for the buttons at the back of her dress, but she stopped me with fingers to my cheek. 'Not tonight. Please. Let's just lie down and hold each other, OK?'

So we lay beneath the spread of stars and I held Philomena, her head on my chest. I made out the glaze of unshed tears in her eyes.

'It's your mother, isn't it?'

'Please.' She begged me to be silent.

'We must talk about it. I know the shrine isn't working.

I know you'll be leaving soon . . .' I wanted to tell her that that was OK, because I had decided to follow her back to Lascaux.

She raised her head from my chest and stared at me. 'No, please. Not that. Let's talk about anything, but not that.'

Tears tracked down her cheeks, and she fought to keep her lips pursed tight in defiance of her need to cry.

'I don't want to leave here,' she whispered then. 'I don't want to leave you!'

'But it's OK, Phil.' I took her shoulders and shook her gently. 'Really, it's OK. You see, I won't let you leave alone. I'm coming with you.'

She blinked through her tears.

'I've planned it all. I'll leave here and book a telemass fare to Lascaux. I'll find work when I get there and we'll be together. That's what matters.' I sounded desperate, even to myself. Perhaps, even then, I realized the impracticality of the suggestion.

She pressed her head to my shoulder and wept, her tears soaking my shirt. I smoothed her back, spoke comforting words.

'Philomena?'

She could not bring herself to speak for sobbing.

I had not expected this response. I had thought she would be overjoyed. I let her spend her tears, then whispered, 'I'm sorry about your mother, Phil. I understand how you feel.'

Her response shocked me. She looked up, anger in her eyes. 'How can you understand?'

'I do. My mother—'

'Oh, God!' coming from the lips of a child, the cry seemed at once comic and indicative of great despair.

'Phil . . .' This in desperation because she had pushed herself from me and dashed to the edge of the clearing.

She turned and yelled, 'Leave me alone! I wish I'd never come here! I wish . . .' but she could not bring herself to finish, and instead dashed off into the maze.

I called after her, 'I know how you feel. I know.' I wanted to tell her that I too had experienced what she was going through. I had watched my mother drink herself to death over a period of years. I had stood at the bedroom door when the doctor told her that if she continued drinking she would not last six months.

She had lasted a year, though it had seemed like ten.

I understood. I understood Philomena's anger, her unfocused hatred at the world in general, at God, at cruel chance that had dictated her mother should die in this way. I understood her outburst at me. In the self-absorption of grief we sometimes hurt the ones we hold most dear.

The following day my father ensured that I had no opportunity to see Philomena. I still cannot decide if the task he set me was intentionally cruel or just thoughtless. He woke me at dawn, before the Duvals left for the shrine, handed me a scythe and nodded to the field of grass beyond our garden.

'But—' I began.

He told me that the farmer wanted it cut, and that we needed the money. 'Start at the back,' he said, 'and work towards the hotel.'

He could have given me the laser cutter, but I suspected then that he wished to add physical distress to my mental anguish.

All day long, under the blistering sun, I toiled in the vast field. I attacked the grass with venom, determined to show my father that his spite would not cause me to surrender. My devotion to Philomena would survive whatever obstacles he chose to put in my way.

I left the flattened area until last. It was dark by the time I came to cut down the grass still standing around our special place. As I swung the scythe and the grass fell to reveal the centre of the maze like a stage upon which great dramas had been enacted, it seemed that I was bringing to an end a special period of my life.

It was late when I finished. There was no light beneath Philomena's door when I climbed the stairs to my room: I had intended to tell her that we would have to meet elsewhere that night.

Just before midnight, I let myself out into the back garden and waited beneath the apple tree. I had so much to tell her, so much to apologize for – I had had no right insisting that I understood how she might feel about her mother. The initial stages of grief are private; only later, when we have distanced ourselves from the bitterest hurt, can we open up and admit that hurt to others.

Midnight came and went. Philomena did not show herself. I cursed myself for frightening her away the night before. I wondered if she hated me for trying to tell her that I understood. Then I rationalized my distress. Clearly she had seen the mown field, and known that we could no longer rendezvous there ... But, surely, in that case she would have waited for me in the garden? Like this, with argument and counter-argument, I worried myself well into the early hours, and then cried myself to sleep. When I awoke, dawn was lighting the far horizon, and I knew what I should do.

I crept silently back to the house. I climbed the stairs to the first floor and tiptoed along the landing to room ten. Holding my breath, I knocked lightly on the door. There was no reply. I knocked again, and this time whispered her name. 'Philomena, it's me.' My heart seemed to be beating loud enough to wake my father. In desperation I gripped the door handle and turned. To my surprise, the door opened. I slipped quickly inside. Dawn light fell between the open curtains and illuminated an empty room. The bed was made, unslept in. Philomena's travelling bag was nowhere in sight.

A hard cold terror expanded in my chest. I wanted to scream denial, but I could not bring myself to articulate my anguish with even a primal howl. It was all I could do to stumble from the room and hurry along the landing to the double room shared by Philomena's parents. I did not stand on ceremony but turned the handle and barged in. The neat bed and absence of personal effects opened a pit of despair in my stomach.

Unable to control my tears, I ran downstairs. I jumped from the porch and stood in the drive. Their roadster was not there. Sobbing uncontrollably now, I sprinted down the driveway between the fields of sunflowers. I had no rational plan – in my anguish at being without Philomena I had to fill my senses with the balm of action. I convinced myself that, if the roadster had broken down, then I still had a chance of rescuing her. It is amazing how we can bring ourselves to believe in miracles when we are sufficiently desperate.

I emerged on the coast road and looked right and left, but the road was empty. I just stood there, staring north through the blur of tears, and in time I was rewarded.

Streaking through the upper atmosphere, a white arc against the blue, was that morning's telemass vector heading for the stars.

I returned home, hollowed out and scoured of all emotion. I must have been in shock. I climbed the stairs to my room, closed the door and began the methodical destruction of my sensorama deck, my computer link-up, my music system and then the furniture. If my father heard me, he left me to it – not that I feared his reaction. Had he tried to stop me then, I would have destroyed him too. At last, the room a scene of chaos around me, I fell to the floor and cried. I asked myself how she could have left without telling me, without even seeing me for one last time. She had told me that she loved me, but she had left without a word of explanation. I could not stop myself from accusing her of betrayal.

I somehow managed to get through the day without allowing my feelings to show. To have let my father see how much I was affected would have been to concede victory. He had me paint the front porch, and for ten minutes stood at the foot of the ladder, supervising. He seemed on the verge of offering an explanation, even, it occurs to me now, of telling me that he was sorry.

The very last time I saw my father alive, when I entered the house to tell him that I had finished painting, I found him seated in the darkened kitchen. He had a bottle of brandy gripped in his right hand, and his eyes were glazed. I backed away without alerting him to my presence.

He did not call me down the following morning. When at last I emerged from my room, he was nowhere in the house. I found the empty bottle on the kitchen floor. His roadster was missing from the drive. He had gone off like this two or three times before, always ending up slumped over the wheel of his vehicle on the greensward overlooking the ocean. Each time I had pushed him into the passenger seat and driven the vehicle back home, and the matter had never been mentioned.

I set off down the track between the sunflowers. I emerged on the coast road and turned right. The greensward was a half a mile away and from that distance my father's roadster was a colourless shape against the morning sky. As I made my way towards the clifftop, I went through what I would tell my father. I intended to leave Earth and make my way to Lascaux, and nothing he could say or do would stop me. The idea had come to me that morning, lying in bed surrounded by the wreckage of my past, but no doubt I had been formulating the plan in my subconscious ever since Philomena's departure.

In the event, I had no need to tell him anything.

The driver's door of the roadster was open, and there was no sign of my father. I found an empty bottle on the seat, and another half-full on the grass. It seemed the obvious thing to do to approach the edge of the cliff. I stared down without the slightest emotion, quite prepared for what I knew I would find. If I felt anything, I experienced a quick surge of relief as I made out my father's broken body on the rocks far below, sluiced rhythmically by the oblivious waves.

It did not strike me at the time that the Duvals' departure and my father's suicide might in some way be linked. In the years that followed, when I thought over that period in my life, I considered the two events to be no more than a coincidence.

My father's death I came to terms with in time, though not without the guilt and recrimination that counsellors and psychiatrists told me was quite natural. The loss of Philomena, however, had a permanent effect.

I stood and retraced my steps through the tall grass. I was still so bound in my reverie of the past that the sight of the house, when I finally emerged into the garden, surprised me. No longer the smart hotel of my childhood, it stood dark and dilapidated against the sunset. A profound sadness coursed through me.

Philomena's laughter echoed in my head.

On the very same day that I discovered my father's body, I was taken to a home in the city where I lived for six months until I was sixteen. The hotel was sold off to pay my father's debts, and what little money remained put in trust until I was twenty. I entered college, studying multi-media, and on graduating found a safe job translating the classics of literature into sensorama programmes. The post was perfect. I could work from home and minimize my social contacts. I was cosseted from the real world and that suited me fine.

For a couple of years I fully intended to buy passage to Lascaux and find Philomena Duval. At first I could not afford the exorbitant telemass fee, and then when I could, with the help of the inheritance, it came to me that it was not that good an idea after all. It was true that I was still besotted with the girl, but I had sufficient wits to realize that if she still loved me, as she had claimed, then she would have returned to Brimscombe and found me ... I often wondered what she was doing now, what kind of woman she had become. I imagined her as cultured and intelligent, working perhaps in the arts and doing well, and still, of course, stunning in red.

In lieu of winning Philomena Duval, I looked for small, dark girls – red dress optional – with gamin-looks, quick movements and intelligence. I found two or three pale substitutes, and proceeded to court them with all the gauche inexpertise of the loner I had become. And then, when I had won the trust and affection of these innocent girls, a defence mechanism kicked in and I would hurt them, and to a lesser extent myself, by contriving to reject them – and in so doing save *myself* from being rejected.

I had soon developed a fine self-loathing.

Now I walked down the garden and paused before the cold house. The sun was going down in strata of burnt-orange and gorgeous scarlet, the very shade of Philomena's dress. The oak beam I recalled from my youth still ran the length of the veranda, but it was rotten now with woodworm and I doubted that it would sustain the weight of my body.

To end my life with sleeping pills was somehow too passive, to shoot myself too violent. It seemed right that I should hang. I looked about for a suitable gallows, and found the perfect place. I made my way to the car for the rope, and then returned to the garden. My pace slowed as I approached the apple tree. It had grown tall and strong in twenty-five years. I recalled Philomena, sitting on the bough and swinging her legs. That same bough was higher now, and stronger, and in that second I knew I should swing from it. I thought back to the boy I had been, and imagined his horror at what I was about to do. He would have seen it as a violation of what had passed between him and Philomena – and perhaps I saw it in the same way now. Perhaps I hated the boy I had been, the relationship that had made me what I was; perhaps I saw what I was doing as a way of destroying not only myself, but the sanctity of what once I had held so dear.

I reached up to cast the rope around the bough, and was stopped by the song of a bird. The notes were high, and regular, and I knew then that it was not bird song.

A strange heat passed though my head, and I felt weakened. I staggered to the gnarled bole of the tree and attempted to locate the source of the chime.

It came to me after long, shocked seconds that she had left me something, that, after all, she *had* thought of me . . .

I found Philomena's pendant in a hollow between bough and trunk, scabbed over with moss so that I had to dig to get it out. The pendant was tarnished, its chain rusted, but the small metal oval still tingled in my grip.

A piece of sunset seemed to detach itself from the sky and dance on the grass before me. My eyes focused and I saw, projected into the air, the holographic image of Philomena Duval.

I dropped to my knees and like this we faced each other across the years. She blurred in my vision. I wiped away my tears. My imagination had done nothing to exaggerate her beauty. She was as I remembered her. She was even crying, as she had been on the very last occasion we had met.

From the pendant in my hand came her voice, synchronized to the movements of the phantom's lips. The sound of her little girl's contralto was almost more than I could bear.

' . . . so much to tell you and so little time to tell it in. Oh, I don't know where to begin!' She raised a hand and pushed it through her short hair in exasperation. The gesture released a flood of memories, and I think I even moaned aloud in pain.

'First of all, I must apologize for yesterday. I'm sorry I shouted like that. I wanted to explain, but I couldn't bring myself to tell you. Not face to face. Like this, it's different, easier. Please say you don't hate me . . .'

She paused then, biting her lips against the tears, her eyes downcast. 'When you said . . .' she began again, 'when you said that you wanted to come with me – oh, you don't know how wonderful and how terrible those words sounded! I love you so much and you've made my life so much better than it ever was.' Her chin on her chest, eyes closed, she cried.

'I . . . I wanted to tell you that you could come with me, more than anything I wanted that. But I couldn't allow you to do that, for your sake. It wouldn't be fair.'

The ghost of Philomena looked quickly over her shoulder, and then faced forwards again, her face twisted in an anguished grimace. 'That was Daddy, calling me. We're almost ready to go. I wanted to come and see you working in the field, but your father stopped me. He knows, you see. He's only trying to protect you . . .' She paused, staring down at her entwined fingers, then gathered herself and managed, 'So . . . this will have to do. I'll leave it where you're sure to find it.'

She turned and called, 'OK, I'm coming. Just one minute!' Then she faced me and I could see that she was fighting to present a brave face.

I had a terrible presentiment of what she was about to say, what she had said to me all those years ago, and I cried out for it not to be true.

'I couldn't bring myself to tell you,' she whispered. 'You thought all along that my mother was ill, and how could I tell you that it wasn't my mother? I've had all the treatment that money can buy, and they brought me to the shrine as a last resort. But it . . . it doesn't seem to be doing any good.' She looked straight at me and smiled brightly. 'But my father's heard about a clinic on Mars. They claim they can help cases like mine. We're heading there now.'

She was silent for a while, then said, 'Please don't hate me for leaving like this. Please don't. I love you,' she said, 'and if I can, I'll come back for you. Whatever it takes, however far and however much it costs, I will. I'll come back for you. OK?' She forced a smile then, and reached out, too quickly, in order to cut the recording before she broke down completely. I held out my arms to her, and Philomena faded against the sunset and was gone.

I sat on the grass as the sun sank over the horizon and the stars brightened overhead. I picked out Vega and smiled through the tears. I remained in the overgrown garden for the long hours of the night, physically in the present but really reliving another life in my head, sorting out the complications, the subtleties of motive, I had been unable to discern as a boy. More than once I replayed the hologram that Philomena had left for me. As she faded for the final time, I even told her that I loved her.

When morning came I stood and stared about me like someone emerging from a dream. I saw the ghosts of a boy and a girl, and I heard our laughter. I thought of the callow youth I had been, in love and without a care in the world, and I thought of Philomena and what our love must have meant to her, and the terrible secret she had kept from me for so long.

As the sun climbed, warming me, I thought back to the day between Philomena's departure and my father's death – the very last day I had spent at the hotel. Had I ventured into the back garden then, and stood beneath the apple tree, how might I have reacted to the knowledge that the girl I loved was dying?

It came to me now that it was perhaps right that her farewell message had been delayed for so long.

At last I moved myself to leave the garden. I walked around the house, leaving for ever the place where I had spent the happiest, and also the saddest, days of my life. I climbed into my car and drove down the track between the gently swaying sunflowers. I turned right along the coast road, the sunlight brilliant on the vast ocean. When I came to the greensward I slowed and pulled on to the side of the road. I stared across the clifftops for a long, long time, towards the rocks where my father had taken his life, and experienced all the emotions I had been unable to summon as a boy.

Then I set off, Philomena's pendant on the passenger seat beside me, and drove north towards the city.

Epsilon Dreams

That evening, the throb of music from the party on the hill drowned out the soundtrack of the film I was trying to watch. I gave up on it with no ill-feeling – I had seen the old black and white movie many times before. I left the lounge and stepped on to the veranda of my A-frame.

The perfect circle of the bay was placid, reflecting the Ring of Tharssos, the band of tiny moonlets that arced overhead and diminished towards the horizon. A warm breeze blew in off the water and a dozen long-billed night-gulls banked on the thermals above the beach. I decided to make a night of it on the veranda, and was stepping inside for a few beers when I heard the screen door in the kitchen slap shut against the frame.

'Mr Henderson? Ben?'

She appeared in the lounge doorway, wearing her shabby pink tracksuit and a wincing I-know-I'm-trespassing-*but* expression. 'Ben, is it OK?'

I smiled. 'Of course, Tammy. Come in.'

I had known Tamsin Challenger for six months; she had emigrated to Addenbrooke from Earth with her father and stepmother. Martin Challenger was a famous surgeon, and had chosen the resort of Magenta Bay as the locale of his semi-retirement. He had bought the villa on the hill overlooking the bay, and had made himself popular in the community by hosting lavish parties to which everyone was invited.

There could be no greater difference between Challenger's brash confidence and his daughter's reserve, her almost pathological shyness. Soon after her arrival on the planet, on hearing that I wanted to rent the showroom I had used as the base of my gemstone business, she had approached me on my morning walk along the beach. She had stammered that she would like to – if it was all right by me – would *really* like to rent the premises and start a gallery to show her artwork.

A combination of her gauche manner, her endearing plainness and evident nerves had made me warm to her. We strolled along the foreshore, and, with much gentle probing, I learnt that she painted cameos on rocks and sea shells, and carved small animal figures from driftwood. She admitted this almost apologetically, as if ashamed of her ability – which, I found out later, was considerable. She told me that her father was funding the venture, and I detected in her manner an undercurrent of resentment of the fact.

Over the months, I had often stopped by to see if I could be of assistance. Her inherent nervousness, no doubt abetted by the stories she heard that I was a cynical old drunkard, had made her wary and distant. It had taken time to win her over, to make her realize that I wanted nothing more than to see her business succeed.

Her gaze alighted on the vid-screen. 'Ben, you never told me you liked old movies!' Her eyes seemed to melt. 'Isn't Garbo wonderful?'

Then she noticed the holo-cube on top of the vid-screen. 'Who's that, Ben?'

I killed the film with the remote control.

'My daughter—'

And before I could explain she rushed on. 'But you never told me you had a daughter! How old is she? Where does she live?'

'She died ten years ago, when she was eleven,' I said, and wished I hadn't.

Tammy reddened and tears appeared in her eyes, and I supposed it was a combination of the fact that she was so easily hurt – and thus gave the impression she required protection – and was the age my daughter would have been had she lived, that made me more than a little infatuated with Tammy Challenger.

She stammered an apology. 'I'm sorry ... I didn't realize—'

'Hey.' I reached out and took her hand. 'Don't worry. It happened a long time ago, and it's true what they say about time, you know.' I smiled. 'Anyway, it's good to see you.'

She smiled and took heart. 'I was just wondering, Ben ... Yours was the only light on along the beach. Everyone's up at the party. My father's celebrating some award he's won back on Earth.' She shrugged. 'Won't you come along?'

I hesitated. 'Your father won't mind?'

A couple of weeks ago Martin Challenger had stopped me outside Tammy's gallery. Drunk, he had muttered some remark about his daughter's celibacy. 'You don't stand a chance, Henderson,' he had said, and hurried off before I could find a suitable reply.

Tammy had overheard him. 'My father's jealous,' she had told me. 'He resents you because you're my friend and he isn't.'

Now she smiled. 'He won't have to mind. He's invited all his friends. I don't know many people up there. We're having a barbecue, and there's your favourite beer – imported from Earth – and later there'll be a laser show.'

There were perhaps a hundred guests on the lawn of Challenger's villa that night. I recognized many faces from the settlement. The entire contingent of the club was present; they had entrenched themselves around the outside bar and were making steady progress into Challenger's stock of drinks. There were perhaps a dozen guests I did not recognize. I later learnt that these were the surgeon's friends and colleagues from Earth, who had telemassed in especially for the occasion. A live band played a selection of mood music. Silver-coated waiters circulated with trays of drinks.

I escorted Tammy to a tesseral patio overlooking the bay and introduced her to a few friends. I caught the eye of the waiter with the beer, and as the evening progressed I drank steadily and listened to Tammy talking shop with the artists who lived and worked on Capricorn Island. Their animated discussion absolved me of the need to contribute. Tammy seemed to be getting on fine, so I left her and sat on the balustrade.

Below, on the first of a series of lawns which stepped down to the foreshore, Marty Challenger and his young wife Rowena stood beside two shrunken figures in floating invalid carriages. The surgeon was a big man whose white suit seemed designed to increase his dimensions and make him appear imposing. His Spanish wife, young enough to be his daughter, wore a silver, backless dress. Her cranial augmentation glinted silver beneath her long black hair.

Tammy crossed the patio and sat on the balustrade next to me. She seemed flushed with the success of her conversation. 'Ben, you're quiet tonight.'

'Quiet,' I said with feigned mysteriousness, 'but taking everything in.' I pointed to the lawn. 'Who are the invalids?'

Tammy peered. Her expression hardened as she saw her father and stepmother. Then she smiled brightly. 'Oh, they're my father's patients. He has a surgery and theatre in the villa and he takes the occasional private patient.'

She paused and gazed at her stepmother with an

expression that might have been wistful. She was quiet for a while.

I took her fingers and squeezed. 'Tammy?'

She shook her head. 'Rowena – she's very beautiful, isn't she?'

I sighed. 'I suppose she is.' I was about to launch into a welter of platitudes about how beauty is only skin deep, and that what matters is what is inside, but stopped myself.

'I'm sorry, Ben. I'm being silly . . .' She faltered, staring over my shoulder. Marty Challenger had left the lawn and joined the crowd on the patio. He circulated, his cultured baritone booming out greetings.

Then he stared across at us, and I recalled what he had said to me the other week, and what Tammy had told me about his being jealous. He ignored whatever it was that someone was saying to him now, tossed down his drink and crossed the patio.

Challenger was incredibly broad across the upper torso, tapering to disproportionately thin legs; his appearance gave the paradoxical impression of absurdity at a distance and looming threat at close quarters.

He towered over me and made a noise in his throat before recalling my name. 'Ah . . . Henderson. I'd like a word.' He turned to his daughter. 'In private, if I may, Tamsin.'

Tammy reddened and hurried off into the crowd.

Challenger snapped at a waiter to refill his Scotch, and then turned his attention to me. His great ruddy face was soaked with sweat and his eyes were glazed with the effects of too many whiskies.

'Henderson – about what I said the other week. I was out of order. I didn't mean what I implied and I hope you didn't take offence.'

The apology was delivered at speed and obviously

rehearsed; I wished Challenger would go away and leave me to my beer.

I shrugged. 'No offence taken,' I said, uncomfortable.

He nodded. 'You get on well with Tamsin, don't you?'

'She's a nice kid,' I began.

'You've been a great help to her over the past few months. She likes and respects you. I was wondering . . .' He paused there, watching me.

I waited.

'You're a regular down at the club,' he went on. 'You know all the locals. I was wondering if you might take Tammy with you now and again – she needs to get out a bit, meet people.' He hesitated, then continued, 'Look, Henderson, what she really needs is an affair with the right person.'

I stared at him, surprised at his show of concern. I muttered something to the effect that I'd be pleased to take her down to the club.

'Good man, Henderson. I'd appreciate it.'

Challenger switched gear, asked me how I was enjoying the party. I think he even tried to tell me a dirty joke. I indicated that I'd finished my drink and required a refill, and escaped. I left the patio and strolled across the lawn.

Tammy was sitting at a garden table with a dozen other guests, waiting for the laser show to commence. She cradled a cup of coffee in her lap and smiled into space. She had not yet seen me, and I took the opportunity to observe her from a distance. She seemed all the more alone for being part of a crowd.

I sat next to her. She smiled. 'What did my father want to see you about, Ben?'

'He apologized for what he said last week.'

Tammy looked bitter. 'He probably said it just to win you over. I wouldn't be surprised if he wants something.'

I saw Rowena Challenger striding across the lawn with

a tall woman in tow. Something about her set, determined expression made me uneasy.

Rowena and the woman paused before us.

Tammy looked up and stiffened.

Rowena smiled at her stepdaughter, and I swear that the expression in her Spanish eyes was one of revenge.

By now the attention of everyone around the table was on the scene that was about to take place between Rowena and Tammy.

'Tam,' Rowena said with theatrical charm, 'I'd like you to meet Sharon. She's staying the night. She'd like to know if you would care to share her bed?'

The woman smiled at Tammy.

Rowena turned to the guests around the table. 'I do hope I haven't shocked you,' she said sweetly.

Beside me, Tammy stood and hurried off into the night. I began to give chase, but Marty Challenger beat me to it. He strode across the garden and around the villa in pursuit.

I turned on Rowena Challenger. 'That was unnecessary!'

The young woman maintained her poise. She smiled at me. 'The little bitch deserved it – as you would know if you had to live with her.'

I found her beauty alone intimidating, but her cerebral augmentation unnerved me. Her head was cupped in an occipital brace of the finest steel, and a spar of Teflon encircled her neck like a choker. It was perhaps the fact that I was ignorant of the reason she was augmented that so daunted me.

I just stared, unable to voice my full contempt, as she turned to the guests around the table and addressed them like the perfect hostess. In seconds she had them laughing.

I left, intending to find Tammy. I walked around the villa and across the extensive garden. The golden aureole of a floating will-o'-the-wisp lamp indicated the whereabouts of

Challenger and his daughter, concealed behind an enclosure of shrubbery. I heard their brief exchange before coming upon them.

'Tamsin . . .'

'Go away.'

'Please, let me help—'

'I said leave me alone!'

I rounded the hedge, stopped and backed off. Tammy was sitting on a marble bench in the shadow of an arbour laden with fragrant nightblooms. Her arms were crossed on her chest and she was gripping her shoulders, head bowed. Challenger stood behind her.

As I watched, he reached out and caressed the nape of her neck with the back of his hand. There was something at once prurient and strangely wistful about the gesture.

Tammy stiffened at his touch, tried to pull away. Challenger grabbed her hair, then pulled her around and up to face him. He stared into her eyes for long seconds, then ground his lips to hers in a kiss of lasting savagery.

Tammy wrenched herself away and fell to her knees. 'I'll kill you!' she cried up at him. 'I swear I'll kill you!' Then she collapsed to the ground, sobbing.

Challenger regarded her impassively, then stalked from the arbour. He must have seen me as I ducked back into the shadows, but, if so, he gave no sign.

I was torn between following Challenger and doing him physical harm – or rather trying to – and rushing to his daughter's assistance. I decided that Tammy was more in need of my attention.

I helped her to the bench and sat beside her, an arm around her shoulders. She cried quietly, my shirt soaking up the tears.

After a while she sat upright, blotted her eyes on the cuff of her tracksuit. 'I'm sorry, Ben.'

'I should have done something when I saw Rowena with that woman,' I began.

Tammy spluttered a laugh. 'Rowena? Do you think I'm bothered about that? I can put up with Rowena. She's pulled that trick before.'

A response was beyond me. Back in the garden, the band was playing. The party was in full swing. The warm air was thick with the cloying scent of the nightblooms. I sat with my arm around Tammy and chastised myself for enjoying the intimacy.

She whispered, 'It's my father I really hate, Ben.'

I tried to think of something to say. She seemed to want to talk about it. 'That wasn't the first time?'

'God, no! Of course not.' She dried her eyes, sniffed. 'Ever since my mother died, three years ago . . . I look like her, you see, except she was beautiful.' She paused. 'I thought it might stop when he . . . when he got *her*.' She nodded in the direction of the front lawn and Rowena. 'But, if anything, it's got worse. The thing is, I understand why he does it, why he's so obsessed. But that doesn't make it any easier to handle . . . It makes it worse, Ben. If *I* understand, why can't *he* – and do something about it?'

I wanted to say something to ease her pain, but found words impossible.

'I wouldn't care, but the worse thing isn't when he touches me, like tonight. The worse thing is when I catch him staring at me. Do you understand that? At least when he touches me I can do something about it. But when he stares. I can do *nothing*. Do you understand, Ben?'

I told her that I understood, not at all sure that I did.

She let out a long sigh. 'I've thought about killing him, I really have. I've caught myself contemplating stabbing him to death, shooting him through the heart.'

The intensity of her words, her sincerity, frightened me.

'It wouldn't be worth it,' I joked. 'You'd be caught and

tried and sentenced to mandatory personality-wipe, and then who would I have to chat to in the mornings?'

She would not be placated by my levity. 'But what a way to go. Quick, painless – I'd just be stripped of my identity, all my worries and crazy thoughts.'

'And your *self*, Tammy.'

'But it'd be worth it!' she said with conviction. 'It'd be much better than suicide – and I'd have the satisfaction of showing *him* how I feel.'

'Tammy,' I said, in a kind of pleading reprimand.

She opened her mouth and began crying again, her face made ugly with anguish. I pulled her head to my shoulder.

'Oh, Christ, Ben. It's so unfair.'

Near to tears myself and utterly helpless, I made soothing sounds as you might to a baby. I could not bear the confirmation that another's emotional life was in more of a mess than my own, especially when that person was someone I cared for.

I have no idea how long we sat like this, on the marble bench in the silver light of the Ring of Tharssos. When Tammy had almost sniffed herself hoarse, she lifted her head from my shoulder.

What she said next surprised me. 'Where's Epsilon Indi, Ben?'

She had asked me the same question often in the past, while drinking beer on my veranda. The enquiry had always preceded a half-joking, half-boastful account of how some day she would visit the star.

I scanned the heavens, indicated a twinkling point of light. 'There, that's Epsilon.'

'I'd love to go there. Have I told you that? Chalcedony, Epsilon II – they say it's the most beautiful planet of all the colonies.'

She stared, the Ringlight reflected in her eyes.

'Have you ever thought of leaving the bay?' I asked.

'What, and go to Epsilon II? It's far too expensive!'

I smiled. 'Not necessarily off-planet. There's Mackinley, any one of a dozen other resorts along the coast. You'd be away from your father.'

Her gaze became introspective, wistful. She no longer saw Epsilon II. She shook her head. 'I have too many ties here,' she said.

'You don't need your father's money, Tammy. You could leave here, get a loan, set up your own gallery.'

She looked up at me. 'I have too many ties!' she repeated. 'You wouldn't understand, Ben. I can't explain.'

I shrugged, hurt that she could be so dismissive.

'Look,' she said, pointing, as polychromatic laser beams sliced vectors through the night sky above the villa.

Once a week I take my hover-car and drive into the foot-hills of the Central Highlands. I spend the mornings prospecting for gems and other features of lapidary interest, and the afternoons admiring the views. In the early days, when I arrived on Addenbrooke shortly after the death of my daughter, I took refuge in the hills perhaps two or three times a week. The grand scale of the scenery, the extensive panoramas to be seen from the meadowed mountainsides which projected above the cover of the rain forest, had the effect of measuring human concerns against the overall scheme of things, and reducing their significance. More recently, when the years had worked to ease the pain, I made the journey less frequently.

I'd spent a restless night, thinking about Tammy Challenger. I was hurt that she felt she could not speak to me in complete openness. At the same time, I reminded myself that she had confided in no one else. This fact in itself spoke volumes about her loneliness, her isolation and lack of trust in those about her. I determined to see more of her, develop our relationship to the point where she felt she could trust me. God knows, she needed someone.

That morning, on my way to the Highlands, I had stopped by the gallery to see how she was, but the showroom was locked and there was no sign of Tammy. I spent the rest of the day at a favourite location in the foothills, my thoughts far from the search for gemstones. I packed up in the early evening and drove to a prominent spur which afforded an uninterrupted view of the vast extent of the rain forest, the entire bay area and the long sweep of the coastline down as far as Mackinley. As I sat in the car, a dazzling bolt of golden light speared through the atmosphere two hundred kilometres south and landed on the deck of the telemass station, the latest demolecularized cargo of people and provisions from any one of a dozen distant colony planets. Five minutes later another bolt appeared, this time streaking away from Addenbrooke. The sight never failed to thrill me.

I climbed out and walked to the edge of the prominence. Perhaps a dozen streams threaded their way through the rain forest, pouring from step to step in great silver gouts like molten silver. Here and there, bodies of water collected in natural sinks to form idyllic lagoons, and it was at one such, perhaps a kilometre below, that I saw the hovercar come to a halt and settle. I recognized the vehicle; it was the crimson, battered run-about that Marty Challenger had bought Tammy for her twenty-first birthday. A small figure climbed from the driving seat – Tammy, distinctive in her pink tracksuit. I raised my binoculars and watched her walk to the edge of the sparkling lagoon. She began to undress, peeling off her tracksuit. I did not lower the binoculars – because it was obvious, as I watched, that she was not alone. She was speaking to someone in the hovercar, its cab concealed behind a stand of flowering shrubbery.

Tammy flung aside the last of her clothing and waded out, her body thin, angular and white. When the water reached her midriff she launched herself forward and swam the length of the lagoon. Then she turned, treading water, and called to her companion in the vehicle, no doubt exhorting whoever it was to join her. Tammy swam back and climbed out, her body bejewelled with diamond droplets. On her face was an expression of joy such as I had never expected to witness. She was a woman transformed. I was overcome with delight that Tammy had found someone, and at the same time I experienced a pang of what might have been jealousy. As I watched, a woman stepped from the cover of the bush, a small, sun-browned figure as naked as Tammy. They embraced in the silver shallows, belly to belly, breast to breast. I lowered the binoculars, my heart hammering, and the two small figures were reduced to a manageable anonymity.

The woman in Tammy's arms was Rowena Challenger.

I spent the next couple of days in my A-frame, drinking beer and watching a succession of old movies. Through the kitchen window I could see across the street to the gallery, but Tammy never showed herself.

In the period which followed my daughter's death, during which my wife and I had first sniped, then argued, and then let go with recriminations we had bottled up for years – resulting in her leaving me for someone I had considered a friend – I had thought that I would never again be amazed by the tortured complexity, the sheer unpredictability, of human motivations. What I saw that day by the lagoon had proved me wrong. I considered the events of the party, re-enacted the confrontation I had witnessed that night between Rowena Challenger and her stepdaughter. Nothing I had seen at the party had prepared me for the scene in the mountains – quite the reverse, in fact. I failed to see why Tammy and Rowena should come together as they had. In the end I gave up trying to work things out, lost myself in the trivial, totally predictable motivations of the characters in one ancient movie after another, and tried to forget.

Two or three days after the incident by the lagoon, I was summoned from the veranda by the chime of the vid-screen. Marty Challenger stared out at me, his face big and florid. 'Henderson?'

'Challenger,' I said, surprised.

'I'm calling about Tamsin.'

I was aware of a sudden tightness in my stomach. 'What's wrong?'

'She's not with you by any chance?'

'No.' I hesitated. 'I haven't seen her since the party.'

He sighed, mopped sweat from his face with a big, red bandanna. 'She went missing early yesterday evening.'

'Went missing?'

'She left the house, didn't come back. She stayed out all night.'

'Did she take her car?'

Challenger hesitated. 'This morning the police reported finding it abandoned in the foothills. I'm going up there now.'

'I'll come with you.'

'That won't be necessary, Henderson.'

'I know the area like the back of my hand,' I said. 'I'm coming with you.'

I cut the connection before he could further object.

Marty Challenger was waiting in the drive, standing beside the big, silver safari truck he took on hunting expeditions into the interior. He was wearing red slacks, a white silk shirt and a fedora. He nodded grudgingly as I drew to a halt beside him. 'We'll take my truck, Henderson. Her car's just ten kilometres up the road.'

I took my place in the passenger seat and Challenger gunned the engine and drove up the winding road into the hills. He steered without saying a word, hands gripping the apex of the wheel, staring straight ahead.

Sunlight flickered through the tall trees as we climbed steadily away from the bay.

I cleared my throat. 'Has Tammy ever done anything like this before?'

He flicked me a glance. 'Of course not. Why should she?'

I sensed his uneasiness. 'Well, after the party the other night . . .'

He opened his palms on the rim of the wheel, closed them. 'Rowena was just playing the fool. Tamsin can take it.'

I chose not to debate the point. 'How do they get on?' I asked. 'It must be hard for Tammy, having a stepmother just a few years her senior.'

I glanced at Challenger. He kept his gaze on the winding road. 'They have their differences. I think Rowena has it the hardest, though.' He hesitated, as if wondering just how much to tell me. 'Rowena's very highly strung, temperamental. She's been very ill the past few years—'

'Hence the hardware?' I asked.

Challenger nodded. 'I worked on her myself. She tires easily. She finds Tamsin's attention somewhat trying.'

'Her attention? In what way?'

'Well . . .' He cleared his throat. 'I think Tamsin resents Rowena. She must see her as someone who has replaced her in my affections, after all.'

I was at once amazed by his ego and amused that he had it so wrong.

A little later Challenger steered the truck off the road and down a rough track. The shimmering surface of a lagoon came into view, its level maintained by a mathematically perfect waterfall from a sink on the step above. Rainbows spangled the mist between the banks of vegetation. I recognized the lagoon as the one at which Tammy and Rowena had had their tryst the other day.

Tammy's hover-car stood beside the water.

I turned to Challenger. 'Something must have happened to make Tammy leave yesterday and stay away,' I said. 'Are you sure she didn't argue with your wife?'

He avoided my gaze, stared up the incline. 'They haven't seen each other for days,' he said. 'Since the party. I don't know what's got into the girl.'

Two pathways led away from the lagoon, winding uphill through tangled undergrowth. I pointed them out to Challenger and suggested that we take one each.

For the next couple of hours we climbed the hillside, calling her name in vain. That Tammy had taken it into her head to run off like this suggested she had been troubled at the time, but right now I was less concerned for her mental health than I was for her physical safety. The paths we followed were steep and dangerous, with long drops to the levels below. I had never before realized how much I might miss Tammy, how much I simply wanted her beside me.

It was mid-afternoon by the time we gave up and drove back to the villa. A servant was waiting in the drive as we drew up. 'Any luck?' Challenger asked.

'I'm sorry, sir.'

'Mrs Challenger isn't back?'

'Not yet, sir.'

I stared at Challenger. 'Where is she?' I asked.

'She spends every Sixthday at some beauty parlour in Mackinley. Wild horses wouldn't drag her away.' He sighed. 'Thanks for your help, Henderson. You wouldn't care to come in for a drink?'

'Ah . . . no. No thanks. I must be getting back.' I climbed from the truck, returned to my own vehicle and drove home in a daze.

Rowena had spent the day in Mackinley, and Tammy was missing – the car by the lagoon leading us to believe that she had taken off into the hills. As I pulled up beside my A-frame, I imagined the two women together in some hotel bedroom. I climbed the steps to the veranda, feeling depressed, excluded and *old*.

I saw the magazine on the chesterfield as soon as I stepped into the lounge. I sat down and picked it up: a travel brochure, open at the page advertising the colony world of Chalcedony, Epsilon Indi II.

I noticed that the bedroom door was slightly ajar.

'Tammy?'

She appeared in the doorway. She had the pathetic, bedraggled appearance of a kitten saved from drowning. Her tracksuit was ripped and grass-stained, her left cheek bruised.

'Hello, Ben.'

I stood. She hurried into my arms and I held her, unable to find the words to express my relief. I stepped back, my hands on her shoulders. Her eyes were red and swollen, but dry now as if she had cried herself empty.

'Ben . . . I couldn't think of anywhere else to go. I spent the night in my car in the hills, wondering what to do. This morning I thought of you. You were out when I got here, but I climbed through the trapdoor in the kitchen.' She began sobbing, then. 'I thought things were bad that night at the party, Ben.' She shook her head. 'But it's *hell* now . . .'

'We've been looking for you all day, Tammy. I thought you were with Rowena.'

She stared at me. 'Rowena? Why should I . . . ?'

'Three days ago, at the lagoon. I saw you there with her.'

'You did?' Tammy actually smiled then through her tears. 'I bet you wondered what the hell was going on, didn't you?'

I shrugged. 'I've had time to think about it. You were seeing each other to spite your father, right?'

She shook her head. 'It's far more complicated than that.'

'It is?'

She looked at me with woeful eyes. 'You see, it wasn't Rowena I was with.'

'But I saw you!'

'Ben, it's a long story. Can I have a beer, please?'

She sat on the chesterfield beside the much-thumbed brochure. I returned from the kitchen with two beers and sat down beside her. She began slowly, haltingly, looking up from time to time to see how I reacted, and punctuating her story with sips of beer.

It all began three years ago, on Earth.

'When I graduated from art school,' Tammy said, 'I moved back to Vancouver and started up as a freelance graphic designer, living with my parents until I could afford a place of my own . . .'

It was not the best of arrangements. She had never seen eye to eye with her mother – Tammy considered her a parasite who had married Challenger for the prestige and riches it would bring – and when Tammy announced that *she* would never marry, and gave the reasons why, her mother told her to pack her belongings and leave within the week.

Tammy rented an apartment on the sea front and, not long after moving in, met a woman called Gabrielle de

Carreras, the arts editor of a local magazine for which Tammy freelanced from time to time. They began seeing each other casually over business lunches, and when it became obvious that they had more in common than merely their line of work, their meetings became more frequent. They had known each other for three months when Gabrielle moved in with Tammy.

One week later her mother was killed in the bayside monorail disaster. The extent of her injuries precluded any hope of resurrection.

Here, Tammy shrugged. 'Fortunately for her, she'd had herself encoded a couple of months before.'

I stopped her. 'Encoded?'

Tammy smiled. 'You've been away from Earth too long, Ben. Encoding is when you have your identity or personality or whatever, your very *self*, recorded on a piece of software like a needle, this long.' Tammy held her forefingers about five centimetres apart. 'My mother was encoded on just such a piece of software. It was strange, going to her funeral – or rather the cremation of her body – and knowing that she still existed and sooner or later would be back with us. If only I'd known then . . .'

Meanwhile, Tammy was enjoying life. She had never been in love before. She'd had girlfriends at college, but had never experienced anything quite like the happiness she felt now. Gabrielle combined the roles of lover, therapist and teacher, and Tamsin Challenger left behind the chronically shy, underconfident girl she had been and became a woman confident of her art and her self.

Tammy looked up. 'It was the best time of my life, Ben.'

'What happened?'

It was a while before she could bring herself to speak.

Gabrielle fell ill, and the physicians diagnosed a rare blood disorder. The condition was curable, but at a cost Gabrielle and Tammy together were unable to afford. The medics gave Gabrielle a year to live, which meant that she would be dead before her twenty-fifth birthday.

In desperation Tammy approached her father.

'He said he could treat her,' Tammy said. 'But only on one condition.'

When Tammy explained the situation to Gabrielle, she jumped at the chance. Anything was preferable to the terrible oblivion she faced if she went untreated. Within one month, Martin Challenger successfully flushed the virus from her system, and then he began the long, delicate programme of neuro-surgery to implant the cerebral hardware required to accommodate an Encoded Identity Insert.

A legally binding contract was drawn up. For three days, Gabrielle de Carreras would live normally as herself; for the next three days, upon insertion of the EII, the body of Carreras would be inhabited by the persona, the identity, of Martin Challenger's wife.

'Christ,' I said. 'Rowena is Gabrielle. No wonder you . . .' I recalled the way Tammy had looked upon Rowena at the party, their (or rather Tammy and Gabrielle's) tryst at the lagoon. And it explained more: Rowena's attitude to Tammy – her resentment that she had to share the body. I even began to understand Challenger's obsession with his daughter, for, although he might have his wife's identity as company some of the time, that other part of her – her physical self – was lost for ever. Tammy sufficiently resembled Rowena to remind him of what he had lost.

'Everything went well for the first few months. All parties were satisfied; Rowena and Gabrielle that they were alive, my father and myself that we had the people we loved, even if for only part of the time. I could put aside the thoughts of what my father and Rowena did together, and as Gabrielle wasn't conscious when all that went on, she could tolerate what happened to her body. It was my mother, though ... she found it hard to accept that Gabrielle and I lived together for the three days as lovers. She'd sometimes come round to my apartment on the third day and scream that what I was doing was sinful and would be punished. It was really scary, Ben – watching my mother's anger, her mannerisms and body language coming from the body of the person I loved so much.' Tammy smiled and shrugged. 'Rowena once even ran away when the three day term was up, so that Gabrielle couldn't resume life in her own body. My mother was always a little unbalanced.'

Then, a year ago, Martin Challenger retired, and he put it to Tammy, Rowena and Gabrielle that they leave Earth and start a new life on one of the colony worlds. They all agreed, and selected Addenbrooke, Altair II. Six months ago the strange *ménage à quatre* took up residence in the villa above Magenta Bay.

Tammy paused there, staring at her fingers. 'Not long after we moved here, things started to go wrong. When Rowena's part of the three day term was drawing to a close, and it was time for her EII to be withdrawn, she'd go berserk. She'd run off for days or threaten to kill herself.' Tammy looked up at me, tearful. 'The thing is, Ben, she got her way. A month ago, my father extended her tenancy to five days in six. He told me that it was safer that way, but I know it was just so that he could have more time with Rowena.'

'But what about the contract?' I asked. 'I thought you said it was legally binding?'

Tammy smiled sadly. 'It is – on Earth. On Addenbrooke, it's worthless. My father can do whatever the hell he wants.'

'So that's why you ran away?'

'After that last day with Gabrielle, when you saw us in the hills, my mother came to my room and told me that she was trying to get Marty to agree to allow me just one day a *month* with Gabrielle. Can you imagine how I felt, hearing this from the lips that the day before . . .' She paused there, then went on, 'I wanted to hit her, Ben. I wanted to hurt her, but how could I do that to the body of the person I loved?'

She was crying again, and all I could do was hold her. At length, when she had calmed down, I asked about the Encoded Identity Inserts.

'They're known as personality pins, Ben. They were introduced on Earth three or four years ago, and bought by people who wanted immortality – even though there weren't enough donor bodies to accommodate everyone. They invested in EIIs in the hope that in years to come androids or cloned bodies would be developed.'

I shook my head. 'That's all very well, but are these inserts the actual person, or just computerized copies? Surely your mother died in the 'rail accident – the encoding of her is just a clever copy, made months before.'

Tammy shrugged. 'What are we, Ben? What are our brains? Nothing but electro-chemical programming. Wipe the brain, and what have you got? Just so much lifeless meat. It follows that a faithful encoding of a person's identity will record everything, their emotions and memories, their very *selves*.' She smiled at me. 'But I understand your objections. Gabrielle refused on religious grounds earlier this year, when I suggested that we should both be encoded in case anything happened to us.'

I stared at her. 'Did you go ahead with it?'

'A couple of months ago I telemassed to Earth and visited a private clinic in Toronto. My father would have done it, but I didn't want *that*.'

We talked for a while about the process of encoding, and all the other technological wonders I was behind on. I was pleased that Tammy was talking about something other than her more immediate worries.

Later, she reached out and took my hand. 'I don't know what I'd do without you, Ben.' She smiled, then looked suddenly stricken. 'Hell, you don't know how much I miss her.'

Later still I made Tammy take a shower and change into a pair of my trousers and an old shirt three sizes too big for her. I told her to stay in the house until I got back, then went to see her father.

I drove from the settlement and up the hill and drew to a halt in the terracotta courtyard outside Challenger's villa. A uniformed servant showed me into the foyer, then down a corridor to a long, sunlit lounge. Marty Challenger stood at the far end of the room, contemplating the view of the bay from a large picture window.

He turned as the servant announced me. 'Ah, Henderson.'

'I think I will take you up on that offer of a drink,' I said.

He nodded. 'What'll it be?'

I asked for a beer, and while he fixed the drinks – a brandy for himself – I looked around the room. On a low table stood a large holo-cube, and within it was the representation of a blonde woman. She was walking along a sea shore, smiling and waving. At first I thought it was Tammy – and then I saw that the woman was older, more made-up and sophisticated. I realized that it was Challenger's wife, Rowena, before the accident.

He passed me the beer and turned to the window, cupping a brandy glass in his palm. 'Still no sign of Tamsin, Henderson. I've had men out searching all day.'

'That's what I came here to see you about,' I said. 'She's at my place.'

He turned. 'She is? Why didn't you bring her back?'

'She doesn't want to come back, Challenger. At least, not yet.'

'How is she?' He seemed genuinely concerned.

'She's in one hell of a state, to be honest. She told me about Rowena and Gabrielle.'

He drew a breath. 'Well, I suppose it had to come out sooner or later.'

His complacency angered me. 'Do you have any idea how unhappy she is?' I asked. 'Why do you think she ran away? You allow her to see Gabrielle for one day a week – less, if your wife has her way – and the rest of the time she's denied the woman she loves. The kid's at her wit's end, for Godsake. She can't take much more—'

'Henderson,' he cut in, a note of pleading in his voice. 'You don't understand. It isn't as easy as you think.'

'All you have to do is allow Tammy a little more time with Gabrielle.'

Challenger was shaking his head. 'As I've mentioned before, my wife is a strong-willed, temperamental woman. Look, Henderson, do you think I don't know what Tamsin is going through?' He stopped there, looking over my shoulder.

I heard the sound of high-heels on the tesseral mosaic.

'Ah, Rowena.' Challenger said.

'You didn't tell me that you had a guest, Marty.' Rowena fixed me with a speculative gaze. 'Henderson, isn't it? Tam's friend?'

She was wearing a black, off-the-shoulder dress, flamenco style, with a rose in her hair – making full use of Gabrielle de Carreras' natural beauty.

'I suppose you've heard about Tam?' she asked. 'If I were you I wouldn't worry. She's prone to these displays of temper.'

'Darling, Tamsin is at Henderson's place on the beach.'

Rowena regarded me. The filigree nexus which braced her neck seemed to hold her head at a haughty angle. 'She is?'

Challenger went on, 'Henderson knows about you and Carreras.'

Rowena's smile was emphasized by the crimson of her lips against the white of her perfect teeth. 'What do you want, Henderson? I take it you did come here for a reason?'

'I've been telling your husband how unfair I consider your treatment of Tammy. If you knew how much she feels for Gabrielle . . .'

Rowena stared at me. 'Tam has the use of her for one day every week. That should be sufficient for her needs.'

I laughed out loud. 'Are you serious?'

The woman almost spat. 'She should be grateful for that! Doesn't she realize that if it wasn't for the skill of my husband, her precious little girlfriend would be dead?'

'Don't *you* realize,' I said, 'that if it wasn't for Gabrielle, you'd be so much data on a personality pin?'

The silence throbbed with the thud of my heartbeat as Rowena Challenger looked from me to her husband. Her eyes blazed. I recalled what Tammy had said about her mother being a little unbalanced. 'I will *not* give in, Marty,' she said, staring at Challenger. 'Let that be understood!'

She turned and left the room.

'Well?' I asked, when she was out of earshot.

Challenger stared at me. 'Well what?'

'Are you going to listen to her, or will you agree to give Gabrielle equal time?'

'That almost sounds like a threat, Henderson.'

'Consider it as such,' I said. 'The contract you had drawn up on Earth might not be binding here, but when what you've been doing to Tammy is made public—'

'You wouldn't—'

'I know a top firm of lawyers in Mackinley,' I said. 'I think Tammy has good ground for litigation – but win or lose, she'll drag your name through the shit in the process.'

He gestured. 'You saw how Rowena feels about it.'

'Then talk some sense into her, for Godsake. Make her see reason. Look, Tammy might even be happy with less than an equal share, just so long as she has more than she's getting now. Is that too much to ask?'

Challenger pursed his lips, stared into his drink. 'Send Tamsin back,' he said, 'and I'll promise I'll do what I can. You can ask no fairer than that.'

I remained staring at him, unsure whether to take his sincerity at face value.

I nodded. 'I'll do that,' I said. 'Thanks for the drink.'

Tammy returned to the villa on the hill and I heard nothing more for a couple of days. She neither called nor dropped by, and I assumed the worst. Then, one morning, as I returned from my daily walk along the beach, I noticed her car parked outside the showroom. I crossed the street and pushed through the door.

'Ben!' She hurried around the counter and hugged me. 'Where've you been? I came around to tell you this morning.'

'Tell me what?' I laughed; her excitement was contagious.

'Marty's allowed me more time with Gabrielle! We can see each other every week – two days in six.'

'And Rowena agreed?'

'She objected at first, but Marty talked her round. Isn't that fantastic? And it's all thanks to you. What did you say?'

I shrugged. 'Just talked to him reasonably.'

Tammy went on, 'The pin's coming out this evening, so I

can spend the night with Gabrielle. Then tomorrow – I've got it all planned. We're setting off into the mountains. We'll take a tent and enough food for two days and lose ourselves away from everything.' She shook her head as if in disbelief. 'I can't wait, Ben.'

'I hope you have a good time. Look, why don't you call when you get back – bring Gabrielle round. I'd really like to meet her.'

Tammy laid her head on her shoulder. 'I'll do that, Ben.'

Two days later I was in the workshop, cutting a pair of gems to set in rings for Tammy and Gabrielle, when the light connected to the vid-screen in the house flashed red. I turned off the cutter, laid down the stones and made my way to the lounge.

I switched on the screen.

'Tammy – how did it go?'

I stopped. She was staring out at me, her face ashen. 'Tammy, what's wrong?'

'We didn't go. Rowena left the villa two nights ago. She's been away ever since. This morning . . . this morning they found her.' Her voice was a monotone, as if drugged. She closed her eyes, then opened them and stared. 'Ben, will you come with me, please? We're driving up the coast now. We'll collect you.'

I nodded, unable to find the words to question her. She cut the connection.

I was standing in the street when Marty Challenger drew up in his safari truck. One of his medics was in the passenger seat.

Tammy sat in the back, as stony-faced as she had been on the vid-screen. She watched me climb in beside her, then took my hand in a tight grip and laid her head on my shoulder. Challenger turned the truck and headed up the coast road, away from the settlement.

We remained silent for the duration of the journey. Beside me, Tammy was rigid, her hand cold. I wanted to question her, ask her what the hell had happened; surely the truth, no matter how terrible, would be better than the ignorance fostered by silence.

Fifteen minutes later Challenger steered the truck from the road and down a rough, unmetalled track to a wide sweep of beach. The tide was out, and we raced along the flats to the opposite headland. A hover-car was parked beside a taped-off area in the dunes. A couple of Challenger's medics were gazing down at something in the sand.

Challenger settled the vehicle, cut the engine and climbed out. Tammy and I just sat and stared.

On the sloping sand inside the cordoned area, Rowena Challenger lay on her back. She had opened her dress and the walls of her abdomen with something very sharp . . .

One of the medics rose from examining the corpse, ducked under the tape and approached Challenger. 'I'm sorry, sir. There's nothing we can do. The two day limit . . .'

Tammy pressed her face to my chest and moaned.

Marty Challenger crossed the cordoned area to the body. He knelt beside it and turned the once beautiful head. I was aware that Tammy was watching him, too; she stiffened, as what he was doing became obvious. With a fingernail, Challenger slid back a tiny panel on the occipital console, and a thin, silver spoke, glinting in the sunlight, ejected itself automatically. He took it in his palm and closed his hand about it in a gesture of ultimate satisfaction. He passed the insert to a medic, who returned to the hover-car.

Then Challenger looked up at Tammy and myself, and smiled.

Tammy cried, tore herself from me and scrambled into

the front seat. Before I could stop her, she had pulled a laser rifle from the door-rack and jumped from the truck.

'Tammy!' I cried.

She staggered forward under the weight of the rifle, myself and everyone around her frozen with fear. She approached her father and halted five metres from him. 'You bastard,' she sobbed, and before she lost control completely she hoisted the rifle and took aim.

Challenger was still kneeling, smiling at his daughter, when she fired wildly and blasted a hole in the centre of his chest.

Then she dropped the laser, and stared at what she had done, and screamed.

The trial was convened one month later and lasted just two days.

I gave evidence to the investigating officers and was called on as a witness. I swore that I had seen Challenger withdraw his wife's EII from Carreras' augmentation, that Tammy had been provoked into shooting her father. But the other witnesses – Challenger's medics – testified otherwise. I was escorted back to the witnesses' enclosure, numbed with shock at the miscarriage of justice.

Then Marty Challenger took the stand, his posture severely upright as a result of the resurrection surgery. He stated that, although Carreras was augmented to accept his wife's EII, she had been herself, Carreras, at the time of her suicide. The judging panel declared that Carreras had taken her own life while in a state of mental unbalance. The prosecution put it to the panel that Tammy's actions in shooting her father had been the result of long-standing hatred and jealousy of Challenger. Tammy's defence claimed that she had killed her father in a fit of mental instability, and because of this should be spared the ultimate punishment.

I sat through the proceedings with a terrible sense of foreboding.

All the time Tammy stood in the dock, immobile, staring straight ahead. If she saw me she gave no sign.

On the afternoon of the second day, the head of the judging panel declared the verdict. Tammy was found guilty of murder and sentenced to cerebral erasure, to be carried out within three days.

Only then did she look across the crowded chamber at me, and smile. Then she closed her eyes and bowed her head as the officials ushered her from the dock.

I left the court in a state of shock.

I spent a lot of time in the mountains, after that. I took a tent and food and prospecting tools and spent days in the Central Highlands, attempting to forget what had happened by losing myself in my work and the splendour of the scenery. I tried to avoid the lagoon where I had seen Tammy and Gabrielle, but every other body of water in the hills – and there were hundreds of them – served to remind me of Tammy and her lover. I reasoned that, but for the insane greed of Rowena Challenger, Tammy and Gabrielle might now be content with their two days in six together. Unlike all those years ago, when the magnificence of the terrain had helped ease the ache at the loss of my daughter, the mountains provided no such balm now. My daughter's death had been a tragic accident, and I had felt anger towards no one but myself; the terrible fact of Tammy's demise was that it was both avoidable and so unjust, and the anger I felt towards Challenger and Rowena and the judicial system consumed me like a fever.

One afternoon, about a month after the trial, I left the

mountains after a sojourn of more than a week. I had a good collection of rocks in my specimen sack, and the time spent away from civilization had put me in relatively good cheer. The sight of Magenta Bay, and all it represented in terms of memories, brought down a sudden depression. It occurred to me that it might be wise to move right away from the settlement.

To reach the bay road and my A-frame, I had to pass Challenger's villa. As I was driving along the road that skirted his property, I caught sight of a small figure sunbathing on the lawn. I pulled up, climbed from my buggy and walked through the knee-high scrub to the immaculate, unfenced lawns. I think I even ran the last few metres, then stopped dead.

'Tammy?'

It came to me that they had not wiped her, after all . . .

She sat up, then climbed to her feet, a hand shading her eyes from the sunlight as she looked at me. She was wearing a bright yellow bikini.

It was Tammy, the same gauche, rather angular body – though browner now than ever before. She had allowed her hair to grow.

'Henderson?' she asked, and although the voice was Tammy's, I detected a hardness, a suspicion. 'What do you want?'

Marty Challenger appeared on the veranda. 'I'm fixing a Martini, darling.'

She turned, and I saw the silver console at the base of her skull . . .

Challenger had seen me. 'Rowena?' he called.

I was almost physically sick.

Rowena hurried away from me and into the arms of her husband. Challenger stared at me over her head, his expression neutral.

I fled. I drove home in a daze of disbelief. I spent the

afternoon in the darkened lounge. I drank beer after beer and stared at the wall, the terrible truth repeating itself in my head like a nightmare.

With Rowena's suicide and Tammy's erasure, Challenger had achieved everything he could ever have hoped for. It was so neat, I told myself – so perfectly neat that it could not be the result of pure chance.

I drank myself to the edge of oblivion. I wanted to strike out, to destroy; only once before had I experienced a time when the thought of the future appalled me, when the prospect of going on seemed unbearable, but I experienced it again now.

I was saved by a knock at the door.

I staggered across the room and snatched it open. 'Yes?'

A middle-aged man in a neat grey suit stood on the veranda. 'Mr Benedict Henderson?'

'What do you want?'

I must have presented an aggressive, dishevelled sight, but he was unflappable. 'I represent Messrs. Delgardo and Graves, solicitors of Mackinley.' I noticed, then, the plastic container the size of a vid-screen at his feet. 'Tamsin Challenger was one of our clients, Mr Henderson. Before her erasure, she was allowed to attend to the dispersal of her personal effects. She wanted you to have this.' He passed me the box. 'If you would be so kind as to sign here, and here . . .'

I scrawled my signature on half a dozen official forms, then carried the container into the lounge and set it on the coffee table. I remained staring at it for a long time, wondering if I could bear to find out what it contained.

I reached out and broke the seal. The sides of the container folded down.

A polished wooden chest, which Tammy had carved herself and which I had admired every time I called in to see her . . .

I unfastened the gold clasp and eased back the lid. The chest contained painted shells and rocks and driftwood, a printed scarf, a small self-portrait in pastel. I lifted them out one by one, laid them on the coffee table.

At the bottom of the chest was a photograph. It showed Tammy and myself on the veranda of my A-frame. I stared at the camera with a glazed expression, while next to me Tammy smiled shyly.

I stared at the photograph and fought back the tears.

Then I noticed the brown envelope, standing upright at the back of the chest. It was weighted unevenly with some small, heavy object. Across the front of the envelope, in Tammy's hand, was scrawled: Ms Tamsin Louise Challenger, followed by the childish capitals: ME!

I ripped open the envelope and tipped the object into my hand.

Then, I did lose my fight against the tears.

I stared at Tammy's personality pin in disbelief.

The following Sixthday I followed Rowena Challenger, at a discreet distance, down the coast road to Mackinley.

She drove her buggy into a right-angled parking space on the main street and entered a beauty emporium. She had made Tammy's body her own. Although she still superficially resembled Tammy, she had added touches of sophistication: she was perfectly tanned and outfitted in a tight, off-the-shoulder mini dress, wore a new hairstyle and the latest cosmetics. She even moved with a brash confidence that her daughter had never possessed.

I waited in my vehicle, going over my plans. Two hours later, she emerged and turned left along the shop-fronts, towards me. As she passed, I jumped from the buggy and grabbed her. Passers-by stopped and stared as, before she could protest, I bundled her into the passenger seat and locked the door. By the time I rounded the vehicle and slipped into the driving seat, Rowena had composed herself.

'Just what the hell are you playing at, Henderson?' she said with cool disdain.

'It's time we had a little talk, Rowena.'

I glanced across at her. I could see Tammy in her face, but the knowledge of who was behind those eyes fuelled my determination.

She sat sideways in her seat. 'It is? And just what would you like to discuss?'

I started the engine, backed from the parking lot and steered up the coast road.

'You had it all planned, didn't you?'

She turned on me a smile of innocent bemusement. 'Had *what* all planned?'

'Your "suicide", Tammy's reaction to Gabrielle's death, your take-over of her body—'

She laughed. 'I don't know what you're talking about.'

We left Mackinley behind us and hit the open country, the wide sweep of the ocean to our left.

'I wondered why you agreed so easily to Tammy seeing Gabrielle two days in six, especially after telling me that one day a week was more than enough. Tammy told me that Challenger had talked you round – but what he'd actually done was to come up with a plan to get *everything* he wanted.'

Rowena watched me.

I went on, 'You killed yourself – or perhaps Challenger did it for you. This got rid of Gabrielle de Carreras, with the advantage that with your Identity Insert you'd be granted continued life.'

Rowena faltered. 'You have no proof.'

'Then Challenger staged that little scene on the beach. No wonder it seemed so theatrical. The body, conveniently undiscovered until after the two day limit, the medics on hand, Challenger's little performance with the pin, to turn the knife in Tammy's wound all the more, the rack of loaded lasers in the truck.'

By now, Rowena's smile lacked conviction. 'You have not one shred of evidence, Henderson.'

'It worked like a dream,' I went on. 'Tammy took the bait, killed Challenger and was duly sentenced to erasure. It was then a formality for Challenger or his medics to make a requisition for the erased body on research grounds, augment it and install your pin.'

I took my gaze off the road and glanced across at her. Rowena Challenger was smiling at me, nauseating in her confidence. There was nothing of Tammy in her expression, now; Rowena's rapacious, scheming sensibilities had transformed it. I recognized the face from the holo-cube in Challenger's villa.

'You've been playing quite the detective, Henderson. It's a pity for you that you cannot substantiate your allegations. The judiciary would laugh your claims out of court.'

It was my turn to smile. 'This case won't be going that far,' I said.

Her supercilious expression wavered. 'It won't . . .?'

I ignored her. I turned off the road and into the drive of a secluded beach chalet. I cut the engine, turned to face her.

She tried to smile. 'Henderson?'

I produced the shock-gun and held it where she could get a good, long look.

She rallied. 'I always thought you were after Tam's—'

'You're not getting off that lightly,' I said. I smiled. 'Though, in a way, it is Tammy's body I want.'

She stared at me, the beginning of fright in her eyes. 'What do you mean?'

I took great delight in telling her, and observing her reaction.

She screamed, attempted to open the locked door. '*No!*'

I hit her with the shock-gun and watched her spasm.

Then I carried her into the chalet and laid her on the bed. I turned her head on the pillow and opened the console. The Identity Insert unscrewed with a high, whirring sound, ejected itself with a final click. I pulled it out all the way and replaced it with Tammy's pin. The hardware in her head pulled it from my fingers, eased it into her cerebellum and screwed it down. I closed the cover.

During the next hour, while Tammy gradually came to her senses, I arranged the various papers I had prepared. I'd obtained a transcript of the court proceedings, and the newspaper report of the trial. Also, I had laboriously written a more subjective account of the trial and the events of the past two months, in the form of a personal letter to Tammy. The account of Gabrielle de Carreras' death had taken me hours and many redrafts.

Tammy moaned. I crossed to the bed and sat down beside her.

With the accession of Tamsin Challenger's identity to its seat of consciousness, the body seemed to undergo a subtle transformation. Despite the suntan, the cosmetics, the hairstyle and the short dress, the awkward, gangling Tammy of old re-established herself.

She blinked, smiled when she saw me.

'Ben . . . Where am I? The last thing I remember . . . I went to Earth to be encoded . . . Ben!' She tried to struggle upright. I held her. 'Ben, my father doesn't know about my encoding, does he? He wanted to do it himself, but I didn't trust him. So I had it done privately.'

I reassured her that her secret was safe.

Then she became aware of her augmentation. She

fingered the occipital console. 'Ben – what's happened?' She panicked. 'What date is it?'

I told her. 'Tammy, two months have elapsed. You're . . . you're using your Identity Insert. A lot has happened since you were encoded.'

I assisted her to the lounger before the picture window overlooking the ocean. I sat next to her and gave her the papers. 'This is the easiest way I could think of to let you know what happened, Tammy.'

First, she read my letter.

'Gabrielle!' she cried, appealing to me to tell her that it wasn't true.

I shook my head. 'I'm so sorry . . .'

She read the account of the trial and the newspaper cuttings, and then began again from the beginning.

We stood on the deck of the telemass station.

Tammy stared at the crammed wallet. 'One hundred thousand, Ben? But I can't take this!'

I smiled. 'You need it,' I said. 'You can't start a new life with nothing.'

'And this?' She held up her passport.

'I arranged it all last week. I made contacts. Don't worry, it's a very good forgery.'

A call went out for all travellers to take their places.

'Ben . . .' She tried not to cry. 'Come and visit me, OK? I'll be in touch.'

Behind Tammy, her fellow voyagers were walking out across the translation pad, prior to being stripped down to their constituent molecules and fired at hyper-light speed through space.

'Ben, what about Rowena's pin?'

I tapped the envelope in my pocket. 'I'll make sure your father gets it.'

'But when Rowena's reanimated, she'll know what you did.'

'Then that'll make us even. I know what *they* did, after all. Don't worry. They won't dare breathe a word.'

'*Will all travellers . . .*'

'Ben!' She flung her arms around me in a hug.

'Goodbye, Tammy.'

She ran across the deck to the pad, took her position and waved. Seconds later, the motionless crowd turned to fire.

I watched the bolt of golden light speed from the deck and arc away into the heavens *en route* to Epsilon Indi II, the glare bringing tears to my eyes.

Then I left the station, posted Rowena back to Marty Challenger and took the coast road home.

Blue Shifting

1

As soon as Janner awoke he cursed himself for having fallen asleep. He lay on his back without moving, feeling at once relief that he was safe, and a kind of retrospective dread at the thought of what might have befallen him. He told himself that, in future, he'd stay awake until five to be on the safe side.

He kept his eyes closed and listened, as if visual denial might make his situation somehow less real. He could hear the distant hum of traffic, an almost subliminal drone interspersed with the sharp sounds of horns, near and far; the ululating cries of women, and what might have been street vendors, in a high, sing-song language.

The air around him was warm and humid; he was sweating profusely. At last he willed himself to open his eyes. He was on the floor of a long, darkened room. He could make out rows of three-tier bunk-beds, occupied by shadowy, covered figures. He climbed quietly to his feet, careful not to disturb the sleepers, and moved towards a high window, one of a dozen ranged the length of the wall.

The sun was rising over a shambles of rooftops – a dilapidated skyline of two- and three-storey buildings. Across from where he stood, a cinema – judging by the posters of overweight film stars placarded across its façade – was washed in faded pink and white pastel shades, like every other building in the long, narrow street. Down below, hordes of foreshortened citizens teemed, their one-way flow snarled by the occasional obstruction of a rickshaw.

Janner turned from the window and leaned against the wall. For the past ten years he had lived a reclusive life, at first in a shack on the lonely western coast of New Zealand's South Island, and then, when his funds ran low, as a country ranger and fire-watcher in the Mount Cook National Park. After so many years with minimal human contact, crowds filled him with dread.

As dawn strengthened behind him and filled the room with its rose-water light, Janner paid more attention to the occupants of the bunk-beds. They were lying absolutely still, laid out on their backs and covered from head to foot with white sheets. He counted a dozen such figures. There was not a sound to be heard in the room not a drawn breath, snore or waking cough. At once, he became aware of the smell in the air, an indefinable sweetness that bordered on the putrid.

His rucksack was on the floor where he had awoken. He snatched it up and hurried down the aisle between the makeshift wooden bunks towards a door at the far end of the room. Before he reached it, the door creaked open and the perilously frail figure of a small old man, wearing a soiled white vest and shorts, hobbled over the threshold. He pushed a brush across the floor, up the aisle towards Janner, who stood immobile, waiting to be seen and anticipating an outraged reprimand. The old Asian halted, reached for a pillar to his right and flicked a switch. Overhead, a line of six large fans swept into motion, stirring the turgid air. The old man bent and pushed his brush ever closer and, as he passed, Janner saw the glaucous membrane that covered his eyes like the skin on boiled milk. Hurriedly, but with care, so as not to startle the janitor, he moved towards the door and slipped out. His last sight of the room in which he'd awoken was of the old man sculling his broom between the silent corpses like a holy man bestowing benediction.

He almost ran down the rickety flight of stairs, turning on three landings before coming to the ground floor and the open doorway. Beyond, a press of humanity surged. Janner shouldered his rucksack and tried to prepare himself for the ordeal ahead. He took a breath and plunged into the flow, and was immediately swept down the street by the bodies around him. The pedestrians poured down both road and pavement, forced on to the latter only when black and yellow taxi-cabs, horns blaring, nudged their way through the throng. He was shoved aside by the first of four jogging bearers carrying a stretcher above their heads, the swaddled corpse jouncing with the rhythm of their steps. As he watched, the bearers cut across the flow and slipped into the opening of an alleyway, and Janner, taking his chance, stepped into the vacuum left in their wake. He found himself in the narrow alley. The cries and calls, horns and engines were modulated to a background hum, though the press of bodies around him was just as intense. The alley was paved with uneven stones, sloping between crazily leaning buildings of tiny red bricks. The pall-bearers put on a spurt and passed from sight. Men and women, children and scrawny dogs pushed past him. A khaki-coloured cow ambled by, its bulging gut forcing him against the brickwork. Janner passed open shop-fronts let into the walls, faces staring out above goods for sale: packets of biscuits and incense, cigarettes and chocolate. He studied the signs and advertisements: the script was joined by a lateral upper bar, with hooks and swirls descending from it.

As he made his way down the alley, adjusting his stride, to the long, uneven steps, a tout materialized beside him and kept pace with a kind of desperate, urgent skip. 'Hashish, sir? Smack? Good smack. You want guide?'

Janner felt himself colour, increased his pace.

It seemed that he was hounded for ten, fifteen minutes, his silence met with an obstinate litany of offers, before the man gave up and vanished as instantly as he'd appeared.

Three times, beggars at ground level thrust stumps into his path – arms or legs, he could not tell: his fleeting glimpse of raw, ill-stitched flesh rendered all limbs alike – and each time Janner turned his head and hurried on. He was at that stage of desperation – the minor troubles he'd experienced since waking indicative of his greater plight – where he felt like stopping in his tracks and yelling out loud. Then, almost before he knew it, the alley debouched on to a broad, sweeping plinth of steps, and he was staring out across the calm, sacred breadth of the Ganges.

The sights and sounds that had harassed him in the alley now decreased to manageable degrees of each: it was as if the expanse of the river soaked up the sound, as if the eye was drawn to it at the expense of the activity on the terraced bank: the scurrying of children carrying racked glasses of tea, donkeys bearing back-breaking loads of timber, the funeral processions following bodies borne aloft on biers, bound in red, white or orange winding sheets and heaped with orange flowers.

Janner had eyes only for the wide, slow river, a cynosure of calm after so much chaos. Slowly, he took the steps down to the ghats and entered a hexagonal belvedere or tower. He sat on the stone seat which ran around the circumference of the interior, and stared through an arched recess at the water, tinted pink and silver in the morning sun.

He unhitched his rucksack, removed his jacket and stripped down to his T-shirt. It was cooler in the thick stone shade, and much of the sound outside was excluded. He worked to control his breathing, calm himself and gather his thoughts.

He recalled once watching a TV programme about the

holy city of Varanasi. The Ganges, on the banks of which the city was built, was considered sacred by devotees of the three major faiths in India: Hinduism, Islam and Buddhism. Millions of citizens every year made the pilgrimage to the Ganges, to be blessed by its beneficent waters, to die within the environs of the city and be cremated and have their ashes scattered on the river . . . Janner wondered if the fact that Varanasi was a holy city was significant to the situation in which he found himself.

From a pouch in his rucksack he withdrew a spiral-bound notebook and flipped it open. He contemplated what he had written on each of the three previous days. He'd scribbled his hasty impression of each city, the incidents of each day – but what concerned him now was not so much the content of his diary but the cities themselves. Surabaya, Alexandria, La Paz, and now Varanasi; was there any link, anything that might connect the cities, however slight or tenuous?

A shadow fell across his notes. He looked up, expecting the attentions of a tout. Instead, a woman – a Westerner in her late thirties – sat down on the stone bench opposite him and admired the view.

He felt suddenly uneasy in the presence of a *bona fide* tourist, as if she might have the ability to see through him and find him out. Self-consciously he returned to his notes. There was, he decided, no possible connection between any of the cities. With the exception of La Paz, none were capitals; he had been to none of them before, or even thought of visiting them. The more he considered his situation, the more ludicrous it became.

He sensed that the woman was watching him. He looked up. She smiled. She wore open-toed sandals, lightweight blue slacks and a white blouse.

'It is so calm in here,' she said, gesturing back towards the terraced incline, 'after the city.' He guessed, from her stilted English and rather outdated, shabby dress, that she was East European.

He nodded uncertainly and pretended to busy himself with his notes.

She persisted: 'Have you been in Varanasi long?'

A quick glance was all he would give her, hoping she might get the message. 'A few hours. I came on the overnight train from Delhi.'

She nodded earnestly, returned her gaze to the view.

He realized that he had broken into a sweat that had nothing to do with the heat. This was the first time he'd conversed with anyone in a long, long time – other than asking directions or booking hotel rooms during the past three days; for the last year the only time he'd heard the sound of his own voice was when he phoned in his daily report to the answerphone at head-office.

He wished she'd shut up and go away. The alternative was that he should leave, but the thought that she might decide to follow almost paralysed him.

'Are you from America?'

He closed his notebook. 'New Zealand.'

She opened her mouth in a silent, understanding, 'Ah,' and lapsed into silence.

He sensed that she was lonely and culture-shocked, and was seeking the affirmation of things familiar. He turned his back on her and stared through the arched opening. On a stone platform ten metres to his left, directly above the water so that it could be swept easily into the river, a funeral pyre was burning fiercely, the thick, acrid woodsmoke hanging low in the humid morning air. Dozens of pilgrims stood on the steps which descended into the water, patiently waiting their turn to submerge themselves and perform obeisance. Directly below him, Janner saw a young man with a red-swaddled bundle in his arms; clearly rigor mortis had passed, and the slumped form might have

been that of an infant asleep, not dead. Beside the man –
and this made the tableau all the more tragic – an old man
carried a huge, square stone. Janner watched them climb
into a boat and row out into the middle of the river.

'Are you religious?'

Janner looked up, surprised. He'd almost forgotten
about the woman.

He shook his head. 'No, not at all.' She was watching
him. He felt obliged to ask, 'Are you?'

She pushed out her lips. 'There are many mysterious
things in the world,' she said.

Once he might have laughed at this. He moved his gaze
away from her steady regard. He decided the time was
right to make his departure, rather than get drawn into
some half-baked religious debate. He stowed away his
notebook, tucked his jacket into his rucksack and climbed
to his feet, making his movements deliberate in lieu of a
farewell.

He felt a surge of relief as he left the stone tower and
climbed the steps towards the alley, a sense of having
escaped an encounter he had neither the will nor the
emotional resources to see through. For so long his life had
been governed by the fear of the new; for so long he
had feigned contentedness rather than face the fact of his
inadequacies.

He retraced his steps up the alley. This time when he
came to the busy street – hard to credit that this press of
humanity comprised a cast completely different from that
which had passed this way one hour before – he had a plan
of action in mind and he was unfazed by the bustle and the
noise. He flagged down a taxi, climbed into its capacious
rear seat and asked to be taken to a good hotel.

He closed his eyes as the car start-stop-started through
the busy thoroughfare. He needed a cool, quiet hotel room

in which to unwind, bathe, eat a leisurely meal and try to come to terms with what was happening to him.

The Excelsior was a grand Victorian building in extensive grounds consisting of long lawns and sparkling fountains. The atmosphere of *fin-de-siècle* calm that pervaded the place was a million miles from the hurly-burly of the city outside. Janner overpaid the cab-driver in US dollars and climbed the steps to the cool, oak-panelled foyer. A young woman in a gold and black sari smiled at him from the reception desk.

Janner requested a single room and the woman consulted a ledger. 'We have a room on the second floor with a western view at one thousand rupees a night.'

'That'll be fine.' He had no idea how much a thousand rupees was in dollars, but what he wanted right now was a room of his own at any price.

'Your passport, sir?'

'Ah . . . is that absolutely necessary?'

'I'm sorry?'

'Why do you need my passport?'

The woman frowned at him. 'Government regulations, sir,' she said.

Bemused, he pulled it from his jacket pocket. She copied his name and passport number into the ledger, then flipped through the pages. Her frown deepened. She looked up at Janner, then back to the passport. She closed it and passed it back without a word.

A bellboy showed him to his room on the second floor; Janner delighted him with a tip of a dollar, then closed the door and collapsed against it. The window was closed against the heat of the day, the curtains drawn. A fan turned on the ceiling. He kicked off his shoes and stretched out on the bed.

For the next couple of hours he attempted to empty his head of all thought, in the manner he'd learned at a Transcendental Meditation course in Auckland over a decade ago. Perhaps, with a clear mind, he might address his situation with greater insight, discern some pattern to the events of the past three days. But his head was a swirling chaos of thoughts which would not be stilled. He glanced at the wall-clock. It was midday. He realized, suddenly, that he'd had nothing to eat for twenty-four hours. A menu card on the dressing table promised Western cuisine. He phoned down for the set meal and two bottles of Kingfisher beer.

He ate slowly, concentrating on the act of eating, savouring every mouthful. If what was happening to him continued indefinitely, and there was no reason to suppose that it would not, then he would be deprived of what could be called a 'normal' life; he would live from day to day, from event to event, with nothing to sustain him in the long term but the assurance of constant change and the small, individual pleasures to be gleaned from such an existence. He had, after all, lived alone for years in the mountains with no ill-effects. He would survive.

After the meal he sat up on the bed, the second bottle of beer in his lap. He was tired, and he decided to sleep until the evening. He wanted to be awake this time when five a.m. came around.

As he drifted off, he wondered if the Park authorities had noticed his absence yet. He'd been gone three days and his failure to report each evening should have been noted by now. They would no doubt ring him, instigate a visit when he didn't respond. He imagined the Bell-Huey landing on the lonely mountainside; what would the forestry commissioner make of the deserted timber lodge, its only door locked from the inside, its windows secured likewise?

Janner was awoken by a knocking at his bedroom door; by its urgency he guessed he'd slept through an initial summons. The room was in darkness. He sat up, fumbled for the bedside lamp and squinted at the clock. It was seven. He wondered what they wanted.

The knocking ceased. 'Mr Janner?'

He snatched open the door. The receptionist faced him, hand raised to knock again. She stood aside, and in the dazzling brightness of the hall Janner saw what at first he took to be two soldiers. Behind them stood curious guests, the bellboy and sundry other onlookers.

A small man in a khaki uniform and beret stood before him. 'Sergeant Banerjee, Varanasi police,' the man said. 'There seems to be some irregularity. If I might inspect your passport, sir.'

I'll say there's an irregularity, Janner thought.

He opened the door to admit the sergeant and his deputy, who closed it on the phalanx of gawping spectators. He pulled his passport from his pocket and handed it to the sergeant.

'I'm sure we can clear up this little matter in no time,' the sergeant said. His English was perfect, though with a lilting intonation which sounded almost Welsh.

Janner almost said: 'I wouldn't be too sure about that,' but stopped himself. He was surprised he was so calm; he had envisaged a similar scenario for a day or two, always with apprehension.

The sergeant was flipping through the passport.

Janner said: 'Is it established practice for hotel receptionists to inform the police whenever there seems to be a problem?'

The officer ceased his rifling, marking his place in the passport with his thumb. 'Of course, sir. India is a powerful country – we have many enemies. We need to be constantly vigilant.'

Janner sighed. 'I assure you that I am no one's enemy.'

'Of course not, sir.' The sergeant smiled. 'In every respect your passport seems to be in order. It is clearly yours; it is valid . . . But in two details it is lacking. I wonder if you might enlighten me, Mr Janner? You seem to have no visa or entry stamp.'

Janner just stared at the sergeant, wondering what kind of response might be appropriate. How about ignorance?

'But . . . surely they're in there somewhere?'

'I assure you that they are not.'

Janner shook his head in feigned incredulity. 'I don't understand—'

'How long have you been in India, Mr Janner?'

'Ah . . . since this morning.'

'And how did you arrive?'

Janner hesitated. 'I flew,' he said.

'You have a return ticket?'

'No . . . It was one way.'

'And you can offer no explanation for the fact that you are without a visa or entry stamp?'

He shook his head. 'I'm sorry. None at all.'

The sergeant was becoming impatient.

'In that case I shall have to ask you to come with me.'

At this, his deputy stiffened. His right hand strayed to the butt of his holstered pistol.

Janner held up a hand. 'OK. That's fine.' He wondered if he would be detained until five the following morning. 'Can I take my rucksack?'

'That won't be necessary.'

Janner could think of no good reason to insist. In the pocket of his shirt was all his money, which was his main concern. He saw his down jacket hanging on the back of the door. On the way out, he casually unpegged it and slung it over his shoulder. There was reason to believe that he'd be experiencing freezing temperatures in the days to come.

After the cool of the hotel, the tropical night air encapsulated the trio with properties more fluid than gaseous. By the time he reached the waiting police car, Janner's shirt was wringing wet with sweat. He sat in the rear seat between the sergeant and his deputy while the driver steered at speed through crowded streets. Janner closed his eyes, grateful for the breeze blowing in through the open front window.

The police station was an ugly concrete building in a compound behind a high wall. Janner was marched down a long corridor, aswarm with civilians and police alike. They halted outside a lacquered wooden door bearing the title, in Hindi and in English, Divisional Superintendent.

The sergeant knocked and entered.

A tall and portly Sikh, his turban the same khaki shade as his uniform, stood beside his desk. He exchanged rapid-fire Hindi with the sergeant, while Janner noted the large map of India on the wall behind the desk. A ubiquitous fan turned lethargically overhead.

The superintendent extended a large hand with a friendliness Janner thought at odds with his rank. 'Ah, Mr Janner. There seems to be a slight problem here.' He spoke in his own language to the sergeant, who handed over the offending passport and hurried from the room.

The superintendent introduced himself as Singh, and indicated a chair before the desk. Singh seated himself and thumbed through the passport, the document reduced to the size of a postage stamp in his massive hands. He turned his attention to a sheet of notes on the desk.

After a period of amazement at the calm he had shown during his arrest – a less experienced Janner would have passed out at the thought of such an occurrence – he now realized that he was confident of his invulnerability. Whatever charges they threw at him, it mattered little. They could jail him and it would cause Janner no concern at all.

Singh looked up. Without preamble he said, 'On which airline did you fly into Delhi, Mr Janner?'

'Ah . . . Air India,' Janner temporized.

'Flight number?'

'I'm sorry.'

'Can you recall what time you landed in our country?'

Truthfully, Janner said, 'Around five o'clock.'

Singh took all this down with an old-fashioned fountain pen, dipping it periodically into a stubby bottle of ink.

'Did you apply for a visa in Wellington, Mr Janner?'

As much as he disliked doing so, Janner thought it best to play the idiot. 'I didn't realize I had to.'

Again Singh flicked through the passport, this time with visible irritation, as if finding it increasingly impossible to believe that a foreign national could enter his country without official verification of the fact.

'Mr Janner, how did you evade our customs check?'

Janner shrugged helplessly. 'I had no idea I did so.'

'I have contacted your embassy in Delhi,' Singh said. 'They are sending someone over. He will be arriving here tomorrow morning.'

'In that case I can return to my hotel?'

'That will not be possible. Absolutely no way, Mr Janner. I am afraid you will be spending a night under lock and key.' Tacked directly to the end of this sentence was a billowed command in Hindi.

The sergeant entered the room and snapped off a salute. Singh grunted instructions, then turned to the phone and busied himself with the process of dialling without so much as a glance in Janner's direction.

He was taken from the office, along the corridor and

down a flight of stairs. His jailer – a scowling Oriental dwarf – gestured him to enter his cell, a narrow space between two other cells, with a whitewashed wall at the back and bars in front. A charpoy covered with a grey blanket occupied two thirds of the floor, and a bucket stood beside it. Janner accepted his incarceration with impeccable grace.

He stretched out on the charpoy and laced his fingers under his head. A clock on the corridor wall opposite indicated that it was almost midnight. Beneath it, a calendar depicted a scene from the Bhagavadgita: a blue man – Vishnu, wasn't it? – enthroned in a garden paradise. Janner smiled.

He closed his eyes, but every time he felt himself drifting off he forced them open and stared at the ceiling. He wanted to be awake – unlike last night – come five o'clock. He was abetted in this by the hourly rounds of his jailer. The small, fat Oriental in flip-flops, blue shorts and vest rattled the bars on the hour with a large dessert spoon, peering into cells to ensure the continued presence of each captive. Repeatedly, Janner started from his sleep to see the man's monkey-like face grimacing in at him.

On the very last occasion, Janner sat up and squinted at the clock on the wall. To his shock it read five minute past five.

He wondered if what he had initially considered a curse – but which this time, he hoped, would be his salvation – had forsaken him.

The jailer waddled past the cell, on his way out.

'Excuse me!'

The man stopped, peered at him.

Janner pointed to the clock. 'The time – is it right? Surely . . .'

The man's face split into a huge grin. 'A-cha! You noticed! Yes, it is right – other times not!'

'I'm sorry . . .?'

His jailer condescended to explain. 'I – Nepalese. Nepali time fifteen minutes before Indian time. I – in command down here. Down here – Nepalese time!'

Janner smiled in relief. 'So the clock's fifteen minutes fast?'

The jailer frowned, his expression as belligerent as it was formerly beatific. 'No, not fast! Time down here right. Up there,' he pointed upwards, indicating the rest of India, 'up there, time slow!'

'Ah . . . I understand. Thank you.'

The man saluted and continued on his way.

Janner sat on his bed and watched the minute hand move slowly towards quarter past. Almost to the second, he felt the curious bubbling sensation, which coursed through his veins like champagne. He was filled with an incredible feeling of euphoria. The faint blue glow, which he had witnessed on two earlier occasions, emanated from every pore of his body, so that within seconds he was encapsulated in a lambent nimbus of lapis lazuli light. It spread outwards, filling his cell, and the feeling of all-consuming peace increased.

Through the haze of the blue light, Janner saw the jailer run into the corridor and stop, transfixed. The Nepali fell to his knees, hands pressed together above his head in supplication. His expression, within the diamond of his raised arms, was one of stupefaction.

The blue light thickened, blotted out Janner's surroundings, and he existed in a displaced void like limbo.

Then the blue light vanished.

Christ, he cried to himself, where the hell now?

* * *

2

Athens – it had to be.

Janner found himself on a rocky knoll, at such an elevation that the city was spread out like an architect's scale model far beneath him. He was on the Acropolis, with the Parthenon below to his right and assorted ruins and statuary occupying the slopes and levels all around, interspersed with sandy paths and olive trees. Unlike in India, here the heat was clean and sharp, almost refreshing. He shucked off his jacket and turned his face to the morning sun. Incredible though his translocation was, he no longer experienced the surge of panic on arrival which had marked his first few transitions.

Until four days ago, his life had been markedly unremarkable. Each day had been like the one before, sixteen hours of rigorous routine with little or no deviation. His job of forest ranger and fire-watching had required an unvarying itinerary, and over the years he had found that his temperament was suited to such a regime. He had watched for fires for hours on end, taken meteorological readings, reported the occasional sighting of a rare bird in the area. When wearing his forest ranger cap, he had erected fences, repaired walls and pathways. It had been a largely uneventful existence.

Then, four mornings ago, precisely seven years to the day since taking up the post of forest ranger in '73, it had happened. He'd risen as usual at four forty-five, fixed himself a breakfast of porridge and coffee, and sat down to eat in his ancient leather armchair before the massive plate glass window. Fortunately, as it turned out, the morning had been cold, and while he had waited for the wood-burning stove to heat the lodge, he zipped himself into the down jacket he'd bought himself as a Christmas present the previous year. Sewn into the lining of the jacket for safe-keeping – he had an eccentric's mistrust of all institutions, banks included – were his life savings, some nine hundred New Zealand dollars, and his passport.

He'd just finished his coffee when the tingling began, followed by the unaccountable sensation of well-being. It was unlike anything he'd ever experienced before, and so at odds with his usual depression that it caused him to sit up and laugh out loud at his reflection in the window. Then his body began to leak a faint blue light. He recalled that he'd screamed – was he about to burst into flame, a victim of spontaneous human combustion? The light had intensified – he leapt from his chair, took a step forward, and then the light had vanished and he'd found himself staggering down a city street in the tropics.

The incident seemed so distant now, his heart-surging fear a thing of the past, that he had difficulty recalling his thoughts and feelings at the time. Certainly his stupefied incomprehension, as he stumbled down the street, had brought him to the attention of the few people about. He recalled a police officer quizzing him in some fast, glottal tongue, other people backing away from him in alarm. He'd wandered through the Indonesian city that day in a daze, had eaten nothing and spoken to no one. Come nightfall, he had found a hostel and booked a room for the night, but had been unable to sleep. At five in the morning he'd experienced a familiar sensation, and when the blue light enveloped him again he gave thanks that at last he was returning home.

Except he had found himself on a park bench in Alexandria.

Curiously, he had acquitted himself well; rather than capitulating to despair, he found resolution in the face of adversity and went about attending to his requirements. He changed his New Zealand currency for US dollars, bought himself a hot meal in a terraced café in the commercial district of the city, and then booked into a comfortable hotel. Later, he went out and bought a second-hand rucksack from a stall in the market, a change of clothes and necessities like razors and soap. He even considered trying to contact his embassy and explaining his bizarre situation, but decided against this. For one thing, he was not likely to be believed – his unstamped passport would prove nothing – and, for a second, he mistrusted all governments. He had visions of becoming the victim of horrendous surgical experiments to locate the source of his strange, if involuntary, ability. Worse, he suspected that, rather than allow him to fall into the hands of those his country considered enemies – and if his country's leaders were be to believed, there were plenty of those – he would be quietly eradicated. So he returned to his hotel, cat-napped until the early hours, and then kept vigil – clutching his rucksack – until he was overtaken once again by the eerie phenomenon which presaged his shift.

La Paz, this time.

He had materialized in a dusty street on the outskirts of the capital city, and his sudden arrival had, at first, startled a band of children and then provoked a hostile response. They'd hurled stones, bottles and Coke cans filled with mud, and he'd taken to his heels and lost himself in the sombre city of skyscrapers and wide, traffic-choked streets, which was like a down-at-heel, Third-World version of New York.

Shaken by his reception, he booked into a hotel, ate paella in his room and slept fitfully, beset by elusive nightmares. He had intended to remain awake during the next period of transition – asleep, who knew what dangers he might fall prey to? – but with his rucksack beneath his head as a pillow, exhaustion overwhelmed him and he slept, waking the following morning in Varanasi.

It had occurred to him, more than once, that he was suffering from an all-time great hallucination – that he was in hospital with terminal brain damage and this procession of cities was no more than his subconscious giving him the world tour he'd never got round to making himself.

Now he sat on a spur of rock and admired the view. Down below, beginning beyond the wall that bounded the Acropolis, a sea of grey rooftops stretched in every direction for as far as the eye could see. To the south, on the horizon, the sea was a slim filament of blue steel, coruscating in the morning light. For the first time in days, Janner experienced a degree of contentment – or perhaps only a cessation of the fears that had haunted him of late. How many hours had he worried himself to distraction over how he might cope when his fund of dollars ran out? Or when his passport was checked and he was exposed as an illegal alien? Well, the latter had occurred, and he had survived. And the former . . . The fact was that, if he was frugal, his money would last him for a while yet. He would worry about his day-to-day survival when it was under threat.

Of more concern to him was the actual fact of the phenomenon which had him in its grip. He might have enjoyed the experience had he known *why* he was undergoing it, how long it might last and in which city he would find himself next . . .

Psychologically, he was well prepared for what was happening to him. It was a corollary of his condition – for some reason, he thought of it as emanating from within him, rather than being caused by some exterior force – that the day-to-day details of his foreseeable future would be transient, ephemeral. He'd arrive in a city, make himself comfortable, and the very next day be gone. It seemed appropriate that for the past ten years he'd lived as a recluse, as if in preparation for what was happening to him now. More worrying was the fact that his life from now on would have no meaningful routine – other than the endless booking into hotels, eating, sleeping, and awaiting the shift in the mornings.

He climbed to his feet and set off down the hillside. His main priority today was to re-equip himself with a rucksack and supplies. He decided to find a quiet hotel, eat, then go for a stroll around the city.

The hillside flattened out. All around him were the remains of ancient structures, the overgrown, single-brick-high outlines of what thousands of years ago had been temples, theatres and other buildings in everyday use. Ahead, beside a gate in the wall, was a concrete kiosk from which an attendant sold tickets to tourists, mainly Americans and Europeans, and the occasional Japanese. Nearby was a stall selling food and drink. Janner decided to delay his search for a hotel. There was something peaceful and timeless – the former a quality lacking in all his other stopping places to date – about the ancient ruins, despite the growing number of tourists, that invited him to linger. He bought two feta cheese pastries and a styrofoam cup of coffee – paying over the odds in dollars – and wandered along a sandy path between bushes decorated with large magenta butterflies. He found a secluded tumble of stones surrounded by olive trees, sat on a truncated length of fluted column and enjoyed his breakfast.

He was finishing his coffee when he caught sight of the girl. She appeared between two trees to his left, breathing hard and looking about her as if in search of a place to hide. She might have been Chinese, was barefoot and wore only a soiled blue smock. As quickly as she'd appeared, she was gone, flitting lithely down a path away from the clearing.

There was something so incongruous about the sight of her that Janner fancied he'd witnessed a scene displaced in time – a Cathay slave girl on the run from her Greek masters.

Then a woman ran into the clearing and stopped dead between the olive trees where first the girl had stood. She stared at him, an expression of disbelief on her face.

The woman wore brown sandals, light blue slacks and a white blouse. 'You . . .' she said, slowly shaking her head.

Janner just stared, unable to find an adequate reply.

The woman gathered herself. 'Did you see a girl run through here one minute ago?' she asked in her heavily accented English. 'Chinese, maybe?'

Janner pointed. 'Through there . . .'

She started down the path, then stopped and turned to him. 'Are you coming?' she asked, then said: 'The girl is one of us.'

Janner hesitated for what seemed like an eternity. Then he followed the women down the tunnel of overhanging foliage. Part of him felt a curious sense almost of jealousy that he was not alone in experiencing the phenomenon of translocation, while another part realized that the woman and the girl might hold the key to what was happening to him.

The path steepened, and up ahead Janner made out the blue of the girl's frock as she darted between bushes into a cleared area occupied by tumbled columns and lintels. Seconds later they gained the clearing. It was bordered on two sides by a precipitous wall of rock, and to the right was a continuation of the pathway which followed the slope. The girl was nowhere to be seen on the exiting path. The woman halted, realizing, like Janner, that their quarry had to be hiding somewhere within the clearing.

She walked towards two great blocks of masonry, knelt and held out a hand. Janner joined her. The girl was crouched in the narrow interstice, hugging her shins and staring at the woman in fright.

The woman glanced at Janner. 'She must be terrified. We have to help her.'

'How do you know . . .?' he began.

'I saw her on the first day, in Surabaya. Of course, then I had no idea she was like us.'

She turned to the girl, held out a placatory hand as if to soothe a frightened animal. 'Come to me. We mean you no harm . . .' She continued in another language, which might have been Russian.

She mimed the action of eating. 'You must be hungry? Eat, yes? Food?'

Staring at the woman, her big eyes filled with tears, the girl gave an almost imperceptible nod.

'Can you get her something to eat?' the woman asked Janner. 'Maybe we can gain her trust that way?'

Janner nodded, set off towards the food stall by the entrance. He bought half a dozen pastries – *tirópetas* – and three cans of cola, and carried them back to the clearing. The girl was still wedged between the masonry, but her posture was less fraught. She had extended her legs and placed her hands on her knees, though her expression was still watchful, suspicious. Janner judged her to be anything between eight and twelve.

The woman passed a *tirópeta* to the girl, who took it and stared at it without attempting to take a bite. The woman sat down casually, cross-legged, smiled at the girl and bit into her own pastry. The girl raised the square of flaky pastry to her mouth, took the tiniest of bites. Finding it to her liking, she ate it quickly, then gestured for a second. They ate in silence, Janner watching the girl and, when she wasn't looking, the woman also. He snapped open the cola and offered the can to the girl. She drank, spilling rivulets over her chin and down her neck.

To Janner, the woman said, 'I thought I saw you that day in La Paz, in the street. Then, yesterday, beside the Ganges – I was sure it was you. But when you said you had arrived from Delhi . . .'

Janner avoided her gaze. 'I thought you were a tourist,' he said. 'I had no idea. I could hardly have told a perfect stranger that I'd materialized in the city out of thin air.'

The woman nodded in a sombre gesture of understanding.

The girl was on to her third *tirópeta*, washing bolted mouthfuls down with swallows of cola. The woman smiled at her, although the girl's only response was to close her eyes as she tipped the can and drank.

'Greg Janner, by the way. Pleased to meet you.'

The woman smiled. 'I am Katia Constantin, once from Leningrad.'

'I wonder who your friend is, and where she's from?'

Katia brushed a strand of hair from her face, held a hand out to the girl. Hesitantly, the girl touched her fingers. Katia smiled. 'Do you understand me? What is your name? From which country do you come?'

The girl just stared at Katia with large brown eyes set flush with the sheer fall of her cheeks.

Katia indicated Janner, then herself. 'Greg, Katia.' She pointed to the girl. 'And you?'

'She doesn't understand a word,' Janner said.

Katia smiled. 'OK – I'll call you . . . What name would suit her? Kim? Do you like that name?'

No response from the girl.

Katia shook her head, glanced up at Janner. 'We three are not alone, Greg. In Surabaya I saw a tall man, I think an American – then I saw him again in Alexandria, but he didn't see me. I decided I would not approach him alone. He seemed angry and loud. Perhaps now the three of us . . .'

Jenner let the silence lengthen. He'd been perfectly happy 'travelling' alone until now; he was not sure how to react at the thought of being part of a group.

Katia looked sideways at him, as if detecting his unease. She changed the subject. 'So, what do we do now?'

'I don't know about you, but I'm bushed – tired,' he amended. 'I need a sleep.'

'I, too, am tired.' She looked at Kim, placed her hands together and mimed sleeping. Kim made no sign that she understood.

Katia looked about her, as if searching for a suitable place to bed down for the day. Jenner sensed a certain tension in her manner.

'Where've you been sleeping the past few nights?' he asked.

Katia shrugged. 'I have not. I was too afraid to sleep, in case . . .' She shrugged again. 'I slept a little during the day, in parks and fields.'

Janner hesitated, assessing the alternatives. 'Look, I've a few hundred dollars left. Perhaps we can find a cheap hotel?'

Katia batted a strand of hair from her eyes, smiled nervously at him. He suspected that, ordinarily, she was not unattractive, but lack of sleep and food had left her looking pale and gaunt. She had a long face with high cheek-bones, elegantly hollowed cheeks and a large mouth much given to smiling.

'That would be nice,' she said.

She stood, held out a hand to Kim. The girl obediently climbed to her feet, smoothing out her dirty blue dress, and took Katia's hand.

Tourists were out in force now – coachloads of well-dressed Germans and Americans filing through the entrance. The sun was climbing in a flawless cerulean sky, and with it the temperature. Janner realized what a disparate trio Katia, Kim and he presented to the oncoming tourists. He was aware of the glances, felt uneasy. At the same time, being seen by others with Katia and the girl gave him a curious sense of belonging. They passed through the gate and strolled along the street; on one side was a row of open-fronted shops selling curios and tourist trinkets, pottery, marble-work and cheap prints. Set up on the other side of the road was a line of tables heaped with junk: boxes full of clockwork parts, old shoes, brass ornaments; records and magazines and paperbacks in English and Greek.

They found a hotel after a walk of ten minutes, a terra-cotta-roofed building around a central courtyard shaded with olive trees. Janner paid for a double room for Katia and Kim, and a single for himself. If the woman who showed them up the marble stairs thought the couple curious – with no luggage and a tiny Oriental girl in tow – she gave no indication. The rooms were old-fashioned, high-ceilinged, marble-floored, stocked with old, varnished furniture and, after the heat outside, gloriously cool.

Janner escaped to his room, took a shower and wrapped himself in a towel. He lay on the bed, stared at the cream-painted ceiling and considered the fact that he was no longer alone in experiencing the bizarre transitions. And there was at least one other, according to Katia – the American she had seen for the second time in Alex. He wondered how many other people were undergoing the daily translocations, and where it might end.

He was amazed, he admitted to himself, at how easily he had come to accept the situation. Had anyone told him a week ago that he would find himself shuttling back and forth across the face of the Earth, he would have considered that the only response in the circumstances would be to go mad – to refuse to believe what was happening.

There was a knock at the door.

He called out that he was dressing, pulled on his cords and his sweat-soaked shirt and opened the door. Katia and Kim stood outside, hand in hand, like penniless mendicants in their old clothes. Janner invited them in. They had bathed – their hair was wet and lank – and their cleanliness pointed up the state of their dress.

He arranged three dining chairs on the balcony overlooking the central courtyard, saying nothing. Kim hugged her legs and squinted at the pigeons lining the opposite rooftop. Katia seemed nervous, as if wanting to talk to Janner but unable to do so.

Ten years of living alone had made Janner rather frugal. He'd shared nothing with anyone for that long. He had worked for what he had earned, spent only for himself and saved the rest. Old habits, he thought, die hard. He found it in himself to be ashamed that he was reluctant to come spontaneously to Katia's aid.

He considered how easy it had been for himself over the past few days – with enough money to cushion himself against privation. How had Katia coped, plucked from Leningrad with nothing but the clothes she stood up in? And Kim – what must it have been like for her?

He returned inside, found his wallet and withdrew two fifty-dollar notes.

He stepped back on to the balcony, shifted uneasily. 'Ah . . . look . . .' He thrust the notes at Katia. 'These are for you. Buy yourself some clothes – you'll probably need a bag, a rucksack. Get some new things for Kim as well, OK? This should cover it.'

Katia slowly accepted the notes, unfolded them and smoothed them on her lap. She squinted up at Janner, the sun in her eyes. 'Thank you, Greg. I appreciate it. Kim, come.' She held out a hand. 'Would you like a new dress?'

When they had departed, Janner sat out in the hot noon

sun and realized that he felt a strange, almost light-headed, sense of relief that he was once again alone.

Later, he left the room and strolled through the streets around the hotel. He changed fifty dollars into drachmas, bought a new rucksack, several changes of clothes, and two bottles of retsina. The streets were crowded, making him uneasy. He saw a tall American at one point, talking to a shop proprietor, and, recalling what Katia had said, he ducked into the nearest alley in an irrational desire not to be seen. He hurried back to the safety of his hotel room, finally closing the door with a sense of accomplishment. He showered again, changed into his latest acquisitions – a pair of light-weight beige trousers and a sports shirt, lay on the bed and closed his eyes. It was not yet three in the afternoon.

He was awoken some time later by a noise from the far end of the room. He sat up. Light from the hallway outside sliced into the darkness. Katia peered through the partly open door. 'Greg, are you awake?'

'What time is it?'

'Almost twelve. Would you like something to eat? I looked in earlier, but you were asleep.'

He turned on the light, splashed his face with water from a basin in the corner.

'Look who's here,' Katia said, dragging a reluctant Kim into the room. 'What do you think?'

Kim stood to defiant attention in the middle of the room. Janner dried his face and smiled at the girl. 'Well, well. A distinct improvement.'

Kim wore sandals and a blue and white striped dress with a big ribbon at the waist. Katia had bought her a small backpack in the form of a koala bear, its arms and legs meeting around her neck and chest.

Katia was unloading a basket of food on to the bed: a cob of bread, feta cheese, tomatoes, olives and apples. She arranged them on the counterpane like a picnic and sat cross-legged on the bed.

'Here is your change,' she said, depositing a handful of crumpled notes on the bedside table.

She had bought herself a pair of green safari shorts and a yellow blouse. Around her neck was a crucifix on a fine gold chain. Janner wondered if it had been there all the time, or if she had just bought it.

Rather than join Katia on the bed, he pulled up a chair and ripped off a chunk of bread. He remembered the retsina. He prised off the caps with the bottle opener on a Swiss army knife he'd bought that afternoon.

Kim remained, unmoving, in the middle of the room.

Katia lifted a red apple. 'Kim?'

The girl gave her head the merest of shakes.

Katia gestured to the rest of the food on the bed.

Kim strode on to the balcony and sat on a chair in the darkness, her hands on her knees.

Janner asked, 'Has she spoken yet?'

'Not one word. She does not understand English.'

'What about in her own language?'

Katia shook her head, moved a strand of hair from her face and manoeuvred a chunk of bread, loaded with a slab of feta, towards her mouth.

They drank the retsina from the bottles.

Janner said, 'How did you eat before, without money?'

Katia was silent, as if reluctant to dwell on the disturbing events of the past few days. 'In Surabaya,' she whispered, 'I was not hungry. I felt too sick to eat. I thought I was going mad. One moment I was in my apartment, ready to set off for work – I am a teacher of small children – and then, *boomf!* I am in an empty building in a strange city. It was an old factory, I think. I had to break a window to get out. I walked around for a long time. When night came I found a park and slept in a small shelter.' Janner glanced up at Katia, alerted by something in her voice; her hands were shaking and tears filled her eyes.

He played with the label on the retsina, turning the picture of Zeus upside-down on the cold, condensation-slick bottle. 'What time was it in Leningrad when you vanished?'

She knuckled a tear from her cheek. 'Around five o'clock.'

'Did you notice the time when you arrived in Surabaya?'

'I saw a clock-tower,' she murmured. 'It was just after five, as if no time had passed at all.'

Janner pointed at her with his bottle. 'Are you sure about that? Surely Indonesia's a few hours ahead of Russia?'

Katia opened her mouth in a silent, 'Oh.' She grimaced. 'Of course. I didn't realize . . . Every time I moved, it was five o'clock in the morning, and again five wherever I landed.'

'I know it's *all* impossible, but this is crazy. I left New Zealand at five in the morning, arriving in Surabaya at the same time, even though New Zealand is an hour or two ahead of Indonesia. It just doesn't make sense – unless all this is an hallucination.'

Katia bit into a tomato. 'This doesn't taste like an hallucination,' she said glumly.

'How did you get on in Alexandria?'

'I didn't like. I thought maybe when the blue light began I was going home. I arrived in a quiet street. I just walked. Many people stared at me. I thought about going to the Soviet embassy and telling them what had happened – but I thought they would not believe me, maybe imprison me. I don't know what I thought.' She tapped her head. 'Maybe I was a little crazy.'

'You didn't eat?'

'I stole fruit from a stall in the market-place where I saw you. That is all. In the night I sat in the doorway of a locked-up shop, sleeping a little. I was asleep when the change came. I woke up in a Spanish city—'

'La Paz,' Janner said. 'Bolivia.'

'La Paz . . . I thought I was in Spain.' Katia smiled sadly. 'La Paz was good. An old lady found me in the street. She took me into her house, gave me meals. That night I slept in a bed for the first time. I woke up just before the change.'

'And yesterday you found yourself in Varanasi.'

'I arrived in the street, frightening many people. They ran away. I made my way to the river. I thought, when I saw you . . . I thought, at last, I might find out what was happening. And then, when I spoke to you . . . I thought I was mistaken and you were just another traveller. I stopped there all day – I was too afraid to move. Then, again at five, *boomf* – and I was here. I saw Kim and knew I had seen her before. So I tried to talk to her, but she ran. Then I met you. I was lucky. I would still be alone right now. When I think how big Athens is I realize how lucky I was.'

Janner shrugged. 'I don't know . . . I think we all come down roughly in the same area – that'd account for you seeing Kim and myself on more than one occasion. The chances of spotting someone twice in two days in cities as big as the ones we've visited must be pretty astronomical. The three of us arrived in the Acropolis, after all.'

Katia was nodding absently, staring at the wall with an olive poised before her lips. She lowered it at last. 'Perhaps, tomorrow, because we are together now, we will arrive in the new city even closer together?'

Janner raised his bottle. 'Who knows?' He concealed his embarrassment by taking a long drink of retsina.

Katia was watching Kim on the balcony. The girl was still on her chair, hands on her knees, staring into the night.

Katia shook her head. 'It was very hard for me,' she said. 'But for Kim it must have been so much more.' She looked at Janner. 'What if we do not arrive together in the next city, what if we are far apart and Kim cannot find us?'

Janner shrugged uncomfortably. 'Always assuming there is a next city. You never know, we might find ourselves back home.'

'Somehow I think not,' she said. She brightened. 'Perhaps we should make arrangements – we will agree to meet at a certain place when we arrive.'

Janner gestured. 'Like where?'

'I don't know. Oh . . . What is always in every city in the world?'

'Banks?'

'Maybe – but banks are usually in certain districts. What if we arrive many miles away . . .?' She stopped. 'What about post offices, Greg? There are always many post offices.'

'So many that we might all end up at different ones.'

'But each city has only one *general* post office . . . OK, we'll meet at the nearest GPO.'

'What about Kim?'

Katia's face clouded over. She shook her head. 'Kim!' she called to the girl, who made no reply. She stared into the night, quiet and melancholy.

From a writing desk in the corner, Katia fetched a pen and a writing pad. Laboriously, resting the paper on her lap, she wrote: 'Can you tell me nearest GPO, please?' And the same, beneath this, in varying standards of French and Spanish.

She held it up. 'This is all I know.'

'Here, I think I can do one.' He took the pad and printed the same message in schoolboy German.

Katia stepped out on to the balcony, took Kim's hand and led her to the bed. She held up the paper. 'Tomorrow, when in new city, show this to people, OK? Greg and myself will meet you at post office.' She mimed licking down an envelope and posting it. Kim watched her closely, then took the note and tucked it into the pocket of her new dress. Though she had said nothing to indicate that she knew what Katia had told her, Janner had the impression that Kim understood more than she was letting on.

Now the girl sat on the bed, picked up a tomato and began to eat. Janner filled his empty retsina bottle with water from the sink and passed it to her.

Katia looked at her wrist-watch and announced that it was four-thirty.

'We'd better gather all our belongings,' Janner said, 'make sure they're with us come five.'

While Katia fetched her bag from the adjacent room, Janner packed his rucksack and set it next to him on the bed. Kim picked through the remains of the meal, turning up her nose at the olives – the most vehement expression, other than her original tears, he had seen from her so far.

At ten to five they seated themselves on the bed in a small circle, facing each other. Janner pulled his wallet from his jacket pocket. He pulled out half of all the dollars he possessed and passed them to Katia. He could not meet her eyes.

She just held the wad of notes before her, staring. 'Greg?'

'Take it. You might need it. There's always the chance that we won't meet up in the next city.'

She counted a hundred dollars, tucked them into Kim's pocket next to her post office note, then wedged the same amount into the pocket of her shorts. 'Thank you, Greg,' she said in a small voice.

She shrugged on a denim jacket she had bought herself.

They sat with their possessions in their laps and waited. As five o'clock approached, Katia reached out and took the little girl's hand in hers.

Janner felt relief that she did not try to take his hand.

The tingling began in his arms, then worked its way around his body. He looked up: already, Katia was beginning to glow. Her body radiated a blue light which surrounded her evenly, then expanded, encapsulating her in a sparkling sphere. As he stared, his own light expanded, along with the sensation of rapture. The last thing he noticed before his own light became opaque was Kim: the little girl was open-mouthed within her own nimbus, like a princess caught in the heart of a crystal.

Then the blue light vanished.

3

He was sitting cross-legged on the grass of a vast sports field. Dawn was brightening a horizon made irregular by a line of one-storey weatherboard houses. On the other side of the playing area was a row of trees Janner recognized as eucalyptus. At either end of the oval, four white-painted timber posts rose against the sky; the two central posts were perhaps thirty feet high, the two outer ones twenty. Janner smiled to himself. He had materialized on an Australian Rules football pitch, which could only mean he was somewhere on that continent. By the parched condition of the grass he reckoned he was in one of the northern states, the Northern Territories or Queensland. He was closer to home than he'd ever been since the beginning of this crazy affair. In theory he could make it to the nearest airport, catch an internal flight to Sydney, and from there fly on to New Zealand. He'd probably make it home just in time to be whisked away again tomorrow morning.

He was relieved that his proximity to Katia and Kim at the moment of transition had not resulted in their arriving here in the same formation. Despite their arrangement to meet at the local GPO, Janner had little inclination to do so. He felt he had discharged his obligations when he had given Katia the money in Athens. He had no responsibility, he told himself, to two people who were almost perfect strangers. Katia would look after Kim, and the money would see them right for a good time yet. He would continue now as he had lived his life for the past ten years.

He climbed to his feet. Perhaps two hundred metres to his left, beside the slide in a children's playground, he saw Kim. She was standing with her back to him. He looked around for Katia, and found her: she was crossing the road towards the playground. She called Kim's name and the girl turned, delight evident in her sudden start of surprise.

Janner scanned his immediate vicinity – if he could see Katia and Kim, then there was a chance that he would be able to spot the American Katia had mentioned. No sooner had he realized this than a tall, broad figure emerged from behind a toilet block to his right, perhaps fifty metres away. Janner looked back towards Katia and Kim. They were hugging, as yet oblivious of him. He still had time to make good his escape. The town proper began on the far side of the football field; he'd be able to lose himself down the side-streets in no time.

But even as he considered this, something stopped him from heading off in that direction. The American – if, indeed, such he was – was walking towards Katia and Kim in the playground. Janner recalled what Katia had said about the American she'd seen in Alex. She'd described him as angry and loud. Janner found himself unable to leave. He knew Katia and Kim to be sane and decent people; he had no such assurances in the case of the American. As much as part of him cried out for the safety of non-involvement, he knew he could not turn his back on Katia and the girl.

The tall, long-haired man had halted some way from Katia and Kim, and stood watching them. Janner hurried towards the playground. Katia looked up, saw the American, and then Janner. 'Greg!' She waved, smiling in delight. 'Look, Kim – look who is here!'

The girl turned – was there a trace of a smile on her face, the slightest sign of recognition in her eyes?

Janner smiled and nodded at Katia, as nervous as if they were meeting for the first time.

Katia was staring around her. 'Where are we, Greg? It looks to me like Africa.'

'Australia.' He glanced across at the watching man. He stood beside a climbing frame; for all his impressive size, he seemed to emanate an aura of uncertainty, even timidity.

Katia followed his gaze. 'Greg, he's the man I saw the other day.'

Janner nodded. 'Another member of our exclusive little club.'

She was shaking her head. 'In Surabaya he was like a crazy man.'

Janner said: 'Maybe he was, but he seems fine now.' Despite himself, he felt something like pity for the man.

Slowly, he lifted his hand in a salute which, to any observer, must have appeared bizarre indeed.

The man returned it and, after a second's hesitation, walked across to join them. He halted three metres from the group. He glanced at Janner obliquely, then at Katia with the same shifting, sliding look.

He was, thought Janner, one of those unfortunate giants that nature has handicapped with a manner debilitatingly meek. His hair was long and greying, but his face, though weather-worn and stubbled, must once have been handsome. Janner judged him to be in his forties, with eyes that had seen much and as a result seemed far older. He wore multi-pocketed combat breeches, a checked shirt and a lumber-jacket.

He bobbed his head at Katia. When he looked at Janner it was fleetingly, with almost a wince in his expression.

It's as if he fears me, Janner thought.

'Saw you in Alex, miss,' he drawled, his voice surprisingly soft.

Katia smiled uneasily. She shrugged. 'This is Greg, and here is Kim. I am Katia.'

The American shook Janner's hand without meeting his eyes, then held out a finger to the girl. She shook it, much to Janner's surprise. 'Hi there, honey,' the man said, then to Katia: 'Friends call me LJ.'

Katia nodded. 'I saw you in Surabaya first, and then in Alexandria.'

LJ gave a half-smile. 'Hope you didn't take no notice of me in Surabaya, miss. I guess I was kinda off my head.'

Janner gestured. 'What's been happening to us is enough to send us all a little crazy.'

LJ ducked him a brief glance. They sat on the grass as the sun came up, casting their long shadows across the playground. LJ removed his coat, folded it neatly and lodged a plastic bag beside it.

'Where are you from, LJ?' Janner asked.

The big man stared at the grass. 'Oregon, USA.'

Katia glanced at him. 'Did you, too, begin all this five days ago?'

LJ smiled. 'Sure did, miss,' he said. 'Had my own place in the woods. I like walking, and that morning I was out taking a trail through some high pines. Then' – he slapped his hands together – 'then I'm smack-bang in the centre of

Surabaya, walking down the main street. Christ! Thought I was flashbacking. Thought I was being punished for fighting in the war – thought a hundred an' one things all at once, and I guess something went snap up here. I set to hollerin' an' creatin' . . . They locked me up – guess it was the best thing they could have done for me. Questioned me about how I got there with no passport an' all.' He shrugged. 'Then round comes five in the morning and it's goodbye Surabaya, hello Alex.' He shrugged awkwardly again, glanced at Janner as if to see how he'd taken the story – Janner smiled and nodded – then started rooting in his plastic carrier bag. He pulled out a map of the world, opened it on the grass between them. He'd marked circles in black felt-tip around the cities they'd hit. LJ squinted around him. 'Now, where the hell is this place? If it were night, I could figure which hemisphere we're in from the stars.'

Janner tapped Australia on the map, then indicated the goal posts. 'I recognize them. I'm from New Zealand.'

LJ nodded. He stared at the map, puzzling. 'Can't seem to see no rhyme nor reason to what we're doing shuttling back an' forth like this. Just plain dumb crazy, you ask me.'

Janner considered the map. 'I don't know. I admit I can't see a pattern – but there is a kind of internal consistency at work.'

LJ squinted at him dubiously, scratching his head. 'There is?'

'So far, we've landed in five cities and this place – what looks like a big town. If we were being moved around the world at random, then we'd find ourselves – I don't know . . . in deserts, at the poles, on mountainsides, even in the sea. A good percentage of the world's surface is wilderness, after all – and yet we *always* find ourselves in densely inhabited regions.'

LJ nodded. 'You got something there.'

Janner smiled. 'But don't try to ask me what it means.'

LJ gave his head a hopeless shake. 'Somebody must know, somewhere. Some expert must have some idea. I mean, it's happening, ain't it? You can't deny that. So, if it's happening, there has to be some expert with an explanation.'

Katia gestured. 'I cannot see how we can ever hope to find out why this is happening to us.'

LJ pointed at her. 'With all respect, miss, I think that's where you're wrong. I'm gonna get to the bottom of this. Tomorrow, next day – when we hit a city bigger than this hick town, I'll find out . . .'

In the silence that followed Katia turned the map around and placed it before Kim. She pointed to Leningrad, then to herself. 'I come from here, Kim. Greg, from here. And LJ, from here.' She indicated the appropriate countries.

'What about you, Kim?' she asked. 'Where do you come from?'

Lips pursed, the girl leaned forward, her koala bear backpack peering over her shoulder. Her finger hovered over central Asia, came down eventually and definitely an inch south of China. Janner peered, along with Katia and LJ.

'Cambodia,' LJ said.

Kim gave the slightest nod to Katia. Janner noticed how her lively eyes darted from one to the other of them, and he wondered how much of the conversation she was taking in.

From his carrier bag LJ pulled a bottle of beer, and for the next hour as the sun strengthened they drank, traded stories, compared notes. LJ lost his nervousness, though even at the end of the hour he still found it hard to look Janner in the eye.

LJ folded his map with a fastidiousness at odds with his

clumsy bulk. He stowed it away in his bag, sneaking Janner a crafty sideways look. 'Shee-it, man,' LJ said.

Janner smiled. 'What?'

LJ shrugged. 'I'm sorry, Greg. It's just that you remind me of an old friend. Guy by the name of Powers. We were together in 'Nam, sixty-nine, seventy.' LJ squinted, again shook his head. 'It's eerie, dammit. You could pass for his twin brother.' He fell silent, staring down at the grass. Then: 'We were out on patrol, Christmas '70. Up at Khe Sanh, filing back to where the chopper was due to pick us up. One minute, all quiet – then all fucking hell broke loose. That was the frightening thing about fighting the VC – you never saw the bastards, Greg. Just saw what they did . . .' He paused there, then finished in a voice no louder than a whisper: 'Powers never made it back.'

Katia murmured that she was sorry.

LJ brightened. 'Now you see why I looked at you like I was seeing a ghost? Goddam it! First I find myself all over the place, then I come across you!'

Janner smiled. 'It's a strange world, LJ.'

'Hey,' the American said, climbing to his feet. 'Let's find a diner someplace and have ourselves a breakfast. I'm buying.'

They came across a café called Robbo's Grill on the main street in the centre of town. A dozen articulated trucks, tractor units and utility vans were drawn up outside. Next door to it was a newsagent's. Janner went in and asked for a local paper to find out where they were. He changed fifty US dollars into Australian dollars and came out with the *Townsville Gazette*.

He met the others in the grill. They were sitting in a booth by the window, checking the menu. Janner slid the newspaper on to the Formica tabletop as he sat beside LJ, who peered at it, took out his map and methodically ringed the town with his black marker pen.

They ordered four mixed grills and coffee. As they ate, Janner covertly regarded the other three. He was surprised at how he was coming to accept the company of these strangers, especially after he had considered leaving them to their own devices just this morning.

A part of him wanted to clear off, strike out on his own, while another part of him realized that perhaps his destiny was linked with these sad waifs and strays . . .

For Kim he felt pity and a curious kind of protectiveness; Katia provoked in him similar sentiments, feelings tempered, though, by her maturity and his inexperience with women. As for LJ . . . Despite his threatening size and marked eccentricity, Janner warmed to the American; there was something hurt and harmless about him, like a lion without teeth.

They finished their breakfast and LJ rooted in his carrier bag and pulled out a huge roll of hundred dollar bills. Kim stared.

LJ laughed. 'I'm not a violent man, understand.' He glanced around the group. 'But I robbed a bank when I was in La Paz the other day. Figured I had to do something drastic if I wanted to eat – and the banks can afford to lose a few grand. I carved a pistol out of a block of wood and demanded all the US dollars they had. Then I ran like hell and buried myself under a pile of garbage in an alley, reckoning they wouldn't begin to look there. I was a long time under all the junk, but come five . . .'

He slapped a hundred dollar note on the tabletop. 'Guess that'll more than cover it.'

The proprietor, a fat man in a white, grease-stained apron, looked from the bill to LJ. 'Last of the big spenders, sport?'

LJ hollered a laugh. 'Plenty more where that came from!'

'Staying in town long?'

Janner said, 'About a day.'

'Found a room yet?'

LJ squinted up at him. 'You recommend anywhere?'

'I'll say.' He pointed over the road to an old, two-storey red-brick building with gingerbread ironwork balconies and gable windows. 'House'll be yours for a hundred a night.'

'Good place?' LJ asked.

'Sure is, sport. I own it. C'mon, I'll show you round.'

One hour later, Janner sat on an upstairs balcony overlooking the football oval. Katia sat on a lounger, Kim stretched out in the sun with her head in the Russian's lap.

LJ knocked on the bedroom door, came in with two six-packs of cold beer and passed the cans round.

Janner had found a chess set in his room, and for a couple of hours he played the American on the balcony, drinking beer and listening to the parakeets in the eucalyptus trees.

After three games – all of which LJ won – they pushed the board aside and sat back in their chairs. Janner lodged his feet on the balcony rail and LJ tipped his chair back against the wall. Kim was sound asleep. Katia sat with her eyes closed, her face tipped to catch the afternoon sunlight.

LJ cleared his throat two or three times, as if he had an important announcement to make.

Janner turned his head on the back of his chair to look at the American. Katia opened her eyes.

'OK,' LJ began, 'I've been giving it a deal of thought, and, no doubt, you all have too. Before I tell you what I think's going on, I'd like to hear what you think. Greg? Katia? Any ideas?'

Janner raised his eyebrows. Katia made an exaggerated shrugging gesture, went back to stroking Kim's hair.

'Greg?' LJ asked.

'If you really want to know what I think's happening,' Janner said, 'then I'll tell you. I'm probably wrong – I'm not sure I even believe it myself – but it's the only explanation I've come up with . . .'

'Well, let's have it.'

'OK . . . Something tells me that I'm hallucinating all this. Everything that's happened to me over the past few days is the product of in here.' He tapped his head. 'I know all this *seems* real – but the brain's a powerful thing.' He shrugged. 'I can't begin to think what else might be responsible.'

LJ was shaking his head. 'Nice try, Greg – but it won't wash. If you were right, why, I'd be nothing but a figment of your hallucination, and I sure as hell know I ain't anything of the kind.'

Janner smiled. 'But if you *were*,' he said, 'then of course you'd say that. From my point of view, everything is an hallucination. There's no way you can verify your reality to me.'

LJ scratched his head. 'Sounds crazy to me.'

'We're in a crazy situation,' Janner said. 'Or rather, *I* am.'

'What about you, miss?' LJ asked.

Katia opened her eyes. 'I do not think anyone is hallucinating this, LJ,' she said. 'I think it is really happening. Nothing happens without the knowledge of God. I think God *must* be doing it for some reason. I do not know, but maybe he is punishing us. Maybe we have died, and we are waiting in purgatory for his judgement.' She smiled. 'I must say, some of these days have felt like purgatory.'

'Interesting thought,' LJ conceded. 'No disrespect meant, miss – but I've never gone for religion in a big way myself. If there was a God, then I don't think he'd fool around with us like this. Seems damned cruel to me.'

'So what do you think?' Janner asked. 'What's your explanation?'

LJ cleared his throat. At this, Kim opened her eyes and watched the big American.

'It's my considered opinion,' LJ pronounced, 'that we're in the employ of aliens.'

Katia made a *have-I-heard-him-right?* face.

Janner replaced the chessman he'd been playing with. He stared at LJ. 'Aliens?'

'Sure thing, Greg. Why not? Look at the facts. We're being shifted around the face of the Earth like mad fools, *and* time's all awry—'

Katia said, 'Pardon?'

'That's right, miss. Time's awry. Listen here, I was in Oregon when all this began. Then suddenly I was in Surabaya. Now Oregon's five hours in front of that area of Asia – I should know, I spent days in 'Nam wondering what the folks were doing back home. Anyways, when I wind up in Surabaya, it's five o'clock *local* time. Means I actually went back five hours. So not only are we a-travelling in space, we're a-travelling in time, too. Space and time. Now, only aliens have the know-how to tinker with space *and* time.'

'But aliens,' Katia pointed out, 'do not exist.'

LJ looked exasperated. 'Of course, we *think* they don't exist, because nothing like this ever happened to anyone before – or else they're keeping mighty quiet about it.'

'I'm not sure I follow your logic,' Janner said.

'Listen, I read a story once, real weird thing. This guy wakes up one morning, only he ain't in his own body no more – he's somehow shifted into the body of this woman he knew. Next time he sleeps, he wakes up in the body of the person he'd slept closest to. It went on like this for a long time as he tried to get home to his own body.'

'I do not see what this has got to do with what is happening to us,' Katia said reasonably.

'But you see' – LJ continued – 'it turns out he's been taken over by aliens—'

'So you think we've been taken over by little green men?' Janner said. 'Or, by aliens, do you mean foreigners – Russians, maybe?'

'I mean *aliens* – aliens from out there,' LJ replied.

'I know that I have not been taken over by anything,' Katia said. 'I am still me.'

'Ah-ha! But that's exactly what the guy in the story thought, too. It wasn't until the end that he found out the truth.'

'Thanks for that, LJ,' Janner said. 'But I'm siding with Katia on this one. There's just some things I can't bring myself to believe.'

LJ cocked an eye at him. 'Would you have believed what's happening to you now, one week ago, say?'

Janner smiled. 'Touché, LJ.'

LJ sat back in his chair, laced his fingers behind his head. 'Show yourselves, whoever you are!' he yelled. 'I know you're out there somewhere!'

Janner looked at Kim. She saw him watching, and quickly closed her eyes.

They remained on the balcony all day, watching the world – or, at least, this small segment of it – go by: people walking dogs, shoppers, schoolkids returning home. Later, a football team practised on the oval, their shouts muffled, at this distance, in the warm evening air. The sun set in a brilliant array of blood-red and tangerine banners.

Katia took Kim to their room at the front of the house, and then LJ announced he was in need of some shut-eye and left. Janner remained in his seat for a while, watching the sun disappear over the horizon. It had been, all told, a successful day – the first such, he had to admit, not fraught with fear and apprehension. He had never known the company of three other people to be less stressful. He wondered if his subconscious was hallucinating these three perfect travelling companions for him. He wondered, too, if he really believed what he'd told LJ earlier, about the last five days being an hallucination. He considered Katia's and LJ's explanations, and dismissed them as even less plausible.

He yawned and decided to get some sleep.

On the way back to his room he heard a noise from LJ's bedroom. He paused by the door, listened. He heard an indrawn breath, followed by sobs, muffled as if LJ was burying his head in a pillow. Janner reached for the door handle, stopped himself. What might he say to ease the American's pain? He hardly knew the man, much less his problems. He remained beside the door for perhaps a minute, then continued to his room. He felt as he had yesterday, when he had given Katia just a hundred dollars to buy Kim and herself some clothes: a feeling of betrayal, that he had not given enough – though, in this case, he had given nothing at all.

He was a good while getting to sleep.

He was awoken almost instantly, it seemed. A hand gently rocked his shoulder. 'Greg,' Katia whispered. 'Greg, it is almost five o'clock.'

He opened his eyes. Two wall-lamps cast meagre illumination across the room. Kim was already seated on the floor, her koala backpack in her lap. Janner got up and gathered his possessions, packed them into his rucksack. LJ shuffled into the room, giving a little wave and a grin to his fellow travellers. His carrier bag tucked under his arm, he joined Kim on the floor. Katia and Janner sat beside them.

'I have tidied the rooms and locked all the doors,' Katia said. 'The owner will wonder where we have gone.'

Janner considered their 'disappearances' from around the world. At least two – his and LJ's from police cells in Varanasi and Surabaya – would have been noted by the authorities. And then there were these disappearances, vanishings from hotels and the like, leaving owners and managers perplexed. He wondered how long it would be before someone in an information gathering government bureau, somewhere, came across rumours, reports, or definite evidence of their mysterious translocations. How long before the CIA were on their trail?

With just minutes to go before five, Katia took Kim's hand, and then LJ's. Hesitantly, Janner reached out for Kim's hand and the American's, to complete the circle.

'See you all at the nearest GPO,' LJ said.

4

Janner shouldered his rucksack and hurried down the alleyway between skips overflowing with garbage. The buildings on either side were high – maybe even sky-scrapers – and, though they shut out much of the morning light, Janner could see from the street at the end of the alley that dawn was breaking. The air was humid, sultry, and the rotting vegetation in the skips was beginning to stink.

He arrived at the end of the alley and halted. The three-lane road was deserted. He stood and listened for a time. The first thing he had heard upon materializing was a series of loud reports like fire-crackers. He heard them again now, closer, and knew the sharp, rapid cracks to be machine-gun fire. He ducked back into the alley as a camouflage-painted armoured car raced along the empty street, three black soldiers riding shotgun. Africa, he guessed; one of the many states suffering internal strife at the moment. When the vehicle had passed, Janner ran across the road to the central, palm-planted reservation. He crouched beside a tree and tried to get his bearings. His immediate worry was Kim. He balked at the thought of her wandering the streets of this hostile city.

He judged that if they had materialized in a similar formation to that in which they'd arrived at Townsville, then Kim would be somewhere across the road – down one of the many side-streets, or even, perhaps, inside a building.

After ensuring that the way was clear, Janner sprinted across the road. The gunfire sounded even closer now, loud in the eerie silence that held the city. Just as he was debating whether to run right or left, he heard a commotion down a street to his right: the squeal of brakes, much shouting, the sound of boots on tarmac. He ran to the corner, peered down the street. Half a dozen soldiers jumped down from an armoured car and surrounded someone, pinning them up against the wall. Four soldiers stood back, smiling to themselves, while the other two attended to Kim. One held her chin in his hand, pushing her head back against the bricks, while the other tipped the contents from her koala bear backpack.

Even at this distance he could see that Kim's eyes were wide open in a combination of terror and entreaty.

When the soldier searching the pack found nothing of interest, he turned his attention to the girl. He kicked her legs as far apart as the hem of her dress would allow and frisked her, running his hands down her body and over her hips. Then he stood, turned and spoke to an officer squatting on the armoured car. At the officer's reply, something changed in the attitude of the six soldiers. It was as if, suddenly, at consent from higher authority, the soldiers had turned from men to beasts. They would be absolved from blame for their consequent actions; the girl would be nothing more than yet another casualty in a conflict to which they had become inured.

Kim screamed – the first sound Janner had heard her utter – and he dropped his rucksack and ran down the street, hands in the air. At the sound of his approach, the soldiers turned, halting him in his tracks with raised machine guns.

'She's my daughter!' he cried. 'Let her go!'

The officer, squatting on his vehicle, stood and snapped an order at the two soldiers who had Kim against the wall. They released her, and she slid to the ground, knees against her chest. The others motioned with their guns for Janner to join her. Hands raised, he edged along the wall. As he came within range, he felt the girl grab his leg and hang on, sobbing.

He tried to see some compassion in the faces of the soldiers watching him, but all he saw was hatred and suspicion.

'Papers!' shouted the officer, jumping from the vehicle.

Janner shook his head. 'I – I'm a tourist. My papers are back at the hotel.' He was stammering.

The officer approached, halted a metre before him. 'What is your name?' he asked in perfect Sandhurst English. Janner released a pent-up breath. It seemed that, with the establishment of communications, the possibility of his murder became less real.

'Janner, Gregory Janner. New Zealand national.'

The officer glanced at the girl. 'And you claim to be her father?' There was a sneer in the question.

'My wife, she's Chinese . . .' Simplify things to eliminate all possibility of misunderstanding, he told himself.

The officer regarded Kim. 'And what is *your* name?'

Kim's grip tightened on his leg. Janner closed his eyes.

These bastards, he thought, will have no qualms about shooting me, raping and killing Kim, and then ditching our bodies on the outskirts of town.

'Your name!' the officer yelled.

Kim replied in a whisper little more than a croak.

Janner opened his eyes, hardly able to believe what he'd heard.

The officer said, 'Louder!'

'Kim Jan-ner,' she called weakly, between sobs.

'And where do you come from?'

A delay. Then, 'New Zea-land.' A tiny voice.

Janner wanted to bend down and hold Kim to him, never let her go – but the machine guns were still levelled on his midriff.

The officer said, 'Where are you staying?'

Janner had anticipated the question. 'At the Hilton.'

'Why did you decide to ignore the curfew?'

'I . . . Kim left the hotel when . . . while I was sleeping. She knew nothing about the curfew. I set out to find her.'

'In future, Mr Janner,' the officer said, 'I would look after your daughter with more care, if I were you. Now get back to your hotel!'

He snapped an order to his men, who retreated, swarmed back on to the armoured car, covering Janner with their guns all the way – and, at that moment, when it came to him in an overwhelming tide of relief that he was going to live, he felt an extraordinary surge of inexplicable gratitude towards the officer who, just minutes before, had calmly sanctioned Kim's violation.

As the armoured car started up and spluttered off down the street in a cloud of reeking diesel fumes, Janner's legs collapsed from under him. He slid to the ground, held Kim in his arms, and wept.

*

Later, as traffic started to appear on the main road, Janner released Kim and helped her gather the scattered contents of her backpack. Hand in hand they walked to the corner of the side-street and Janner shouldered his own rucksack. An old man was raising the shutters of his grocery store, and Janner asked him for directions to the GPO. It was close: a hundred metres down the main road, turn left, and the building was fifty metres along the street, opposite the park. Janner took Kim's hand and they walked slowly, saying nothing. He thought of Katia and LJ, hoped they had made the rendezvous point without mishap. He realized, suddenly, both how hungry he was, and how tired. He was beginning to shake from the delayed shock of what had happened in the side-street. He wondered how many more life-threatening situations he might find himself in before this cruel test of nerves was over.

The street outside the post office, when they arrived, was deserted. From across the road, in the park, Janner heard, 'Yo, Greg!'

LJ stood and waved over a short hedge. Janner and Kim crossed the road and entered an enclosed lawn dotted with circular, white-painted tables beneath Campari parasols. Katia and LJ sat at a table, food stacked before them.

'You guys certainly took your time,' LJ said, tucking into his breakfast.

Katia, sensing something amiss in Janner and Kim's attitude, was on her feet, her face ashen. 'What? What is wrong?'

LJ halted his fork in transit to his mouth, a *what-have-I-missed?* expression on his face.

Kim launched herself at Katia, almost knocking her off her feet. 'Soldiers – soldiers got me!' she sobbed. 'Greg saved me! Soldiers wanted shoot me!'

'Kim?' Katia stroked the distraught girl's hair, looked up at Janner.

He sank on to a chair. 'She was stopped by a patrol for breaking the curfew. It was pure luck I heard them. I managed to convince them she was my daughter.' He found himself laughing edgily, overcome with the thought of how close they had been to tragedy.

'Greg saved me!' Kim said, staring at Janner with tear-filled eyes.

'You saved us both,' Janner corrected her. 'An officer asked her who she was, where she came from. Christ, I thought that was it – but she spoke, she actually spoke . . .'

Katia held the girl at arm's length. 'Where did you learn to speak English? Why did you not speak to us before now?'

Kim lowered her eyes, silent. Janner took her hand. 'What's your name? I mean, your real name? Can you tell me?'

She looked up, shyly. 'My name is Tan Yung,' she said.

'Hey,' LJ called, his mouth full of food, 'pleased to meet you, Tan.'

They ate for a while in silence, making in-roads on the pile of food LJ had ordered. Around them now, the city was like any other; distant traffic droned, people strolled through the park.

Janner said, 'I guess we're in Africa somewhere?'

LJ flapped a paper, the *N'Djamena Times* – Chad. Banner headlines proclaimed continued civil unrest, a six till six curfew. From the sublime, Janner thought, to the ridiculous.

Katia indicated a multi-storey hotel overlooking the park. 'LJ said we should stay there today.'

'I reckon we deserve a little luxury,' LJ said. 'It's gonna get hellish hot later.'

*

They booked into a suite of adjoining rooms after break-fast. Janner lay on his king-sized bed after taking a shower, luxuriating in the cool acres of cotton sheets. But every time he closed his eyes and tried to sleep, his mind re-ran that morning's sequence of events. His imagination enlarged upon them, took off into unscripted, alternative possibilities: what if he hadn't happened along when he had? What if Tan had been unable to speak English?

He saw her lying dead in a pool of blackened blood . . .

Someone knocked on the door. It was Tan. 'Katia wants you come quickly. She argues with LJ!'

Tiredly Janner hoisted himself from the bed, hurried into the next room. Katia and LJ were facing each other, silent and staring as if in some kind of impasse.

Katia flicked a glance at Janner, as if reluctant to take her eyes off LJ.

'What's going on?' Janner asked.

'You ask him!' Katia snapped.

Janner looked at the tall American, who was shuffling uncomfortably in the middle of the room. 'LJ?'

'Like I told Katia,' he mumbled, 'I'm going to my embassy. I'm gonna tell them all about the crazy shit going on—'

'I said no,' Katia interrupted. 'I do not trust people in power. Who knows what they might do with us? I stopped LJ from leaving. I locked the door.' She indicated the door to the hall behind her.

Janner said, 'Why tell your embassy, LJ? What do you think they'll be able to do about it?'

LJ looked uneasy. 'They might have experts.'

'Experts?' Janner sneered. 'Experts in what's happening to us?'

'It might've happened to others before us, only it was covered up then. They might know how to treat us.'

Janner nodded. 'Too right. They might just consider

us all too much of a security risk and bump us off. I'm with Katia on this one. I don't trust governments, and I especially don't trust yours.'

LJ gestured feebly. 'I don't know how much longer I can go on like this, Greg. Never knowing what's gonna happen tomorrow. Jesus, it's as bad as 'Nam. The uncertainty from day to day . . . How long will it be before we hit some war zone? What the fuck do we do then?'

'And you seriously think you'd help us by telling your government?' Janner asked. 'Do you think they'd believe a word you tell them? "Excuse me, but overnight I've been mysteriously granted the ability to travel across the face of the Earth in an instant." They'd probably lock you up!'

LJ grinned. 'Good. Then they'd soon find out I was telling the truth. And the next city I find myself in, I'll go tell the embassy there, and soon they'll have all these reports on me from all over the world.'

'And they'll round us up and cut us up into small bits just to see how we do this miraculous thing.'

LJ hunched his shoulders. 'Are you two gonna try to stop me?'

Janner sighed. 'I'd like to, LJ, for your own good. I don't want to see you hurt. But I can't stop you—'

'Greg!' Katia remonstrated.

'If he doesn't tell them today, then he'll just not meet us tomorrow and inform the embassy then.' He looked back at LJ. 'You can go, but do me a favour. Don't mention us. Tell them about yourself if you must, but leave the rest of us out of it.'

LJ nodded. 'Fine. OK.'

Reluctantly, Katia dropped the keys into his palm, stood aside as he made for the door. He turned. 'I really need to tell someone about this,' he said. 'I want to know if they can do something for me. I want an end to it.' He closed the door behind him.

Janner appealed to Katia. 'What else could I have done?'

She smiled. 'I just hope he keeps his promise and does not tell them about us.'

Hours later, Janner opened his eyes and rolled over in bed. The room was in darkness. Beyond the curtained windows the city, under curfew, was still and quiet. Janner dressed and made his way to the next room. The smell of food made him hungry.

Katia was sitting on the floor, the remains of a meal before her. 'Greg, here is some for you.' She indicated a serving trolley. 'I ordered enough for everyone.'

Tan was stretched out on the bed, intent on the comics page of the paper LJ had bought that morning.

Janner yawned. 'What time is it?'

'Almost ten.'

'Have you slept?'

She nodded. 'I am feeling awake and ready for a new city.'

Janner selected a plate from the trolley, sank down beside her and ate. The chicken salad was good, and he was famished. He had to admit that he'd eaten better over the past few days than when he'd cooked for himself over the last ten years.

'No sign of LJ?'

Katia shook her head, without comment, and poured two glasses of red wine.

Suddenly, Janner felt uneasy, no longer safe – as if expecting a dozen CIA agents to invade the room at any second.

'It'll serve him right if they've locked him up,' he said.

'You do not really mean that, Greg.'

Janner looked up. She was watching him. 'No, actually, I don't.'

'Why do you try to hide your feelings so much?' she asked.

Because, he said to himself, not to hide my feelings would be to admit that I have feelings – and that would make me vulnerable. It was difficult, after ten years, to discover things about himself which he thought he'd long since lost.

Perhaps sensing his unease, Katia asked, 'Tell me about your job as a forest ranger, Greg.'

He shrugged. He told her about his job, the daily routine, the natural beauty of the mountains. By the time he'd finished, he realized he'd compressed the highlights of years into just thirty minutes.

'That sounds so exciting,' Katia said.

Janner laughed. 'Don't you believe it. You probably had more excitement in one week at school than I had in a whole year.'

'Oh, no – you cannot be serious. If only you knew what it was like.'

'You sound almost glad to be out of it.'

'In a way, I suppose. Since my father died, I threw myself into it. It was my whole life. Perhaps it was unhealthy.'

He asked her to outline a typical week in Leningrad, and she laughed and fell to the task with humour. Is it, Janner wondered, merely the fact that Katia is the first woman I've spoken to seriously in ten years, or do I really find her – as a person – attractive?

She was interrupted by a quizzical grunt from the bed. Janner looked around. Tan was sitting up, staring at them. 'I not understand,' she said.

'What do you not understand?' Katia smiled.

Tan shuffled off the bed, dragging the *N'Djamena Times*

and the *Townsville Gazette* with her, the pages like sails in her small fists.

She wafted them on to the floor, smoothed them out. 'Look,' she said, pointing at the dates on the masthead of each paper.

Janner looked.

The date on the *Townsville Gazette* was 15 July.

The date on the *Times* – today's newspaper – was also 15 July.

'Something is wrong,' Tan said.

'But it's impossible,' Katia said. 'It was the fifteenth when we first . . . shifted. That was five days ago.' She looked up, her eyes wide – and Janner saw something of his own shock reflected in her expression.

The fifteenth of July had been the day, ten years ago, that Janner had turned his back on civilization.

He said, 'Everything's impossible – our shifting around the world, the fact we arrive at five *everywhere*, and now this.'

'Perhaps the *Times* made a mistake,' Katia said, standing and moving to the phone.

'*And* the *Townsville Gazette*?' he asked.

Katia got through to reception and asked for today's date.

She waited, Janner and Tan watching her.

Silently, she nodded. She replaced the receiver.

'It is the fifteenth,' she whispered.

Tan frowned down at the newspapers.

Katia sat next to the phone, her expression stricken. When someone knocked on the door of the far room, she stood and hurried off to answer it, as if to distract herself from her thoughts.

Seconds later LJ staggered into the room, a concerned Katia behind him. He reeled against the wall, slumped to the floor and regarded them. The neck of a whisky bottle protruded from the pocket of his lumber-jacket.

Janner helped him up and into a chair. The big man came compliantly. Katia knelt beside him. 'What happened, LJ?'

He stared straight ahead, drunkenness giving him a lugubrious, hang-dog expression.

'Did you get to your embassy?' Janner asked.

'They wouldn't listen to me,' he said at last. 'The bastards wouldn't even listen!'

Katia clasped his hand. 'Perhaps that is just as well.'

'No!' LJ bellowed, frightening both Janner and Katia. 'No . . . We need help, all of us. If it is aliens . . . we need help. We can't cope alone, just the four of us. What can we do against all these . . . these *aliens*?'

Janner and Katia exchanged a look.

'I will make you some coffee,' Katia said.

'I don't want any fucking coffee!' LJ cried.

'LJ,' Janner said – if he couldn't reason with him, then perhaps he could shock him to his senses – 'LJ, does the fifteenth of July mean anything to you?'

LJ looked up, focused on Janner with difficulty. 'What d'ya mean?'

Janner grabbed the papers, thrust them at LJ. 'It's the fifteenth LJ. Every day, for the past five days, we've been living through the same day – or rather the same date.'

'The fifteenth,' LJ repeated, and closed his eyes.

Janner wasn't prepared for what happened next. LJ exploded to his feet, knocking Janner off balance. Raging and roaring, he strode out of the room, through the connecting door to his own room. Janner picked himself up and gave chase. The American had flung himself on his bed, face down. Janner reached out. 'LJ, look . . . It's the same for all of us. If you can talk about it—'

LJ roared and lashed out, catching Janner a sideswipe across the cheek. 'Leave me alone. Just get the hell out!'

Janner stared down at the big American as LJ sobbed into his pillow. He left the room silently, closing the door behind him.

Katia looked up as Janner emerged. 'Perhaps we'd better do as he says, leave him alone,' he said. 'He'll be sober by morning.' He wanted to ask Katia what significance the fifteenth had for her, but he was shaking from the exchange with LJ – sorry that he'd provoked such an angry response from the American. He had no desire to cause any more emotional trauma.

He was about to return to his own room when he saw Tan's expression. She was kneeling on the floor before the spread papers.

'Tan?' Janner said. 'Tan, what's wrong?'

The girl's mouth was open and tears streamed down her cheeks.

Katia moved to her side and took Tan in her arms. 'Tan, please, tell me . . .'

In barely a whisper, Tan said, 'On the fifteenth of July, '76 or '77, my mother, father – they were teachers . . .' She stopped there, unable to go on for the sobs that constricted her throat.

'What happened?' Katia asked.

Touching the newspaper before her, Tan said, 'My mother and father . . . When Khmer soldiers came to my town, they kill many people. They come in my house one morning. We were eating, all together. My father, he sees soldiers coming, he tells me to hide. So I go into small cupboard. A long time I wait, and then soldiers come into house. They take my mother and father . . .'

She hung her head, her mouth open in a silent sob. Katia stroked the girl's hair, looking up at Janner with pain on her own face.

Tan took a deep breath, and went on, 'Soldiers, they take my mother, my father into the street and make them kneel and shoot them – *phitt, phitt* – in back of head. I stay in house a long time, but soldiers find me . . .'

Janner closed his eyes, recalling Tan's terror that morning when confronted by the soldiers in the alley.

'I think, they will kill me now, like they kill my mother and father. But they don't. They beat me and throw me in river again and again so that I nearly drown, so that I think each time I will die, but they pull me out and ask me questions. They ask me who were my parents, and I want to tell them – more than anything I want to tell them – but I know if I do, they will kill me too.' She gave another sob, her shoulders shaking.

At last she went on. 'They take me in truck a long way, then leave me with many other people in prison camp – a re-education camp. I no speak, never. In Khmer camp they kill me if find me educated, like they killed my mother, my father. So I keep quiet. Say nothing. Later I escape with other people, walk to Thailand. I live three years in refugee camp, say nothing.'

Katia whispered, 'You've never said anything, until now?'

Tan nodded. 'Nothing I say, until now. Too frightened.'

Katia pulled Tan to her chest. 'It's OK, it is all OK now. You are with friends.' She lifted the girl on to the bed.

'I will set the alarm for four-thirty, Greg,' Katia said in a whisper. 'I will give you a call.'

Janner nodded and retired to his bed.

Later they emerged from their respective rooms, sat on the floor knee to knee without a word. LJ quietly joined them, avoiding their eyes. Only as they linked hands at one minute to five did LJ speak. He squeezed Janner's fingers. 'Hey, I'm sorry, man. OK?'

When the blue light took them, Tan's seemed brighter

than ever before. Janner stared into the light that emanated from the little girl, and saw that she was laughing, as if in rapture. He was overcome by an intense surge of sadness, and then joy.

5

The sun warmed his skin, and when he opened his eyes the blue sky dazzled. A formation of wild geese flew high overhead. He was sitting on the bank of a rolling green-sward. Perhaps a kilometre away was a stretch of sparkling water, and beyond it the high-rise blocks of a futuristic-looking city, a million windows returning the morning sun-light in a fiery furnace glow.

Two hundred metres to his right sat LJ, looking around him. He saluted when he saw Janner. There was Katia, perhaps three hundred metres directly before him, on the opposite bank of the hollow. Janner looked to his left, to where Tan should have been – but he had an intimation as he looked for her that he was searching in vain.

Katia climbed to her feet, set off in the direction of the fourth – Tan's – corner. She halted when she reached the approximate position where Tan should have been, and looked about her. She called Tan's name.

Janner shouldered his rucksack and walked though the short grass, down into the hollow and up the other side. He approached Katia.

'Greg . . .' She gestured around her. 'Where is Tan?'

'She didn't make it this time, Katia.'

She began to cry. 'I want to know where she is! I want to know that she is safe!'

Hesitantly, Janner drew her to him, held her while she sobbed against his shoulder. 'I think she is safe,' he said.

She stared at him. 'What do you mean? How can you know?'

Janner shrugged. 'I think that Tan had to go through the catharsis of reliving the events of the fifteenth all those years ago. For the first time, she could speak about what happened. As a consequence, as a reward or whatever, she left this repetitive cycle. Didn't you feel it, back in the hotel room? Didn't you see her glow?'

'I felt her joy, but I didn't know what it meant.'

LJ was shuffling uncomfortably from foot to foot. 'Ah . . . I'll go and try to find out where we are, OK?' He moved off up the greensward.

Janner and Katia sat on the grass in the morning sunlight, arms around each other. It was a paradox too strange to plumb, he thought: in real terms he hardly knew the woman, yet in terms of knowing how she felt, of communicating with her on some subconscious, maybe even intuitive, level, he felt as though he had known Katia Constantin for a long, long time.

She dried her eyes on the cuff of her blouse, drew a strand of hair from her face. She gazed out across the water to the city. 'Where do you think we are, Greg?'

There was no one about to give them a clue by the colour of their skin, no hoardings or other advertisements in sight. 'Europe?' he guessed.

'Paris? London?'

'Not London. Too many skyscrapers. It could be Paris, or what about somewhere in North America?'

Katia laughed, covering her mouth with the back of her hand.

'What's so funny?'

'Often at home I dreamed of travelling the world, of visiting the USA.'

'Your dream's come true, then.'

'I suppose it has,' she said, and asked him if he had ever dreamed.

I dreamed once of living in the mountains and never seeing another human being for as long as I lived, he thought. 'When I was a boy I dreamed of visiting Nepal, climbing in the Himalayas. You never know,' he said, 'I might make it yet.'

He lay back on the warm grass, and Katia joined him. He closed his eyes against the sunlight, aware of Katia beside him, the scent of her hair. He dozed off.

He was awoken by the sound of someone clearing their throat. He opened his eyes, grimacing as he tipped his head forward and squinted at the perpetrator. LJ grinned back at him, hoisting a litre-carton of milk in salute.

Katia awoke beside him, sat up.

'Breakfast!' LJ called.

Janner stretched, yawned. 'What time is it?'

'Almost eleven. You've been asleep for hours.'

LJ had a cardboard box beside him, stacked with fruit juice, apples and oranges, and small white bags containing bacon and egg sandwiches. Janner smiled at the American's reliance on the reassuring balm of food.

'You've done well, LJ,' he said, biting into a sandwich.

'Even found out where we are, too,' LJ said, pulling a newspaper from his pocket. He held it to his chest, hiding the masthead. 'Any ideas?'

Katia prised open a carton of orange juice. The writing on the side was in English. 'New York?'

'Chicago?' Janner guessed.

'Not far off, both of you. Ottawa, Canada.' He passed Janner the *Ottawa Tribune*. Janner looked for the date. It read 15 July, as he'd expected.

LJ hadn't mentioned it so, remembering the American's outburst last night, Janner kept quiet.

Katia took a covert peek at the masthead, frowned to herself.

Cheeks bulging, LJ waved a half-eaten sandwich in the direction of the water. 'See those A-frames on the shore? Thought it'd be kinda great to rent one, so I did. The middle one of the three down there. We can move in any time.'

Katia shook her head. 'It's beautiful,' she said.

LJ shrugged. 'Had to rent the damned place for a whole week. Guy in charge wouldn't let by the day. I guess if I go on spending like this I'll have to rob another bank in . . . oh, say, a month or two.'

Janner smiled to himself. LJ had obviously not realized that Tan's non-appearance signalled the beginning of the end.

When they finished the meal, they packed up their belongings and walked down to the A-frame. It was luxuriously appointed on the water's edge, with a large veranda overlooking the lake and a motor-boat moored alongside for their use.

That afternoon, Janner took them out for a spin around the bay. They tied up at a downtown wharf and dined at an expensive restaurant, joking and laughing about nothing in particular – everything today, for some reason, seemed funny. It was as if they knew that their time together was coming to an end, and that they had better make the most of the few hours they had remaining.

They arrived back at the chalet as the sun was setting behind the erratic skyline of the city. A little drunk and clutching bottles of wine, they clambered on to the veranda and settled themselves into comfortable chairs to watch the sun go down. Janner found a corkscrew and glasses, and they toasted each other in the warm summer night.

As the sun finally sank and the stars appeared, LJ ceased his chuckling and grew quiet. As if he had been considering it all day, but had been unable to broach the subject until now, he said, 'It's the fifteenth again today.' His words hung heavily in the air between them.

'I know why this is happening to me,' he said. 'It's punishment.' He stopped there, collecting his thoughts, ordering his words.

'I never told no one this before,' he said, then stopped.

Katia leaned forward, touched his hand. 'Go on, LJ,' she said.

He took a deep breath. 'It was the fifteenth of July when we went out on that patrol. We took the chopper low over the jungle, and, like, I just knew something was gonna come down . . . I was high on fear and I just wanted to get in there and out again in one piece.' He snorted a laugh. 'Christ, I can't recall now what the fuck we were doing out there – don't know rightly if I knew too well at the time.'

LJ paused. Janner didn't move, not even to lift his glass. LJ held him and Katia in the grip of his words.

'So we dropped and the chopper left us – saddest sound you ever heard, sound of blades fading away . . . We filed through the jungle and heat and shit, jumpy and thinking every second some gook was gonna jump out and blow our balls off. So we patrolled all day and saw nothing and made it back to the rendezvous point, only the chopper didn't show. Like, an hour passed and Powers on the radio was yelling, screaming for the fuckers to hurry it up – and then we heard the sound of the blades, coming for us. It was sunset. The chopper came down, stirring everything around us, and then something flashed from the jungle and hit the chopper and hell it just went up in one fucking big ball of flame and hit the ground and set everything alight all around and we, like, just ran, got the fuck out a there. A miracle we stayed together. We found cover and Powers got through to base to send us another chopper. Fear, man? Fear? The VC were out there and we didn't stand an earthly.'

He stopped there, swallowed, gathered himself.

'When the firing started it was every man for himself. Twelve of us and I saw six buddies ripped open in the first five minutes. We fired back, of course – but it was like firing at ghosts. All I really recall is running and emptying my machine gun into the darkness . . .

'That's when I shot Powers. We were heading for a back-up rendezvous point, and I thought I saw this gook shape on the path ahead of us, beyond Powers. So I just opened up and I cut Powers in half before I knew what I done, and I can't remember much more, except me and this other guy got back to the clearing and waited till another chopper came in for us.'

LJ stared into his glass. 'That was '70,' he said in a whisper, 'and I never told no one I was responsible for Powers's death. I mean, we all feared dying. We feared the VC killing us all that way from home, but for Powers it was his best buddy did it to him . . . He'd've got out, but for me. He'd still be alive today . . . Man, you see now why I'm living through the fifteenth again and again? Do you see?'

Janner reached out, took LJ's hand.

'I think you might be right, Katia,' LJ said. 'It ain't anything to do with no aliens. It is God – God's punishing me for what I did.'

'LJ,' Janner said. 'You didn't mean to do it. It was an accident, right? It just happened.' Janner paused, aware of how inadequate his words were. 'It was a filthy war and accidents happen and Powers would've done the same were he behind you.'

'But he wasn't! I killed him and I'll never forget it . . . that sick, gut feeling—'

'LJ,' Katia said, 'you've told us now. You have gone some way to atoning for what you did.'

LJ held his head in his hands and sobbed. 'But why the fuck am I reliving today? Why? It's driving me crazy!'

'I don't think this will go on for very much longer,' Janner said. 'Don't you see? It was as if we all had to go through this . . . We all had to meet and trust each other enough to face the fears that haunt us. From today, LJ, you can put the past behind you.'

At five in the morning, the light that surrounded LJ radiated a blinding, sapphire brilliance. The last Janner saw of the big, sad American, he had his head tipped back in rapture, smiling.

6

Janner panicked.

He was sitting in a red-bricked courtyard surrounded by tall, four-storey buildings of the same baked brick. Wooden shutters were closed over windows. There was the smell of dung and woodsmoke in the air – the stench of Asia.

For a second he feared he had materialized alone, that Katia had vanished like Tan. Then he realized that it had been LJ's light which had shone like Tan's – that, if this phenomenon followed its logical course, then LJ would no longer be with them.

A plump, brown-skinned old woman in a *shalwar kameez* waddled into the courtyard from the street, a brass urn slopping water balanced on her hip. She saw Janner, hissed like a goose and hurried past him.

He shouldered his rucksack and made his way through

the arched exit into the street. He turned right and halted when he came to a main road. Battered blue and white single-decker buses carried citizens to work, and grey cars pumped fumes into a grey dawn. Across the street, a poster advertised a brand of cigarettes in a script strange to Janner. Asia, almost certainly. But which country?

Then his curiosity was displaced by the need to find Katia.

He entered a shop selling electric fans, asked an old man behind the counter the directions to the nearest GPO. The old man stared at him, nodded animatedly and disappeared through a doorway hung with strung beads. He appeared seconds later with a young boy in a school uniform.

Janner repeated his question.

The boy pointed. 'Down street, yes? Turn left, first street. Two minutes, you see.'

The old man patted the boy on the head, saluted Janner.

He left the shop and followed the directions, realizing as he turned down the street that his heart was hammering.

Katia was waiting for him outside the GPO.

They embraced, held on for longer than was necessary, like lovers reunited after years, not just friends meeting again after a separation of – what? – five minutes?

'Christ, I thought I'd arrived here alone!'

'I, too. I thought you had gone with LJ.'

He pulled away from her, aware that she was crying. 'Come on, let's find a hotel.' He put an arm around her as they set off. 'Any idea where we are?'

'Istanbul, Turkey – it said so above the door of the post office.'

'We'll head for the old part of the city, find somewhere quiet and . . .' He trailed off. Had he been about to say 'romantic'?

They booked a room on the top floor of a guest-house overlooking the chocolate brown waters of the Bosporus, choked this morning with every conceivable kind of sailing craft, from barges to junks, ferries to what looked like coracles, piled with produce and steered by old men in khaki capes and white lace skull-caps.

All day they lay on the bed with the louvred windows open, and talked. They questioned each other minutely about their pasts, their parents and childhoods, hopes and fears, likes and dislikes – the catechism almost frenzied at times, as if they realized that, unlike conventional lovers with all the time in the world in which to get to know each other, their time together was limited, circumscribed by the rigorous logic of the phenomenon which had brought them together and would soon tear them apart.

They left the room in the early evening and strolled along the banks of the river. They dined at a local restaurant, hurrying the meal when they were both overcome suddenly by the need for intimacy.

They made love on the bed with the louvres open and the wind blowing in from the river, the experience for Janner an expression of physical gratitude after so many years of self-denial.

Later, he asked Katia why the fifteenth was significant to her.

She was a long time before replying.

'I nursed my father for the last fifteen years of his life, and then five years ago, on this day, he passed away. I did not grieve for him – he was ill and in pain, and death was merciful. But I was resentful of all the years I had ceased to live, never doing what I wanted to do, wasting my life. For the past five years I have taught at school, but it is like I have missed a part of my life, of learning and maturing, that was vital to me. I found it impossible to make friends, to trust people. I could speak to no one about my pain.'

They were silent for a time. Then Katia said, 'For Tan

and LJ this day was terrible, and in its own way, so it was for me too.' She paused. 'And for you?'

'For me it was different,' Janner told her. 'The culmination of many years of . . .' How could he put it without sounding maudlin? ' . . . of unhappiness.'

'Tell me, Greg.'

He wondered where to begin.

Later, as five o'clock rapidly approached, they gathered their belongings and sat face to face on the bed. Katia tried to return the dollars he had given her.

'No, please – keep them.'

'I think I will not need money, where I am going.'

Janner laughed, gently. 'And where is that?'

She whispered, 'I truly think we are being judged by God. Maybe this is a hallucination which everyone on Earth goes through in the seconds before they die. Perhaps we are being judged by the most significant incidents of our pasts, made to confront the consequences – and having confronted them, pass on.'

'Pass on . . .?' he said. 'To where?'

'Oh,' she smiled, shrugged. 'You know – Heaven, Hell . . .'

He reached out and thumbed tears from her cheeks. The religiosity aside, he asked himself, was she perhaps right? Perhaps we are being judged – *by ourselves* – and will pass on to . . . to *what*?

The thought of oblivion terrified him.

He felt his entire body tingle.

They held each other in an embrace almost aggressive.

'Don't go!' Katia cried. 'Please, Greg . . .'

Her light glowed, like diamond with blue fire at its heart. For a second he could look through the light encompassing him, watch Katia as she was taken. From an expression of anguish, her face calmed suddenly, and then she smiled in joy. Her light became blinding, and Janner closed his eyes.

He knew that, when he opened them, he would be alone. Katia had gone to confront whatever fate had in store for her, a fate that still awaited him.

7

He felt warm sand beneath him, hot sun on his exposed skin. He heard the gentle lapping of waves. He envisaged a scene of tropical paradise, and when he opened his eyes the view before him perfectly matched his vision. He was on a golden beach with the brightest of blue seas before him, a blue sky arching overhead without a cloud to mar its perfection. He turned his head. Behind the island, destroying the illusion that this was a sequestered desert isle, was the foreshore of a town or city. Tall buildings rose against the sky.

He climbed to his feet, left his rucksack in the sand. From the acute curve of the beach he guessed that the island was small. He moved from the deep, fine sand which impeded his step, to the dark expanse made firm by the incoming waves. Then he set off to circumnavigate the island.

Half-way round, he stopped. He stood and stared across the narrow channel of bright water to the mainland. Now he could make out a multitude of small figures on the street that ran the length of the waterfront. They appeared busy to him, absorbed in their own activity – oblivious of his presence. He looked for a means by which to cross to the mainland, but there was neither a causeway, nor a bridge, nor any other way of leaving this tiny isle. Janner turned and began walking again.

Thirty minutes after setting out, he observed irregularities in the sea-darkened sand ahead. As he approached, he realized that they were his own footprints. There is nothing more lonely, he thought, than a set of footprints marching off by themselves into the distance. Or, rather, there is – when those same footprints join up to form a cycle that is forever one and continuous.

His heart ached for something he had never, until now, realized he was without.

He made himself a shaded canopy from broad fern leaves in the margin of undergrowth bordering the shore. Fitfully he slept all day, as the burning sun rose, arced overhead and set behind the city. Tan haunted his dreams, the size of her eyes in the sheer fall of her cheek, the sound of his name on her lips in the side-street in Africa. LJ was there, too; his clumsy, childlike demeanour filling Janner, even in sleep, with a compassion that was almost painful. And Katia . . . Katia was so real in his dreams that, when he awoke beneath the stars, he grieved anew at her absence.

He had no watch with which to mark the passing hours, but when five o'clock approached it was as if his body, his metabolism, was aware of the fact. For a panic-stricken second it came to him that he did not want to die – that he had many years ahead of him, and much to do. How cruel it would be to die now, to end a life so unsatisfactorily spent.

Then he felt a subcutaneous boiling sensation, as if his blood was charged with dancing particles of fire. The sense of well-being, which had visited him at this time before, returned now, multiplied. He raised his arms as the blue light poured from him, brightened and occluded the sight of his surroundings. He threw back his head and cried out in rapture.

8

When Janner opened his eyes, he found himself sitting in his old leather armchair before the plate glass window with a view of the forested mountainside below. A bowl of porridge and a mug of steaming coffee sat on the low table before him. The clock on the window-ledge read one minute past five. He glanced to his right, at the digital calendar on the wall.

It was 15 July.

He looked around for his rucksack, the other possessions he had gathered on his journey – this time, they had not come with him. But his memories had; he thought of Tan and LJ, and he thought of Katia. He wondered if she, too, had returned to her point of origin, and, if so . . .

Janner climbed from his chair, moved to the window and stared out, as he had done for so many years in the past. Winding down the mountainside between the firs and the pines was the rough track that left his lodge and led, eventually, to the nearest township, and beyond.